"I would prefer to speak alone with Lady Frederica. My time is limited and there is a question of great importance I wish to ask her."

The duchess gave him a dazzling smile and left the room as if she were leaving a pair of young lovers and not childhood enemies.

"I suppose I ought to apologize for putting the bear cub in your room when last I saw you," Frederica said in a completely unrepentant tone. She may have grown into a beauty, but her personality had not changed one whit. Something about her had always irritated him.

"Freddie, do not bother apologizing," Samuel said sardonically. "I should not wish for our relationship to begin with a lie."

She let out a crow of laughter and gave him a beguiling grin. "You are not as stupid as you used to be, and no one calls me Freddie anymore." She laughed again and more color came into her cheeks. She was an attractive woman with curves even courtesans would be jealous of.

"Do you wish to marry me?" he asked bluntly, hoping by some miracle that she would release him from this unwanted obligation.

"No," she said honestly, raising her eyebrows. "Do you wish to marry me?"

No, but I wouldn't mind kissing you.

Author Note

I am so delighted to share another Stringham story! Frederica has been one of my favorites from the very beginning. She is headstrong, fiery, intelligent, adventurous and brave. She will require all these qualities to survive the Battle of Waterloo. Her childhood nemesis turned fiancé, Colonel Lord Samuel Pelford, needs her help to spy on the French before their upcoming attack. Will their temporary truce turn into something more, or will the merry war between them continue?

Alas, because Lady Frederica Stringham is a fictional character, she did not discover or invent carbolic soap nor sell it. Chemist Dr. Frederick Crace-Calvert (1819–1873) is credited with inventing and producing the first carbolic soap in 1857.

The Prince of Orange (later King William II), of the Netherlands, went to school at Eton and served with the Duke of Wellington in the Peninsula wars. He was briefly engaged to Princess Charlotte of Wales before she called it off. He was known to his friends as "Slender Billy." Lord Arthur Wellesley, the Duke of Wellington, was an international hero after Waterloo. He later served as prime minister of England, and it was not until then that he was dubbed the "Iron Duke." Lieutenant-Colonel Colquhoun Grant was Wellington's top intelligence officer for the Battle of Waterloo. He always wore his uniform behind enemy lines and did not consider himself a spy. Colonel George Scovell oversaw communications during Waterloo and he did find a wounded officer in a cowhouse.

SAMANTHA HASTINGS

—

Wedded to His Enemy Debutante

HARLEQUIN
HISTORICAL

HARLEQUIN®
HISTORICAL™

Recycling programs for this product may not exist in your area.

ISBN-13: 978-1-335-59596-6

Wedded to His Enemy Debutante

Harlequin Enterprises ULC
22 Adelaide St. West, 41st Floor
Toronto, Ontario M5H 4E3, Canada
www.Harlequin.com

Printed in U.S.A.

Samantha Hastings met her husband in a turkey-sandwich line. They live in Salt Lake City, Utah, where she spends most of her time reading, having tea parties and chasing her kids. She has degrees from Brigham Young University, University of North Texas and University of Reading (UK). She's the author of *The Last Word*, *The Invention of Sophie Carter*, *A Royal Christmas Quandary*, *The Girl with the Golden Eyes*, *Jane Austen Trivia*, *The Duchess Contract*, *Secret of the Sonnets* and *A Novel Disguise*. She also writes cozy murder mysteries under Samantha Larsen.

Learn more at her website: SamanthaHastings.com
Connect with Samantha on social media:
Twitter @HastingSamantha
Instagram @SamanthaHastingsAuthor
Facebook.com/SamanthaHastingsAuthor

Books by Samantha Hastings

Harlequin Historical

The Marquess and the Runaway Lady
Debutante with a Dangerous Past
Wedded to His Enemy Debutante

Visit the Author Profile page
at Harlequin.com.

To: Susannah Holden

Chapter One

London, March 1815

'The London Season is abominably dull,' Lady Frederica Stringham said, to no one in particular.

Her mother had once again refused to let her go to the factory with her that morning. It was scandalous enough that a duchess owned a perfumery and actually oversaw its day-to-day dealings. But working there or at the fashionable shop on Bond Street was quite out of the question for an unmarried debutante of the *ton*.

Frederica stood next to a window as tall as a person and three times as wide. She stared at the rain pouring on the cobblestone street of the exclusive Berkley Square—brick and stone mansions in the best part of London. Wishing instead that she was in Greece with her sisters and their father. Papa had accompanied them on their journey, but only planned to stay for a month or two to get them established in a good place. Frederica had spent over a year with her married sister Mantheria in Italy, but Mama now insisted that she attend the London Season. She was one and twenty after all and *unmarried*.

Perish the thought.

And whilst flirting with dandies was delightful and playing cards with Corinthians was charming, no suitor had captured her heart. Although, she did enjoy kissing several of them. Another thing debutantes were *not* supposed to do.

Frederica yawned, walked back to the sofa, and slouched down in her seat. Stacked beside her on the side table were all the Maria Edgeworth books from the lending library. Picking them up, she saw the titles *Belinda*, *Castle Rackrent*, and *Tales of Fashionable Life*. She had read them all. If only she could return them and select more without her mother coming with her. Debutantes in London were guarded more closely than treasure. Listening to the raindrops pelt against the window, she let out another sigh.

A footman with a white-powdered wig opened the door for her mother, the Duchess of Hampford. Her mother was an older version of herself, with the same hazel eyes and brown hair, although showing some grey now. She was an inch or so shorter than her daughter, yet her figure was still trim where it ought to be and generous where she would wish it to be. The fragrant smell of lilacs and rock rose clung to her. She gave her favourite daughter a look of reproach.

'Lawson, you may shut the door,' the Duchess said majestically. 'Frederica, sit up at once. I will not have you slouching like a hoyden. You would think you were a chit out of the schoolroom, instead of a young lady in her twenties.'

Frederica sat up stiffly. All right then. This was going to be a business meeting. 'Yes, Mama.'

Her mother sat on a chair beside her and said in a

more coaxing tone, 'My nerves have been in shreds these last few weeks, but at last, all of my worries for you are over.'

Stretching out her arms, she smiled. 'I do not think I am about to die. In fact, I am in perfect health.'

'Stop it, Frederica,' Mama said in a sharp tone. 'This is no time for funning, Samuel is finally coming up to scratch.'

That wiped the smirk off her face and she lightly touched her throat. 'But his father only died less than a month ago.'

Mama brushed a finite piece of lint off her beautiful pink morning dress in what appeared to be silent frustration. 'Lord Pelford will be arriving this afternoon to make you an offer of marriage.'

Frederica's mouth fell open. 'I cannot believe it! He has not seen me in seven years and he did not like me much then. He was always criticising me and prosing on about proper behaviour.'

Her mother sighed and folded her arms. 'You are acting like this is a surprise. You were named after his mother and a union has been planned between our two families for years.'

Squeezing her hands into fists, Frederica stood up and walked to the window. Her heart palpitated and black spots blocked her vision. 'I thought... I thought after Mantheria's disastrous marriage to a duke, that you would have changed your mind. Glastonbury was not faithful to my sister for even six months.'

Dropping her eyes to her folded arms, her mother sniffed. 'Samuel is not like Glastonbury. I have known him his entire life and he is a steady, intelligent young man. He would never be unfaithful to you. Glastonbury was too old for Mantheria and I was too foolish to realise what a mismatch it would be. I admit that I was blinded to his many weaknesses by his wealth and position.'

'Including Lady Dutton?' Frederica asked, knowing full well that her mother knew about Glastonbury's long-time mistress before he married her sister.

Mama closed her eyes and inhaled sharply. 'We assumed wrongly that he would give her up. You have no idea how much both your father and I regret giving our consent to the match. We resolved to not bring out a daughter at seventeen again, deeming it too young to make a good choice for a spouse. You are more mature at one and twenty. You are well-educated and well-travelled. I believe you will make the right choice.'

Her blood boiling, Frederica threw her hands up in the air. 'But you are not giving me a choice! You are marrying me to a man who will disapprove of everything I say and do.'

'If you had found another young man who caught your fancy when you debuted at nineteen, we would have supported you,' she said slowly as if Frederica was still a small child. 'But after two years, you have not. And I will not attempt to deny that I did everything in my power to secure for my daughter a husband of the highest rank.'

Frederica's hands shook and fluttered. 'Have you bought me a husband?'

'I bought you a title—the husband comes with it.'

A giggle escaped Frederica's lips. Drat her mother for making her laugh when she was trying to throw a proper tantrum. 'It is all about town that Samuel inherited very little beside debts and mortgages from his father, besides a younger brother and mother to keep.'

Mama got up and walked to where Frederica stood by the windows. 'A union between our two families was planned almost from the day of your christening. Lady Pelford has been just as determined as myself for this day to come. She has invited us to stay countless times at Farleigh Palace to improve your acquaintance with her son.'

'Little good it has done either,' Frederica said, folding her arms across her chest. 'I was eight years of age and he eleven, when Samuel and I learned that we could not endure each other's company. And since then when forced together, we have done our very best to make each other miserable.'

'Well, I suggest that you stop trying to make him miserable when he is your husband.'

Frederica let out an airy laugh, but quelled it quickly. 'The last time I saw him, I was fourteen years old, when he stayed with us that summer at Hampford Castle. Samuel gave me a box of chocolates and told me I was immature and badly behaved.'

Mama put her hands on Frederica's shoulders. 'As I recall that summer, you and your little sisters put your papa's pet bear cub in his room in the middle of the night and scared the poor fellow out of his wits.'

Frederica grinned fondly at this memory. 'He didn't have many wits as I remember.'

'But you have both wits and talent,' her mother said, squeezing her daughter's shoulders lightly before releasing her hold. 'And I can think of no better person to leave my perfume company to.'

Her heartbeat raced in her chest as warmth radiated through her body. She grabbed her mother's arm and tugged it. 'You are leaving Duchess & Co. to me?'

Mama smiled like a lioness after a successful hunt. 'I am leaving Duchess & Co. to another duchess. Mantheria is not interested. Please tell me that you will accept Samuel and become a *duchess*.'

Frederica dropped her mother's arm and turned back to the window. She breathed in slowly and exhaled, but it did not slow down her racing pulse. There was nothing in the world she wanted more than her mother's company. She had always been afraid that Mama would leave it to Matthew, one of her elder brothers, who was a fine businessman. Frederica had little experience with running a company, but she had grown up practising languages and mathematics to prepare herself. She even planned to expand her mother's perfume business into red scented soaps with phenol. Adding phenol to the sodium tallowate, sodium cocoate, and glycerine had helped her scratches heal without infection. Three fragrances went well with it: camphor, rosemary, and eucalyptus. Trying different combinations, she had made at least one hundred cakes of them as she waited for something to happen during the early Season.

Gulping, she turned back to her mother. 'When do I get your company?'

The look on Mama's face was triumphant, she knew that she had won. 'I will deed half of it to you when you marry and the other half when I am dead. It is slightly less profitable currently, for I used a large portion of the savings to pay Lord Pelford's family debts.'

Frederica did not want her mother to die any time soon and she knew that she still had a lot to learn from

Mama about how to run her own business. She held out her hand. 'It's a bargain.'

Her mother shook her hand tightly, not letting go. 'You will dress in your blue sprigged muslin and have Wade thread flowers through your hair. Do not forget to put a dab of perfume on your inner wrist. And perhaps if you still look as pale as a ghost, tell Miss Wade that she has my permission to add some rouge on your cheeks.'

Her mother finally released her hand and Frederica threw her arms around her mother's neck, hugging her tightly. She kissed her cheek. 'I won't disappoint you, Mama.'

'With the business or with Samuel?'

Frederica laughed. 'Either.'

'I only met your father once before I married him,' she said, 'and we were not even alone. But any marriage can work, if both parties are committed to its success.'

She thought of Samuel and sobered. She was willing to commit, but she could not be certain that he would be. When they were younger, the harder she'd tried to get his attention, the more he'd ignored her. It had been infuriating. He'd had the unique ability to get underneath her thick skin. No person had ever aggravated her more.

'Yes, Mama.'

Her mother sighed. 'If you wish to love your husband, choose to, as I did. Love is not a feeling, but a choice.'

Frederica nodded again and left the room. She could try to love Samuel, but she doubted whether he would do the same. Was a perfume company worth a lifetime without love? Slumping, she walked up the grand staircase to the second floor. She opened the dark mahogany door to her room and found Wade waiting for her. The lady's maid had already laid out the sprigged muslin day dress that flattered Frederica's figure and colouring. Miss Wade was not yet thirty, but her thin face seemed older because of her perpetual frown. She wore her vibrant brown hair in a severe bun, and her plain dress emphasised her slender figure. She stood and executed a sharp curtsy to her mistress.

'I suppose Mama has already spoken with you.'

Wade curtsied again. 'Yes, my lady.'

'Well then, do your best to make me presentable,' Frederica said, sitting down heavily on the bed. 'For as you, and undoubtedly every other servant in the house, already knows, I am to be engaged to be married today.'

Wade assisted Frederica out of her morning gown and into her prettiest dress in the palest shade of blue. She added fresh white flowers to Frederica's coiffure and carefully added a bit of powder to her cheeks. Frederica held still as the lady's maid put on her gloves, silk stockings, and slippers that were dyed the same shade of blue.

'Thank you, Wade. That is all. I should like to be by myself for a little while.'

Once Wade closed the door, Frederica opened the top drawer of her dresser and pulled out her pistol and powder. It was time for some target practice in the garden.

Chapter Two

When Colonel Lord Samuel Corbin's father died and he'd succeeded to his dignities, Samuel had every intention of selling his commission in the British Army and returning to civilian life. Unfortunately, Napoleon Bonaparte escaped from the island of Elba on the same day. Samuel could hardly desert his friends and his country on the brink of war, despite his bereft mama's many pleadings in her letters. But he had asked for a short leave of absence to return to England and put his affairs in order.

It was seven years since he had last set foot on English soil. His memories of home and his father were still painful. He'd run away from them as a youth of seventeen, but he must face them now as a man.

Samuel fought fearlessly during the Peninsular Campaign, as only a young, stupid officer could. His foolhardiness had come with several rank risings and eventually the Duke of Wellington made him a member of his staff. After the war, Samuel had not returned to England with his regiment; instead, he'd accompanied Wellington to France and to the Congress of Vienna.

There he'd stayed quite happily until the little emperor decided to rule the world again.

Not that Samuel had been avoiding England.

He loved his home, Farleigh Palace.

No.

He had been avoiding his father and a certain young woman: Lady Frederica Stringham.

Samuel knew that if he returned home, he would be expected to make her an offer of marriage. Wisely, he had stayed on the Continent. But with his father's death, followed by insistent letters from his father's many creditors, he'd returned to his encumbered estates and distraught mother. He was relieved to learn that his father was already buried six feet underneath the ground when he arrived. His corpse couldn't be deep enough for Samuel. His sire had made his mother miserable and destroyed his childhood. Samuel only hoped that he could shield his little brother from the entire truth. It was a burden no schoolboy should have to carry.

Donning black gloves, he strolled into his mother's private sitting room, where she sat with her embroidery work. Mama was bedecked in black from her cap, which covered her thick brown hair, to her leather boots. Her face was round and dimpled. She had large pale blue eyes, a pointy nose, and a generous mouth with thick red lips. Placing the hoop and needle on the table beside her, she patted the seat next to her. Samuel dutifully sat beside her and was overwhelmed by the smell of her lavender perfume.

'You asked to see me, Mama?'

She gave her son a fond smile and smoothed a crease out of his coat with her gloved hand. 'There, you look very handsome.'

He grabbed her hand and pulled off the glove. The pale skin was unmarred. 'You are still well?'

Swallowing, his mother nodded and tugged back on her glove. 'As well as can be expected and much better now that you are home.'

'Thank you, Mama, but I do not have time to chatter. I am riding to London to meet with our solicitor and steward. The three of us are going to sort through the tangle of our finances before I return to Wellington's services.'

'Perhaps a little refreshment,' she said, picking up a bell off the table. But before she could ring for her servants, he took the bell.

'Mama, I have no desire for tea and commonplaces. Tell me why you sent for me.'

His mother gave him a tremulous smile as if she was trying to hold in her tears. In the past, he would have promised her anything when she cried, but his years at war had hardened him.

'Oh, Samuel, I hope that you will not dislike it. Before you see Peterson and Fuller, I must tell you something of great importance.'

'Do,' he invited.

She brought a trembling black gloved hand to her mouth and sniffed. He placed a comforting arm around her round shoulders. His mother might be a duchess, but she had endured a long and unhappy marriage.

'The Duchess of Hampford owns all the mortgages to the estate,' she said at last. 'Actually, it is her company, Duchess & Co., that holds them.'

He dropped his arm from her shoulders. 'What? How could that be? Why in heaven's name is Hampford involved in the business?'

A large tear came out of his mother's left eye and slowly fell down her rounded cheek theatrically.

Mama could always cry upon command, he thought. Then chided himself for his callousness. He was one of the few people in the world who knew how much she had suffered and how much she would continue to suffer for his father's choices.

Chagrined, he put his arm back around her and gave her a gentle squeeze. 'Mama, I have been gone for seven years and when I left, I was but a lad. Please explain why Hampford is involved in the business.'

'The Duke of Hampford is not at all involved,' she said, biting on her lower lip as if to stop it from trembling. 'You know about your father's—illness.'

He gave a curt nod. The less that was said about that the better.

'About a year after you left for the Peninsula, he took out another mortgage on the estate and lost a fortune on cards and low company. Before we were entirely ruined, I was able to have him incarcerated for his own protection and that of others. But our finances were in a very bad way. I was forced to order a new gown to placate my dressmaker and additional supplies that we could ill afford to keep them at bay, causing us to fall even deeper into debt.'

A feeling of guilt tightened his chest and Samuel gave her another side hug. He should have been there for her. 'I do not blame you at all for our financial state, Mama.'

His mother exhaled a wobbly breath. 'Your father could not help me and you were not here.'

Samuel's chest felt tight and sweat was forming on his forehead. Guilt settling over him like a sash across his chest. He should have supported her better. Instead, he'd joined the army to escape his family problems.

Sighing, Mama put a hand on her chest. 'So, I confided in my dear friend Selina, Lady Hampford. She brought her son Matthew, and they called in Peterson and Fuller. They went through all the bills and mortgages and established a plan to get rid of the debt. Selina assured me with a little economy, we could be free of encumbrances in around twenty years.'

His ears were ringing and he was seeing black spots. 'Twenty years!'

'Fourteen now. Indeed, Samuel, I know I ought to have consulted with you then, but I did not wish to burden you further,' she explained, pausing to sniff into her handkerchief. 'Selina redeemed half of the mortgages and, with my permission, instructed Mr Peterson to sell the London house and most of the unentailed property to pay off all the moneylenders, tradesmen, and the remaining mortgages. You cannot know what a relief it was to me not to have the knocker banged at all hours of the day, with tradesmen and bailiffs begging for their bills to be paid.'

'I am sure it was very disagreeable,' Samuel said, his skin tingling with discomfort. 'Do you recall the entire sum?'

His mother took another shaky breath, bringing her handkerchief to her dry eyes. 'Two hundred thousand and three pounds, five shillings, and four pence.'

He swore underneath his breath, clenching his fists but still feeling helpless and vulnerable. Swallowing the lump in his throat, he asked, 'And how much money do I still owe Lady Hampford or her company?'

'I am not entirely sure,' his mother said, not looking

him in the eye. 'I believe the total to be over one hundred thousand pounds.'

Samuel's pulse thundered against his skin. His heartbeat quickened as if he were about to face an enemy army with cannons and guns. 'One hundred thousand pounds! My commission is not worth a tenth of such a sum.'

Mama took his fisted hand and stroked the top of it. 'Lady Hampford, Selina, told me that the estate, even without the unentailed property, was worth around ten thousand pounds a year. And if we did not entertain, reduced the staff, and sold the best horses from the stables, we could contrive to live on less than half of that amount and slowly pay back the remaining mortgages. I have enforced the strictest of economies on the estate these last six years and we are in a much better financial position than we were.'

Samuel released his hold on his mother and stood, walking briskly around the room, holding his elbows tightly to his sides. 'Is there anything else I should know?'

Another tear fell down his mother's cheek. 'I hope you know that everything I did, I did for you.'

'I do not doubt that.'

More tears fell down her cheeks, but his mother made no attempt to wipe them with the handkerchief in her palm. He was supposed to see these tears. 'Selina saved our family from ruin and she suggested that you need not pay back the mortgages held by her company... That they could be a part of your wife's dowry in addition to the money from her father of thirty thousand pounds. You would only need to repay the initial mortgage on the estate.'

An unsettling heaviness overcame his body and he felt cold all over. His mother and Lady Hampford were forcing his hand. He knew that they had planned such a union from the time he was a small child, but these sorts of family arrangements were not legally binding and he had never intended to marry Frederica. He'd wanted to choose his own bride.

His mother tried to touch him, but he recoiled. 'Lady Frederica Stringham is the last woman on earth that I should wish to marry.'

'Now, Samuel, you haven't seen her in seven years, and she has become a prodigiously pretty girl and very accomplished,' his mother protested, no longer feigning tears. 'Even your father was quite set upon the match before he went mad. And you could hardly do better than a duke's daughter… Lady Hampford expects you to call on her this very afternoon to ask for her daughter's hand in marriage.'

He felt a sharp pain as he sucked in his cheeks, biting down on them in anger. 'I will not.'

Mama picked up her fan that was attached to her wrist and gently wafted it as if this were an everyday sort of conversation and not the end of his hopes and plans. 'Is there another lady you prefer?'

Gritting his teeth, Samuel shook his head. 'No.'

His mother got to her feet and placed a hand on his arm. 'Dearest son, people of our rank rarely make love matches. And those few like myself who marry for love, are not always happy. Not that it was strictly a love match, for our parents did bring us together several times. As you know, after we were married, your father did not remain faithful to me for very long. Samuel, I beg you to consider Lady Frederica. The Stringhams can trace their line back to William the Conqueror. And I know that I can trust you to be a good and faithful husband to her.'

His own father had been anything but good and faithful. Whenever Papa had been in London, which was most of the year, there was always a prostitute on his arm, usually two of them. His father had also frequented every whorehouse and bawdy club in the city. He'd even brought them into their family's townhouse. Samuel did not regret that his solicitors had sold it to pay his family's debts. He never wished to step foot in that building again.

Samuel tried to swallow again, but was unable to. His throat felt thick. 'For all that Lady Frederica is the daughter of a duke and a descendant of the Conqueror, everyone knows that her grandfather is a wealthy London merchant who purchased Lady Hampford's way into the peerage.'

'That is all forgot,' his mother assured him with a coaxing smile. 'Selina has been the Duchess of Hampford for over thirty years, and her children have married into all the best families. Think of the connections you would acquire. And you would save your family from further disgrace and penury. For how are you to provide for your brother, Jeremy, if you have not a farthing to spare? And you would have to repay the additional mortgages held by the Duchess's company.'

Clenching his fists, every muscle in Samuel's body quivered with anger, resentment, and frustration. 'I take it that both Peterson and Fuller are aware of my approaching nuptials? And no doubt they have already met with Lord Matthew Stringham to discuss the wedding settlements.'

Mama held up her hand. 'Only a preliminary meeting. And Matthew is the Earl of Trentham now.'

He let out a forceful breath. 'What if I were to be killed fighting Napoleon? What would Lady Hampford do with the mortgages then?'

Clearing her throat, Mama said, 'Selina was wishful that you sell out of the army immediately, and we had not yet heard of Napoleon's escape when we initially discussed your marriage. After we learned of Napoleon's uprising, she did say, *most delicately*, that if you were not to come back from war, that perhaps Jeremy might become fond of her youngest daughter, Rebecca. Such a dear girl. She is quite a favourite with me.'

'By Jove! That beats all,' he said, digging his fingernails into his palms. He would not force his little brother into an unwanted marriage. 'Lady Hampford is a fool if she thinks I will go down without a fight. I'll find a way without her money.'

Samuel left the parlour, slamming the door behind him. Passing several servants, he walked through the long portrait gallery of his ancestors. He resented each and every painting.

'Oi, Samuel,' his younger brother, Jeremy, hailed.

Jeremy had inherited his mother's pale blue eyes and pointy nose. At the age of fifteen, he was an ungainly youth with large hands and feet. A smattering of freckles sprinkled over the top of his nose, and his hair and eyebrows were so blond that they looked white.

He gave Samuel a quizzing smile. 'Is Mama still weeping? By golly, I never knew one woman could retain so much water inside her. I daresay she has been weeping for three weeks together, which is perfectly ridiculous, because she did not even like Papa. No one did.'

Samuel grasped his little brother's shoulders for a moment and then let go. 'Have no fear. Her endless stream of tears has finally ebbed. When are you back to Eton?'

Shrugging, Jeremy raised his pale eyebrows. 'Ought to have gone back a week ago, but I was afraid that I would miss your visit.'

Samuel touched his chest. 'I am flattered.'

His little brother laughed, shoving Samuel's shoulder. 'And the food is ever so much better at home and no one expects me to do anything. I am the spare after all.'

Jeremy was not a spare to him. He was Samuel's only sibling and he would not let anything bad happen to him. He loved his brother, and unlike Papa, Samuel would take care of him. 'Well, pack your trunk, I will have Mr Kent drive you back to school tomorrow with a hamper full of Cook's best pastries.'

Leaning his head to one side, Jeremy frowned at him. 'Is there any money for school? Some of my friends at Eton heard that our family was all but rolled up. I thought I could perhaps join the army or the navy?'

Samuel's insides felt knotted and he couldn't get enough air into his lungs. He'd hoped to spare his younger brother the weight of their family problems. Such worries were crushing to a schoolboy, as Samuel had learned all too well and too young. Yet, how was he to raise enough money to take care of his brother's future and keep the family estate? And would he be able to do so in the brief time of his military leave? He didn't wish for his brother to join the army or navy. He'd lost too many friends on the battlefield and couldn't lose Jeremy.

At least if he married Frederica, his little brother would never want for anything. It stung his masculinity and his pride to allow the Duchess of Hampford to win, but there was nothing he would not do for Jeremy. Even marry a badly behaved termagant to pay his family's debts. Samuel pulled Jeremy into a tight hug before letting go. A rare sign of affection. 'We are not destitute and you will return to school. We were obliged to sell the London house and some land, but we are quite well to pass, and since I have no taste for cards, you have no need to worry for your future.'

His little brother did not appear convinced. 'Are you sure?'

Samuel took out his coin purse from his pocket and tossed it to Jeremy, who deftly caught it. 'Don't spend it all in one place.'

His little brother's worried expression turned into a grin. 'I won't!'

He gave his brother a nod, before heading out a side door. Samuel ordered the head groom to saddle his horse—he was to ride to London today. Turning back, he looked at his home, Farleigh Palace. It was one of the few edifices built in the English Baroque style and was as ostentatious as it was ornate. The grey stone building had countless arched windows and looked like three enormous houses connected by covered halls. The centre building was a storey taller than the others and had a great domed roof. The farthest right building connected to the pleasure gardens through several archways. From the outside, Farleigh Palace was cold and stately, but to Samuel, it was the only place he had ever called home. It would have been a wrench to lose it, but to keep it, he would have to marry Frederica.

Samuel had always tried to behave in the opposite manner that his father would have. Serious. Responsible. Thoughtful. Frederica had once called him 'stuffier than a stuffed animal head nailed to a wall'. Perhaps as a young man he had come off as a bit uptight. But he'd had to grow up at a very early age. His mother and his little brother had depended upon him for their emotional well-being.

Frederica had always been his opposite: light-hearted, mischievous, and fun-loving. He worried that she shared some of the same wild traits as his father. She didn't care for society's opinion or approbation. She would always do what she wanted and hang the consequences. And what was worse was that she made *him* feel unsettled and out of control.

He had never been foolish enough to believe that he would marry for love. Dukes didn't. But he had intended to make his own choice. To select a young woman of good birth and family that he both admired and cared for. One that returned his preference. A woman that he could be faithful to for the rest of his life.

The head groom handed him the reins. 'Here is your horse, Your Grace.'

Samuel blinked, still getting used to his father's title. 'Thank you, Jepson. Please advise my valet that I no longer have a London house, so he had better meet me with my gear at Grillon's Hotel.'

'Very good, Your Grace.'

He mounted his stallion and cantered off at a spanking pace. At last being able to work out some of his frustrations.

Chapter Three

Samuel stopped first at his club, Whites, where he freshened up after his ride and had a couple of glasses of ratafia. He next stopped at Manton's, where he shot clay pigeons for over an hour and left no longer feeling as if he was going to backfire like a cannon. His final stop was in Berkley Square. He rubbed his temples, trying to release some of the tension from his body. It didn't help. The butler, Mr Harper, bowed painstakingly to him and asked him to come in. The smiling butler then requested that His Grace follow him upstairs. He had known this man all his life and Harper was clearly aware of what was supposed to happen on this auspicious day. Samuel couldn't help but wonder how many unions planned from the cradle actually resulted in marriage. He wished the number were one fewer.

The butler opened the door to a well-lit room. It was decorated in shades of yellow and the sounds of Beethoven floated from a grand pianoforte. Samuel's eyes alighted on Lady Hampford, who stood to meet him. He sucked his cheeks in. He'd always liked her. She was everything his mother was not: strong, determined, and independent. He'd wished his own mama had half of her resolve. Except now that selfsame resolve was coming for him and he no longer admired it. He resented it and her, greatly.

Lady Hampford raised a white-gloved finger to her lips and looked meaningfully at her daughter playing the instrument. He followed her gaze and saw Frederica. He would have recognised her face anywhere. That stubborn nose. Determined mouth. Slanted eyebrows with diabolical intent. But there were subtle and beautiful changes about her. Even sitting down, he could tell that her figure was tall. Her hair was a rich brown and her lips generous enough to kiss. The fashion for high-waist dresses emphasised her ample chest and trim waist. It was the figure of a woman. A diamond of the first water. He wished that his palms didn't feel sweaty in his gloves or that his collar wasn't quite so tight around his neck.

Her face was slightly flushed as she finished the crescendo and ended the piece with a laugh of triumph, 'Ha!'

His heart jumped, as did his pulse.

Frederica's hazel eyes met Samuel's blue ones, and she immediately stood up from the piano bench. 'I did not hear the door open. Please forgive me, Lord Pelford, for not rising immediately to meet you.'

Samuel was an honest man—especially with himself. He could not deny that the young woman before him was very attractive. Somehow Frederica had managed to grow into her long limbs, for the last time he had seen her she was all knees and elbows. She walked towards him gracefully, with a light step. She held out her hand, and he bowed briefly over it. He caught a hint of her scent, an attractively earthy combination of linden and conifer.

'Why do not we all sit down?' Lady Hampford suggested, smiling at him. 'Shall I ring for some tea?'

He shook his head, holding up one gloved hand. 'Not on my account, please. And if you will forgive my abruptness, I would prefer to speak alone with Lady Frederica. My time is limited and there is a question of great importance I wish to ask her.'

Lady Hampford gave him a dazzling smile and left the room as if she were leaving a pair of young lovers and not childhood enemies. Samuel sat on a chair across from Frederica, where he could readily observe her features. He smiled slightly when he realised that he was not the only one surprised at what he saw. The colour in her cheeks was high and her lips upturned into the slightest of smiles.

'I suppose I ought to apologise for putting the bear cub in your room when last I saw you,' Frederica said, in a completely unrepentant tone. She may have grown into a beauty, but her personality had not changed one whit. Something about her had always irritated him like a rash on his skin.

'Freddie, do not bother apologising,' Samuel said sardonically. 'I should not wish for our relationship to begin with a lie.'

She let out a crow of laughter and gave him a beguiling grin. 'You are not as stupid as you used to be, and no one calls me Freddie any more.'

'And you are not as skinny as you used to be,' he retorted.

She laughed again and more colour came into her cheeks. She was an attractive woman with curves even courtesans would be jealous of. 'I suppose I am not. But then, neither are you. You seem twice as broad as before.'

'Do you wish to marry me?' he asked bluntly, hoping that by some miracle she would be the one to release him from this unwanted obligation.

'No,' she said honestly, raising her eyebrows. 'Do you wish to marry me?'

No, but I wouldn't mind kissing you.

Where had that thought come from? He pulled at his collar, feeling rather hot and betrayed by his own body.

'Heavens no! I do not even know you.'

And I've never liked you.

Frederica laughed loudly at this and his lips twitched. Earlier in the day, he would have thought that there was nothing humorous in his situation. But he'd forgotten that Frederica could be funny; unfortunately, in the past, he'd been the butt of most of her jokes.

She sobered first, clearing her throat. 'Perhaps we could become better acquainted now that we are no longer children? I long for adventure and purpose. And no doubt you have had many adventures and political intrigues whilst on the Continent.'

Samuel stiffened. He hated how the aristocracy glamourized war with their fancy uniforms and formal parades. There was nothing adventurous or exciting about a battle. It was loud. There was so much blood, the wounded, and the burying of your friends. 'Those stories are not fit for a woman's ears.'

Her lips tightened into a straight line. 'Quite a setdown.'

He could not help but smirk back at her as he watched Frederica struggle within herself to be civil. As a child, she would not have even tried. She would have yelled at him, hurled an object, or got her revenge when he least expected it. Usually with a dead rodent or a live snake whilst he was sleeping. Still, he had loved the summers he'd spent at Hampford Castle with her older brothers, avoiding Frederica whenever possible. Her brother Charles had been his best friend and closest companion. He was also the first person he'd seen buried. After his death, Samuel had resented how Frederica had tried to take her brother's place as his friend. She was a poor substitute for Charles, who had been a good listener, clever, and kind.

Little had Samuel known then how many friends he would lose in the war. How many pieces of himself he would bury with them.

After a few moments she said in a lighter tone, 'Shall I receive many set-downs as your wife?'

'I haven't asked you to be my wife,' he pointed out.

Frederica lifted her eyebrows in an arched look and talked with her hands. 'No, you have not. And I have not said yes, but somehow, I believe we will both find ourselves arrayed in finery and in front of the Archbishop of Canterbury before too long.'

'Dreadful thought.'

'I know. It quite gives me the dismals.'

She was so quick-witted. Samuel was smirking at her, as if they were friends instead of old acquaintances who shared a keen dislike of each other. But there was little choice but to make her his wife, so he'd have to make the best of it.

He got out of his chair and kneeled before her. 'I have found in the army, that if something has to be done, it might as well be done at once: Lady Frederica, will you do me the honour of becoming my wife?'

Frederica covered her mouth with her hands and fell into a fit of chuckles.

He caught his breath in surprise, his heartbeat quickened in annoyance. Shaking his head, Samuel asked, 'Why can you never be serious?'

She laughed harder and tears began to form in her lovely hazel eyes. Unexpectedly, her mirth warmed his heart and Samuel struggled to keep his own mouth from forming a smile. Maybe he needed a little lightness in his life.

It was a ridiculous situation that they had found themselves in. Engineered by their meddlesome mothers and his dead father's extravagance.

He handed her his handkerchief embroidered with his initials and the Pelford crest and said in the same exaggerated formality, 'Dearest Lady Frederica, please accept this small token of my high esteem.'

Frederica snorted and giggled harder. Eventually, she stopped laughing and took the handkerchief and dabbed at her eyes, breathing in and out slowly. Her gaze met his and it felt like she was seeing through his ragged soul. He was not sure that he wanted her to see the darkness that raged inside of him now. The terrible secrets that he held in his heart. The burdens he carried.

Taking her hand in both of his, he said, 'Am I to receive an answer, or shall I spend the afternoon kneeling on the floor?'

'My lord duke,' she said with mock formality. 'I should be most honoured to become your wife.'

He kissed her hand before standing up. 'Well, it is about time, my knees were getting sore.'

Frederica got to her feet, as well. They stood eye to eye inches apart, for she was a very tall young woman. Samuel impulsively leaned towards her, placing a hand on her cheek. Frederica did not startle, nor move away. If anything, she leaned towards him. Considering that enough encouragement, he placed his mouth on hers. Her silken lips were cold at first, but warmed quickly. And to his great surprise, Frederica returned his kiss with ardour. Her arms wrapped around him, pulling him closer. Samuel's heart beat fast as his free hand found the dip of her waist and pressed her against him. She tasted of mint and honey, everything that was fresh and wonderful and bright. He was not sure which one of them deepened the kiss, but neither of them seemed to want the embrace to end. Perhaps they had been using their mouths wrongly with each other all these years.

Lips were not made for fighting, but for kissing.

At last, he lifted his mouth from hers. They looked at each other, both breathing heavily. His mind whirled. Frederica put her delicately gloved hands on the lapels of his green coat and pulled him to her for another open-mouthed kiss. He couldn't believe that *she* was kissing *him*! This time her lips were wet, warm, inviting, and deliciously familiar. Samuel put his hands over hers on his chest. Wanting to keep them there. To hold her close. His tongue slipped into her mouth and her tongue tangled with his. If this was another fight, for once he would let her win.

The footman coughed. Samuel and Frederica dropped their hands and quickly parted. He felt more flustered than a raw recruit on the first day. The footman opened the door for the Duchess of Hampford to walk into the room. He stood up taller and nearly saluted her like a general. Lady Hampford had not seen the embrace, and Samuel hoped that she presumed the heightened colour in both of their cheeks resulted from the embarrassment of the situation.

'Have I returned too soon?'

'No indeed, Duchess,' Samuel said, bowing to her. 'Your daughter has been kind enough to accept my proposal of marriage, and I was just begging her leave to write to her father and send an announcement to the newspapers. I do not have much time. The Duke of Wellington demands I return with all possible speed.'

Lady Hampford bit her lower lip, nodding. 'To Vienna?'

Swallowing heavily, Samuel shook his head. 'No, ma'am. I am to meet General Lord Wellington in Brussels, where he will take command of the coalition army.'

'Ah,' Lady Hampford said, tipping her chin. 'I will not detain you any further, Duke. But if you have time to visit us again before you leave, we would be honoured to receive you at any time.'

The Duchess of Hampford held out her gloved hand, and Samuel bowed briefly over it. He then turned back to Frederica and surprised both ladies, and himself, by kissing her on the cheek. Frederica flushed a deeper shade of red and brought her hand to where his lips had brushed her skin. He left the room, escorted by the footman who had opened it.

Feeling lighter than he had all day, Samuel slipped the man a coin and touched his hat. 'Thank you for the cough.'

Chapter Four

'Samuel has certainly become quite broad-shouldered since he went to war,' Mama said after the Duke of Pelford left. 'I scarcely know if I would have recognised him on the street.'

Frederica walked to the window, watching Samuel below hail a hackney coach and get in. She was relieved to see him go. She'd tried to unsettle him with the kiss and it had backfired most dreadfully. Her pulse beat faster than if she'd run a mile. Samuel had changed. Or she had. Perhaps them both.

He was neither short nor tall, but a stocky fellow with thick dark brown hair that he wore shorter than was fashionable. His eyes were a pale shade of blue and his chin jutted out, giving him a determined look. He had left England a boy and returned a man with a powerful upper body. He was too muscular to be shown to advantage in skintight cream pantaloons, nor in the green coat made for him. She thought he would look best in uniform, where his brawn was intimidating.

She turned back to her mother. 'His appearance has changed, but he is still as stubborn and stupid as ever.

He informed me that his adventures on the Continent were not fit for a woman's ears. As if a woman's ears were any different than a man's! Clearly, he has never dissected a cadaver. I can assure you that they are precisely the same.'

Mama raised one eyebrow. 'You obviously did not mind too much, or you would not have let him kiss you.'

Frederica felt a blush suffuse her cheeks. Her mother was too sharp by half. 'It was only on the cheek, Mama.'

Her mother shook her head, a smile on her lips. 'You are not my eldest child. I know the look of someone who has been thoroughly kissed.'

His kisses had been knee-weakeningly wonderful, Frederica admitted to herself. Not that she would admit as such to her mother. 'Samuel's kisses were not as good as the Italian count's.'

Mama snickered, a funny sound, coming from her. 'It would be unfair of us to compare our Englishmen to their Latin counterparts. They will always be deemed inferior.'

Frederica laughed and took a seat next to her mother on the sofa, trying to calm the wild beating in her heart. She didn't want to admit to liking anything about the match. She would lose negotiating ground. Leaning her head on her mother's shoulder, she said, 'Sacrifices must be made in all battles.'

Her mother put an arm around her and sighed. 'That horrid Napoleon has quite overturned all of my plans with his wars.'

'Perhaps he was not considering your convenience.'

Mama chuckled again. 'He certainly was not, or he would have waited to escape for another month or two. The nuisance! Now we must be serious. I do not think we should purchase your wedding clothes until we are able to set a date, which I suppose again will be at the little emperor's convenience. It is bad enough that he has kept most of Europe in war for twenty years, quite making it impossible to visit all my favourite cities. Or sell them my perfumes.'

Frederica sat forward, struck with an idea. 'Mama, why do we not follow Samuel to Brussels? Lady Jersey was bemoaning the other day how so many of the best families are abroad and my dear friend Georgy Lennox is already there.'

Her mother took a deep breath, clearly thinking about Frederica's suggestion. 'I cannot deny that your idea does find favour with me. Like yourself, I wish we were in sunny Greece with your sisters and father, instead of rainy old England. And I do believe a trip to Brussels would alleviate some of the tedium. However, I must have your word that you will behave with the utmost propriety at all times. And that you will do everything in your power to further your match with Samuel. Nothing is final until the vows have been said and the marriage papers signed, and I do not wish for you to do anything that might jeopardise your future.'

Leaning back against the sofa, Frederica put her hands behind her head. 'Sign over half the company to me first and I will behave with perfect propriety.'

Instead of being affronted, her mother smiled. 'I will have Matthew draw up the contract at once, giving you fifty percent of the stocks in Duchess & Co. And we will bring all the soap cakes that you have already made to Brussels with us. I can think of no better advertising than the soap used to tend our wounded, brave soldiers.'

'Thank you, Mama,' Frederica said, kissing her on the cheek. Then she ran up a flight of stairs to her bedroom. She scrambled onto her enormous four-poster bed and jumped up and down—giggling. She would own half of the company and her mother would produce her red scented soaps. At last, her life would have meaning and purpose.

Chapter Five

Brussels, May 1815

They'd settled into their Brussels lodging just the day before, with barely enough time for her maid to unpack her belongings before preparing for their first invitation. Frederica entered the ballroom in a crimson gown with a high waist and a matching crimson gauze overlay, delighted that she was no longer required to wear white like a young debutante. It was a dull colour. Frederica's brown curls framed her face and Wade had intertwined fresh red roses into the chignon on the back of her head. For jewellery, she wore only a single round ruby surrounded by a cluster of diamonds. It hung on a thin silver chain around her long throat. She was not surprised when several eyes focused on her. Both she and her mother were taller than the average height and some of the highest-ranking guests of the party.

Next to them stood the Duchess of Richmond. Lady Richmond was a short woman with large green expressive eyes that missed very little. 'Lady Frederica, may I introduce my nephew, Captain Mark Wallace, as an amiable dance partner?'

A young man not much older than Frederica walked out from behind the Duchess of Richmond. He was tall and fashionably slender. He had curly black hair, dancing blue eyes, and an engaging smile. He bowed to Frederica, and she curtsied. Her mother nodded, giving her permission, and Frederica held out her hand. Captain Wallace took it and led her back to the dance floor. Frederica had more time to study her partner while they performed a country reel. He really was quite devastatingly handsome.

Quirking up one eyebrow, she asked, 'Are you going to speak to me or just smile at me?'

The young captain threw back his head and laughed. 'I am trying to make a good impression. Cousin Georgy suggested that I not say a word.'

Frederica grinned back at him, wrinkling her nose. 'Would you make a bad impression if you spoke?'

'Indubitably,' he said, with a slight Scottish accent and another grin. Both were very attractive. 'I invariably say the one thing that I ought not.'

She laughed out loud as she took his hands in the circular figure. 'You need not worry about my good opinion.'

'No?' he said with a wink, releasing her hand for the turn and then taking it again. 'Has some malicious person already told you that I am a second son?'

Frederica touched her chest and pretended to be shocked for only a moment, before spinning to the correct place to take his hand again. 'No indeed, if they had I would not have danced with you. For I make it my policy to only dance with older sons, in full possession of their fortunes.'

He pulled her closer, his hand on her waist. 'And

I usually only dance with heiresses. But I thought I would make an exception tonight, and dance with the most beautiful lady in the room.'

Nodding her head, Frederica smiled at his compliment. 'Perhaps I am an heiress. How much money do you require for a young lady to be considered for courtship?'

Captain Wallace twirled Frederica around and around. 'Oh, not much more than one hundred thousand pounds.'

'Just a little pocket money.'

He let out another guffaw of laughter and gave her another devastatingly attractive smile. 'I should like to be kept in the same style I have grown accustomed to, when married.'

Her body shook with silent laughter. Frederica turned and saw two people standing on the side of the dance floor giving her a stern gaze. The first was her mother and the second her betrothed. Heat pumped through her body like blood. She had been right. A uniform suited Samuel's muscular form perfectly. He wore a scarlet coat with a high collar, gold braid on the shoulders, and a navy sash across his broad chest. He looked formidable and a bit frightening. He positively glared at her. She hoped that he felt jealous. Growing up she had chased him, wanting to be included with the older children. He'd left her behind over and over again. This time she wanted *him* to do the chasing and she would decide when and if she allowed him to catch her.

Captain Wallace glanced in the same direction. 'Who is that stocky officer over there on the left side of the room that is scowling at me?'

Turning away, she said, 'Colonel Lord Pelford.'

'I have heard of him. He is an aide-de-camp to the

Duke of Wellington. My cousin Alexander has mentioned him several times. Alexander says that he is a positive demon in action. No better man on the field. Do you know the fellow well?'

'When we were children, we hated each other with a passion,' Frederica said, and added conscientiously, 'but not now we are betrothed to be married.'

The captain clenched his fist and struck his heart, his eyes downcast. 'How is it that every beautiful girl is already taken?'

'I have two younger sisters.'

'A poor consolation,' he said with a mournful sigh.

Frederica gave him another beaming smile. She had not met such an amusing fellow in all her London Seasons. 'And how do you know? They could be much prettier than me. You would get along famously with them if you don't mind snakes or mice.'

He stopped mid dance step. 'What?'

Gurgling with laughter, she tugged him to the right place in the line. 'My sisters are both naturalists and extremely fond of all God's creatures. Particularly the animals that no one else seems to like.'

The music ended and they bowed to each other. The captain still grinned and Frederica thought he was either playing at being a fortune-hunter or that he was the most skilled one that she had ever come across.

Captain Wallace took her hand to escort her to the side of the room, not ten feet from Samuel. The captain did not release her fingers; instead, he bent over her hand and kissed it. Thanking her profusely for being his partner. Frederica glanced to her side, to see Samuel looking like he had swallowed an ostrich egg whole. His cheeks were as red as his scarlet coat. The two gentlemen could not have been more different. Samuel scowled and Captain Wallace smirked.

Her betrothed strode purposefully towards her and slightly bowed. 'Lady Frederica, may I have this waltz?'

'Yes.'

He tightly gripped her right gloved hand in his large left one. He led her back onto the dance floor and then put his right arm around her waist and led her in perfect circles around the room. For all his strength and bulkiness, there was a gracefulness to his dancing. A precision that she would expect from a high-ranking officer in the army. She breathed in his scent of leather, boot-blacking, and musk. He wore no cologne, but that did not surprise her. The clean and natural scent suited him very well.

Frederica leaned in a little closer to sniff again— she was going to be a professional perfumer after all. She breathed in deeply before saying, 'You are an accomplished dancer.'

'Wellington requires all of his staff to be adept at the art.'

The corners of her mouth tilted upward. 'And do you always frown at your partners? Or only the ones you are betrothed to?'

Samuel reluctantly returned her smile and nodded his head in the direction of the captain. 'You seemed to enjoy dancing with young Wallace. A Scot, I believe, and the younger son of the Earl of Inverness.'

'I did,' she said in her sauciest voice. 'He is so handsome and there is something irresistible about an accent. I could listen to him speak for hours.'

He snorted, his lips forming a grim line.

If he were one of her unwanted suitors, she would

have allowed him to remain jealous. But he was not. Like it or not, without love, but with a company and a dukedom, they were getting married.

Leaning closer, her nose brushed his. 'Captain Wallace was describing what he is looking for in a wife— a pair of lovely eyes and pots of money. I, alas, do not qualify. Not being nearly rich enough to meet his basic needs as a second son.'

Samuel's lips twitched as if he were fighting them not to grin; his military training must have won out, for he kept his mouth straight. 'Are you ever serious?'

'Occasionally, when the time requires. And never while dancing. I love to dance.'

'Well, I would seriously like to take you outside.'

Was it a challenge? She could not and would not back down. She was not a green debutante, she knew exactly what her betrothed wanted to do out there. Perhaps if they talked less and kissed more, they would have a rather good relationship on the whole. Not that she was eager for his embraces. Of course not. This was a battle for dominance and she intended to win it. 'What a pleasant thought. I should like that very much.'

He turned her abruptly and led her to the opposite side of the room near the door to an antechamber and into the courtyard. They walked past the gravel walkway to the green grass in the centre to a secluded nook behind a statue and shadowed by a large circular bush. Samuel stopped, still holding her hand.

Ignoring the fluttery feeling in her stomach, she shook her head. 'Surely, a seasoned officer like yourself knows better than to stop at the first bush? It is always wiser to go farther back. You are less likely to find a previous occupant, or to get caught kissing by a chaperone.'

One corner of his lips tilted upward. 'Is that why you think I brought you out here?'

'Of course!'

Frederica pulled his hand, leading him farther into the dark garden. She did not stop until they were in a corner that was blocked on one side by a stone wall and the other by a prickly rose bush. 'Now this spot is quite secluded.'

Samuel's grip on her hand tightened slightly. 'Have you been to many secluded spots?'

Wrapping her arms around Samuel's neck, she pressed her body against his. He was all firmness and tight muscles. His brawn made her feel small, a rare thing for a voluptuous woman. 'A lady never kisses and tells.'

'Neither does a gentleman,' he said, before slanting his mouth to hers.

She could feel him everywhere, for he was about her same height. His muscular thighs pressed against hers. It was wickedly exciting. His lips moved over and over hers in a beautiful rhythm, almost like music. Frederica ran her fingers through his short, thick hair, eliciting a soft moan from Samuel. She pulled his hair slightly, before opening her mouth and deepening the kiss. He responded by tightening his hold on her. The pressure of his lips matching the pressure of his arms. It was heaven. Even better than kissing Conte de Ferrari, the fiery Italian she had met whilst her family were staying in Rome.

When he nibbled on her lower lip, it was more exciting than reading the most sensational Gothic novel. Her imagination was nothing on the reality of his embraces. Samuel moved his mouth from hers and made a trail of kisses to her throat, still holding her tightly in his arms. She could hear his heart thundering in his chest. Her own heart was just as loud and wild.

Frederica placed her two hands on his chest and pushed him away slightly, but stayed encircled in his strong arms. 'Why did you bring me here?'

'A singularly stupid question,' Samuel answered, pulling her back to him and kissing her neck in a sensitive spot below her ear.

She could not help herself, she purred like a kitten. She'd always enjoyed kissing and Samuel was rather good at it. She allowed him several more kisses before she gently pushed him farther away from her. 'One more singularly stupid question—have you ever been in love?'

'I think every man of four and twenty has at least imagined himself to be in love once or twice,' he replied lightly. 'And you?'

Raising her eyebrows and shrugging her shoulders, Frederica grinned. 'Oh, several times.'

'Really?'

'The first a footman when I was thirteen. Then an under groom. His name was Jacob, he helped me put the bear cub in your room. Helen and Becca helped, as well. Then there were a few lords and an Italian count.'

He creased his forehead. 'So, you haven't been waiting for me all these years.'

Biting her lower lip, she shook her head. 'No. Did you think I was?'

Samuel stiffened. She could feel the tenseness of his leg muscles. The tightness of his entire body. 'No.'

Frederica gave him a playful shove on his shoulder, before kissing his cheek. 'You are jealous. How deli-

cious! But you need not be. Truly. I never fancied myself in love longer than a fortnight. How about you?
Was there a dark Spanish beauty? Or a saucy German
baroness? No. I know, a young French comtesse with
an elderly husband.'

He stepped back from her and she immediately
missed the warmth of his body against hers. The con-
tours of his shape and how they fitted so perfectly
against her own curves.

Samuel cleared his throat, then swallowed heavily.
'I suppose I should bring you back to the party before
your presence is missed by your mother.'

She linked her arm with his and leaned her head
against his shoulder. 'Spoil-sport. I merely wish to
know you better. Next time, I will make you confess
before we kiss.'

He returned them to the ballroom and they were met
at the door by her dear friend Lady Georgiana Lennox.
She was a short brunette with large brown eyes. Her
hair was a darker shade of brown than Frederica's and
her skin was a paler cream. Georgy took Frederica's
arm from Samuel's and led her to another antechamber that led to a retiring room.

'What are we doing, Georgy?'

'Fixing your hair,' she replied, deftly arranging several curls in Frederica's hair that had fallen into disor-
der. 'Did you want the whole room to know that you
dallied in the garden with your betrothed?'

'I do not know what I would do without you, Georgy,'
Frederica said earnestly. She looked around for a mirror,
but could not see one. 'Am I presentable now?'

'Yes.' Georgy linked arms with Frederica again and
they walked back to the party. 'Your Colonel Lord Pel-

ford certainly looks strong and—do not eat me when I say this—very handsome.'

Frederica's nostrils flared. 'I suppose he is pleasant to look at. Especially from behind.'

Blushing easily, Georgy laughed. 'Am I to understand that you are more reconciled to your engagement?'

She winked at her friend. 'Of course I am. Why else would I be kissing him in the shrubbery?'

'Sport,' Georgy answered and they both laughed as they left the retiring room.

Captain Wallace walked up to the ladies and bowed. If she had not just kissed Samuel, she might have been tempted to see how the Scots compared to Italian counts.

Bowing her head, Georgy curtsied. 'Cousin Mark.'

'Captain Wallace,' Frederica said, giving him a nod of acknowledgement.

The captain smiled at them and somehow placed himself between them with a lady on each arm. He was certainly a smooth manoeuvrer.

'Any luck finding an heiress?' Frederica asked coyly, squeezing his arm.

Georgy giggled and swatted at her cousin's shoulder. 'You didn't tell her, did you?'

'Lady Frederica,' he said in mock surprise. 'I am shocked that you would treat a fellow's delicate confidences thus.'

Grinning, Frederica tapped his arm with her fan. 'Oh, I am sorry. But it is only Georgy after all, and she is your cousin, so I assumed she was already aware of your matrimonial plans. And is possibly a co-conspirator.'

The captain flashed them both a knee-melting smile. 'If she is "only Georgy" can I be "only Mark"?'

Georgy let go of her cousin's arm. 'I can see that I am not needed for this conversation, I shall go beg a partner for the country dance.'

She walked away from them and 'only Mark' asked Frederica for the next dance. She nodded, looking around the room for Samuel. She saw him making one in the circle of men around the infamous Caroline Lamb, who'd had a public affair with Lord Byron. Lady Caro had a small pixie-like face, surrounded with a mass of short dark curls. She had big brown eyes, a little nose, and a petite red mouth, which she often wore in a pout when she was not laughing. Frederica thought that Lady Caro looked practically naked in her thin white gauzy dress. She must have dampened her chemise. The lady's form was willowy, as unlike Frederica's full figure as possible. Samuel's face was animated when he spoke and Frederica heard Lady Caro's unmistakable high shrill giggle ringing across the room. Frederica scowled across from Mark as they lined up for the country dance. Samuel had not looked so happy speaking with her.

'Is something wrong?' he asked, leading her through the next form.

Frederica gave a ready laugh. She was not some love-struck miss. She had known Samuel her entire life and she was not about to beg for his favour now. 'You tread on my foot!'

Twirling her around, he shook his head. 'Nay, that is impossible. All fortune-hunters are great dancers. It is one of the rules.'

She did not have to fake a smile this time. 'And pray, what are the other fortune-hunter rules?'

'The first,' he said, pulling her towards him. 'You

must be handsome. The second, charming. And the third—'

'Insolvent,' she supplied.

Mark stuttered and missed his step for the first time that night. He grinned at her sheepishly and she thought that he was indeed handsome, charming, and a great dancer. She did not stop smiling until she saw Samuel promenade by with Lady Caro on his arm. Frederica had never liked Lord Byron as a person, his poetry was rather good, but she did not blame him for dropping Lady Caro. She could have happily dropped the woman into the English Channel at that very moment.

Jealousy, she discovered, was a most unpleasant perfume. There was nothing for it, but to ignore Samuel for the rest of the night. She flirted in French when she danced with Belgian nobles, and in English with officers from the British Army. She never lacked for a partner. Unfortunately, neither did Samuel.

Not that she was watching him.

She was not.

Because she did not care about him at all.

Chapter Six

There had been balls in the Peninsula. Parties in Madrid, but nothing like the endless string of entertainments in Brussels. Samuel could have happily missed most of them, but the Duke of Wellington insisted that his staff attend in full dress uniform. He had already attended a picnic that afternoon and he would have preferred an early rest to another night dancing. Being an aide-de-camp to the general kept him busy all day.

Taking a deep breath, he walked up the steps to the rented house where Lady Snow was throwing her ball. He was met at the door by none other than the Prince of Orange.

'If you had any more feathers in your cap, I would have shot you for a bird,' the prince said in a slow English drawl, with only the slightest of accents.

Samuel bowed formally before the young prince. 'I doubt you could hit a bird with your aim. Even one of my size, Your Royal Highness.'

His friend barked out a laugh. 'Only the English know how to insult with pomp and circumstance. You can keep your fine bows for the ladies.'

'I should not wish to steal them all from you, Slender Billy.'

The nickname was one only close friends were allowed to call him. Samuel and the prince had attended Eton together as boys and they'd both served in Spain under the Duke of Wellington. Although they were the same age, they were not at all alike. Samuel was broad, while Billy was angular. Samuel had a thick thatch of dark brown hair, and Billy's thin brown curls had already begun to recede. The prince was a heavy drinker and sometimes silly, while Samuel was known for being sombre. Despite their differences, there was a steady friendship between them.

'You must not steal ladies from me, you know. I have already lost one royal bride,' Slender Billy said, with a curl of his upper lip. 'To lose a second would smack of carelessness.'

'At least you will not have the Prince Regent for a father-in-law.'

The prince sneered. 'Nor the mad grandfather. I wonder if insanity runs in families. I quite thought that Princess Charlotte suffered from it.'

Raising an eyebrow, he asked, 'When she ended your engagement?'

Billy shook his head. 'No. When she entered it in the first place. Completely mad.'

Samuel tried to hold in his laugh, but it came out in several snorts. His friend grinned broadly.

Swallowing his mirth, Samuel said, 'She would have been lucky to have you as a husband, my friend. Just think how envious Princess Charlotte will be when you become the hero of the Napoleonic Wars.'

Billy shook his finger before pointing. 'She will lament the loss of me, I am certain. But over there. Isn't that your filly?'

His gaze followed the direction of the prince's finger. Frederica looked nothing like a horse. Her net gown was a celestial blue that clung to her generous curves and dipped rather low in the front. Samuel quite enjoyed the view, but wished that no other men in the room could. Not that her neckline was at all scandalous, there was simply so much beautifully rounded skin on display. And he knew how she felt pressed against his chest. A surge of desire shot through his body to his belly. He wanted to take her to a secluded spot in the garden again. He needed to feel the soft texture of her lips moving over his.

'For a fellow forced into an engagement,' Billy said, 'you do not seem overly upset by it. I nearly drank myself into a stupor when I had to pay my addresses to Charlotte.'

Shaking his head, Samuel retorted, 'Of course, I don't wish to marry her.'

'I do not claim to read minds, but from the expression on your face, I am pretty sure what you were thinking about her would require marriage banns to be read. She is certainly a goddess of a woman, a pocket of Venus. Ah, and you do not like when other men compliment her either. Am I to understand that you do not want her, but you do not want another man to have her?'

Samuel's hands clenched into fists and his school friend laughed merrily at his expense. 'Of course not.'

'A piece of wisdom, Duke,' Billy said, the first time he used Samuel's new title. 'Lie to others, but never to yourself.'

Clapping him on the shoulder, the prince left for the

card room. Billy was overly fond of drinking, gaming, womanising, and, if the rumours were true, male lovers. He did them all with the enthusiasm of a king. Turning back to see Frederica, Samuel noticed that Colonel Scovell was by her side. The colonel was a man of lower birth who had risen in the ranks with his excellent cryptography skills. In the Peninsula, he'd decoded the Great Paris Cipher and employed army guides as intelligence officers.

Samuel sauntered over to them. Scovell was around forty years of age and quite bald on top with thick sideburns running down his cheeks. His small eyes were keen and Samuel doubted that the man missed any detail. He was Wellington's spymaster after all.

The colonel bowed to Samuel. 'Colonel Lord Pelford, I was just becoming acquainted with your betrothed. I would never have guessed that Lady Frederica was English. Her French is flawless.'

His betrothed gave the spymaster a beaming grin and Samuel doubted that the man was thinking about her French conjugations.

'I am a lucky man, Colonel Scovell,' Samuel said slowly. 'Lady Frederica is a very accomplished young lady.'

Frederica's eyes danced with mischief. 'And you have not even seen me with a pistol, sir! Back at Hampford Castle, I could even best the duke in marksmanship.'

He had expected the proper gentleman, with an even primmer wife, to be shocked by Frederica's unfeminine talent, but it was interest and not censure in the man's countenance. He appeared pleased.

Contrarily, Samuel did not want Frederica to please any man but himself. Taking her elbow tightly, he nodded to Scovell and tugged her towards the dance floor. Like most insipid English balls, it started with a quadrille. He did not release his hold on her arm until she was standing in the right formation and he took his place next to her. The musicians began to play and Frederica weaved through the figures with him.

'That was a cavemanlike manoeuvre,' she whispered when their hands met. 'A gentleman, even a duke, is supposed to ask a lady to dance before dragging her onto the floor.'

Clearing his throat, he felt the blood rush to his face. Frederica did bring out the basest parts of his personality. His spite, resentment, jealousy, and uncontrollable desire. He wanted to grab her and tell everyone in the room that she was his.

They were not allowed to look at her.

Or touch her.

Mine.

Samuel had never known himself to lose control of his emotions or his body before. He did not wish to be a wanton like his father, giving in to his primal lusts to the point that he ignored his responsibilities as a duke and his duties to the family. Samuel wanted to be better. He needed to be the sort of duke and father that his brother could look up to.

Like the Duke of Hampford.

While his own father had been whoring in town, Frederica's father had taught him how to ride a horse, fish, shoot, hunt, swim, and race a curricle. He'd loved going to Hampford Castle in the summers and helping care for the menagerie of animals. He had enjoyed every part of it except for a loud, irritating girl that had followed him around like a golden retriever. She'd demanded to do whatever her brothers and Samuel were doing. And no matter how hard he and Charles tried to shake her, Frederica always found them. She even parroted what they said like their annoying yellow macaw with a missing claw, Mademoiselle Jaune. But what was worse, she always beat him at everything. She was a faster swimmer. A lighter rider. A better aim and swifter on her feet, but that was before she had grown in quite the opposite directions.

Frederica's gaze met his.

'Please forgive my rough handling,' Samuel said, holding her hand for an instant longer than he should have. 'I promise that it will not happen again.'

He would not be like his father. He would remain in control of his body. His emotions.

Wrinkling her nose, Frederica grinned at him. 'I was only teasing, Samuel. I rather liked your caveman treatment.'

'Shall I throw you over my shoulder and drag you to a nearby cave?'

She held her breath. A beautiful blush growing up from her neck and into her face. For all her talk of love and kisses, she was still innocent in the ways that mattered. 'I would say yes, but I do not think we would make it past Mama. As you can see, she has placed herself near the door to the gardens. We will not escape so easily this time. It will be difficult for you, I'm afraid, but you'll be forced to speak to me using real words, instead of grunting like a gorilla.'

His entire body bristled at the comparison to a great ape.

'Alas,' Samuel said in a voice barely above a whisper. 'Talking with you is like speaking to a magpie.'

Frederica shook her head. 'Unoriginal. I expected better from you. But since we cannot converse politely, I suppose we will have to dance instead.'

The hair rose on the back of his neck. Waltzing would have to do, but he wanted to be closer to her. To silence her saucy mouth by tasting her sweet flavour on his lips. Making polite conversation with Frederica was nearly as agonising as a battlefield wound and twice as deadly.

Chapter Seven

Rubbing the sleep from his eyes, Samuel yawned again. He had stayed up too late dancing the night before and keeping an eye on his badly behaved betrothed. Frederica had flirted outrageously with every man she met. From fortune-hunters to generals. She even blew Samuel a kiss when she was dancing with the Prince of Orange. He tried not to react to her blatant attempts to infuriate him. Even as a little girl, she had always been able to get underneath his skin and get him into trouble.

He kept thinking of their stolen kisses from the first ball she'd attended in Brussels, wishing to repeat the experience. Dreaming about it. Her lips were more practised than any incognita. Her shapely figure would be the envy of any woman. And Frederica was too clever by half. All the mischief that she could get up to in Brussels kept him tossing and turning all night long with his desire for her. Frederica was strong, independent, and completely beautiful. He would have to keep an eye on her to save her from falling into scrapes. They were not in England any more and she couldn't rely on her family or her name to keep her out of trouble.

'A word, Pelford,' General Lord Wellington said.

Samuel followed him to his office. Wellington was a tall man with brown hair and brown eyes under thick brows. His nose was rather large and had a distinctive bump. His lips were thin and pressed tightly together. Despite his air of authority, he was a warm, kind man who cared deeply about his staff members. He made Samuel feel like family. Like he was wanted. Like the words that he spoke mattered.

'In the situation that we are placed at present,' the general said, 'neither at war nor at peace, we are unable to patrol the enemy and ascertain his position by view, or to act offensively upon any part of the French line. All we can do is put our troops in such a situation as, in case of a sudden attack by the enemy, to render them easy to assemble, and to provide against the chance of any being cut off from the rest.'

Samuel sighed, nodding. Their position felt precarious.

Rubbing his nose, Wellington cleared his throat. 'Colonel Scovell has an idea, and after ruminating on it, I think it is rather a good one. I should like for you to travel farther into Belgium and meet with Lieutenant-Colonel Grant and bring back his findings.'

He forced himself to keep in a groan. Samuel had worked with the surly Scotsman before. He was a fine intelligence officer, but he made no attempt at stealth. Dignity or not, Samuel's life would be in danger if he was seen in that man's company. At seventeen, death did not scare him. At four and twenty, there was so much he still wished to do.

Samuel took a sharp intake of breath. One did not say no to the general. 'Of course, Duke.'

General Lord Wellington pressed his two hands to-gether until his fingertips turned white. 'I have also heard that congratulations are in order. It took a few weeks to arrive, but I saw the notice of your nuptials in *The Times*.'

He could feel his cheeks growing hot and his collar shrinking around his neck like a noose. He pulled at it. 'Thank you, Your Grace.'

'And I believe that your betrothed, Lady Frederica Stringham, is now in Brussels with her mother.'

'Yes.'

An unwanted and unexpected wave of jealously swept through Samuel. The general was known to like beautiful women. More than like them. Despite being married, he collected mistresses wherever he went. And women seemed to be drawn to a man with power.

Wellington's smile did nothing to ease his discomfort. 'I hear she is a spirited young lady and Scovell suggested that you might wish to bring her with you, when you meet with Lieutenant-Colonel Colquhoun Grant to pick up his reports. It should allay suspicion from your intelligence activities. Hopefully, people will assume that you are going on pleasure rides with your betrothed.'

He did not know if spending more time with Frederica would be a good thing or not. When he was with her, Samuel could never decide if he would rather wring her neck or kiss her. Or both at the same moment. She loved to infuriate him, and even after all this time, she knew how to press all his buttons. Even if Frederica drove him to the brink of madness daily, he still did not want anything bad to happen to her. It would be dangerous to travel farther into Belgium and be seen in the company of a British Army officer. And he doubted Frederica understood the meaning of the word *caution*.

Swallowing heavily, Samuel said, 'I think Scovell's idea is a clever one, but I do not wish to put a lady in danger.'

'Scovell remarked that Lady Frederica spoke French flawlessly,' the general pressed. 'I do not think the danger will be too great. He believes, as do I, that you both will be able to blend into your surroundings. And if anyone notices you, they will only see a young couple devoted to each other.'

Desiring each other was more like it, but he would not dream of telling his superior that.

'Yes, sir.'

Wellington cleared his throat. 'I should like for you and Lady Frederica to meet Grant tomorrow at midday in the town of Genappe. At a public house called The King of Spain Inn. There, he will give letters for me and perhaps more instructions for you.'

Samuel tried to swallow again, but could not. It was as if there was a ball in his throat obstructing his breathing. He saluted the general. 'We will be there.'

He left Wellington's office and went to the room that had a map of the Continent. He placed one finger on Brussels and the other on Genappe. It was close to seventeen miles by road—it could hardly be considered an afternoon jaunt. Even cutting through fields the journey there and back would take nearly seven hours. Not that he thought Frederica wouldn't be more than able to do it. The Stringhams were a hardy set that swam in freezing rivers and wrestled with wild animals. A thirty-four-mile ride would be nothing to her.

After fetching his hat and gloves, Samuel called for his horse and rode to the rented house on Rue de Lombard where Lady Hampford and her daughter were staying. It did not surprise him that it was one of the nicest and most opulent townhouses in Brussels. The Stringhams spared no expense when it came to their own comfort, or that of their guests.

Harper, the Stringhams' butler who had once helped him down from a tree after Frederica dared him to climb it, opened the door. When Samuel asked to speak to Lady Frederica privately, the man grinned and acted like he was assisting in a grand love affair. But the butler could not have been more wrong—this meeting was strictly army business. Harper ushered him into a sunny parlour and bid him wait for his betrothed.

Frederica opened the door a few minutes later, wearing a thin wrap over what appeared to be her nightgown. Only his betrothed would meet a visitor thus arrayed. Or rather, disarrayed. The prim garment buttoned up to her neck, but it did not hide her gorgeous figure or the fact that she had recently risen from bed. Her lustrous brown curls were falling in waves over her shoulders and down her back. Her hair was as untamed as she was. And there were no cosmetics on her face, but her countenance appeared fresh and fetching. Samuel's fingers itched to touch her skin.

She yawned widely, stretching her arms out. 'I hope someone has died. Otherwise there is no good reason for you to have got me out of bed before I have even had time to drink my hot chocolate.'

Samuel's lips twitched. 'Alas, no one has cocked up their toes. I am here at the Duke of Wellington's request. He wants you to do something for him.'

Frederica raised both eyebrows and stepped closer to him. Her breath smelled like mint. He wondered if she had just eaten some. Samuel would not have put it past the proper Harper to give her the herb. The butler thought that this was a romantic interlude after all.

She pinched his left arm sharply. 'If you're having me on, I will murder you.'

Raising his eyebrows, he lifted his free right hand. 'I swear that I am not jesting or pranking. General Lord Wellington requested you by name.'

Moving her hands, she grabbed his lapels and pulled him closer to her until her body brushed his chest. She was most certainly not wearing a corset and a wave of longing shot through him. He took a sharp inhale of breath and tried to think of England. It did not work.

'Tell me. Tell me. Tell me,' she repeated, her lips close to his.

For a moment, Samuel could not think of anything except for how much he longed to kiss her lips. Touch them. Suck them. Bite them.

Frederica pressed the full length of her body harder against his and he could have spontaneously combusted right there on the spot. 'Samuel, please tell me!'

Shaking his head, he managed to clear his mind enough to say, 'The general would like for you to accompany me to pick up letters from an intelligence officer in Genappe.'

She blinked her long eyelashes twice before squealing loudly enough to wake the entire house. 'He wants me to be a spy!'

Most people thought spies were dishonourable; trust Frederica to want to be one. She threw her arms around his neck and hugged him roughly. His whole body was on fire for her.

Trying to keep his wits about him, Samuel said, 'You are not a spy. The appropriate term is an intelligence officer and you would not be one. You are simply going to accompany me to get the letters. Your presence is to allay suspicion from locals.'

Frederica laughed and pressed a hot kiss underneath his ear. 'Oh, Samuel, I have always wanted to do something truly important and I would love to be a spy for the army.'

She nuzzled his neck and he found himself placing his hands on her waist, pulling her closer to him. Frederica's lips made a slow burn from his neck to the corner of his mouth, pausing a hair before reaching his desperate lips.

'Say that I am a spy and I will kiss you.'

'Companion.'

Giggling, she kissed the other side of his face, near his mouth. 'Not good enough.'

'Intelligence officer,' he whispered.

Frederica kissed his chin with a giggle. 'Spy or nothing!'

Looking into her hazel eyes, he knew he would tell her anything when she was in his arms. 'Fine. You are a spy.'

Her lips pressed against his open ones and her tongue entered his mouth. Her lips ravaged his as her tongue stroked his, finding the most sensitive spots in his mouth. When she moaned against his lips, Samuel knew that she was going to be the death of him. Her fingers moved from his neck to his hair and roved through it, claiming everywhere she touched. He knew when her silken mouth slanted over his again, that Frederica was not a novice kisser, but an experienced one with great technique. He had never felt such a thrill. Not on his first horse ride or sailing with the wind in his hair. It was like learning how to kiss all over again. Frederica had remade the art into her own.

Unmarried young ladies were not supposed to be experienced, but Samuel did not care. No, he enjoyed the fact that she knew how to set them both ablaze. Nor did he care about any of the men she might have kissed or the women that he had. They were all in the past. And not worth remembering.

Frederica broke the kiss, but stayed encircled in his arms. They were both breathing heavily. Her face was beautifully flushed from the kisses. Samuel felt a surge of possessiveness that he had never experienced before. She was his now.

'When do we start?' she asked breathlessly. Her breath against his lips.

'Tomorrow morning at nine o'clock,' he said, kissing her neck beneath her ear. 'And we probably won't be home until four or five o'clock in the afternoon. Be prepared for a long and hard ride.'

'I look forward to it,' Frederica said with a giggle, and he realised that his words had a double meaning. A proper young lady would never make such a euphemistic jest, but he had always known that his betrothed was anything and everything but proper. Which in this particular moment did not seem like such a bad thing.

He forced himself to step back from her, his control already slipping, and the butler was just behind the door. 'Try to be dressed next time when I come.'

She smiled at him saucily. 'Are you sure that you would prefer that?'

Rendered speechless, he left the room without a word and was escorted to the door by Harper. Touching his swollen lips, Samuel realised that the butler had been right after all: it had been a romantic rendezvous.

Chapter Eight

Frederica descended the narrow wooden stairs thirty minutes to nine o'clock the next morning. She wore a lavender riding habit with two rows of brass buttons down the bodice, giving the article of clothing a military look. It was all the rage in London fashion this year. She donned a matching lavender bonnet with feathers that looked more like a sailor's tricorn than a feminine hat. Clutching her reticule, she ensured that her pistol was there and loaded.

Frederica politely asked Harper to call for her horse to be saddled.

The butler bowed to her. 'Shall I have a groom saddle up a horse, as well?'

She shook her head. Spies did not bring along servants. 'No, thank you. Samuel, I mean Lord Pelford, will be my escort.'

The good man raised only one eyebrow. 'Are you sure your mother would approve, my lady?'

Huffing, she hated when Harper caught her behaving badly. Frederica shrugged her shoulders nonchalantly. 'He is my betrothed. It is quite unexceptional for us to go on a ride together.'

'How long will you be gone?'

Holding in her groan, she realised that whilst it might be perfectly acceptable for a suitor or a fiancé to ride with a young lady in the park, it was quite another thing to travel for several miles across country with her. They would not be home until late in the afternoon. And Harper was her friend and not a fool.

'Harper, Samuel has asked me to help him with secret military business. I might be gone for seven or eight hours. Could you cover for me?'

The butler gave her a studied look. Harper had known her since she was a child and could usually tell when Frederica lied. Luckily, this time she was not. 'Very well, Lady Frederica. But be very careful.'

'I am always careful.'

Harper raised one eyebrow again and gave her a dubious look. He knew her too well.

'Fine,' she said with another huff. 'I will be *very* careful. The soul of caution.'

Frederica thought she heard the dear butler mutter that she was *the soul of mischief.* But that did not stop him from calling her a horse and holding the door open for her when it arrived. Jim, her favourite groom, helped her into the side-saddle just as Samuel came down the street. He was not in uniform today, but dressed in a dark riding coat with five shoulder capes. It was severely cut and made him look very handsome. She thanked Jim and gave the butler a wave goodbye, before urging her horse towards her betrothed.

She winked at him saucily. 'I am clothed and ready as requested.'

A little colour stole into Samuel's tanned cheeks. He was obviously attracted to her and Frederica liked having this power over him. When they were younger, he had treated her like an annoying fly that buzzed around him. He either ignored her or tried to swat at her. Now he was practically drooling over her. That Samuel was equally desirable to her, she did not focus on. Or that she had spent the rest of the day after he left thinking about his kisses. He did not need to know that. Being a man and a duke, he already had the upper hand in their arrangement.

'You look—fine,' he said, his eyes avoiding her entire person.

Frederica grinned, directing her horse near his. 'We haven't got all day.'

Samuel nodded, turning his horse around in a circle. Together they weaved through the streets until they had left the city of Brussels. She made to turn onto a small gravel path. Wisely, Frederica had consulted a map for the location of Genappe after he'd left the day before, but Samuel checked her. He told her they would save a mile by cutting through a few fields. She allowed him to lead the way and Frederica revelled in jumping over several fences. They returned to the road and passed the small village of Waterloo. It was not much to look at and nothing worth stopping for.

Over three and a half hours later, Frederica reined in her horse outside of The King of Spain Inn. The building was two stories high and had been painted a crisp white. The only colour was a small black sign, three feet by three feet, that proclaimed the name of the inn. She was relieved to have finally arrived, for her thighs were becoming a bit sore. She was not used to riding this far or hard during a typical London Season. But she would have died rather than admit her weakness to Samuel. He could use it to tease or mock her.

Frederica allowed Samuel to assist her down from her horse and she had to bite her lower lip to keep from groaning. Together, they strode into the taproom of the bar. She tried to walk as normally as possible. A small Belgian man who was several inches shorter than Frederica bowed deeply to her, his long nose almost touching his knees. Samuel requested a private parlour and tea. The owner bowed lowly yet again and directed her to a side chamber with a large window that filled the room with natural light. A round table was placed in the centre of the room and had six chairs around it. The walls were whitewashed and simple, without adornment, but the parlour was clean.

'Monsieur, my betrothed and I are expecting a British gentleman. He is going to help us with our marriage contract. Could you please bring him in here when he arrives?' Samuel asked in French.

The small man nodded vigorously and executed another low bow. Within five minutes, a young waiter with fair hair and innumerable red freckles entered with the tea tray. He set it on the table and asked if the gentleman and lady required anything else. Frederica replied in French before Samuel could that they did not. She wanted to show her fiancé that she spoke French as flawlessly as he did.

Frederica prepared the tea and poured Samuel a cup and then herself. She enjoyed the hot sensation down her throat as she drank it. Somehow, she felt the comfort all the way down to her sore inner thighs. She hoped the British spy would be slow to arrive. She wasn't ready yet for another long and hard ride.

Samuel drained his own cup. 'You're still a bruising rider.'

She could only be glad that she had not mentioned how stiff she was. She realised that it had been seven years since he had seen her ride. 'Did you really join the army to get away from me? My brothers said that you did.'

His cheeks turned as red as a soldier's coat. 'You shouldn't mention that I am a soldier whilst we are here.'

Blushing, Frederica realised that she was not being a very good spy. 'You still have not answered my question.'

Picking up the teapot, he poured himself another glass. The colour in his cheeks fading. 'Believe it or not, Freddie, not all of my life decisions were based upon you.'

She hated that nickname which Matthew sometimes called her and Samuel knew it. She wanted to growl at him like a wolf, but then she would have childishly risen to his bait. She refilled her own teacup. 'Nor have I based my life decisions on you, my sweet baby angel Sammy.'

It was the endearment his mother called him and he hated it more than anything. Hence, Frederica had loved to call him that as children.

Wincing, he took another sip. 'Shall we call a truce on names? I won't call you Freddie and you will refrain from calling me Sammy?'

'Bargain,' Frederica said, holding out her hand. 'Shall we shake on it?'

'I'd rather kiss on it.'

She cursed her fair cheeks, for her body agreed that

was a *much better* way to seal a bargain. But before Samuel could kiss her, there was a knock on the door. They leaned away from each other, both a little breathless.

'Come in,' Samuel said in French.

A gentleman in his mid-thirties entered the small private parlour. He wore a wide-brimmed hat that hid his eyes. His nose was large and straight and his lips a thin straight line. He was neatly dressed in a scarlet uniform with a white cross on the chest.

Samuel and Frederica rose to their feet.

'Lieutenant-Colonel Grant,' Samuel said, bowing. 'Please allow me to present my betrothed, Lady Frederica Stringham.'

She beamed at the man and gestured to the chair. 'Do please sit down. I have never met a real spy before.'

He sat at the table next to Samuel and accepted a cup of tea from her, but his body stiffened at the word *spy*. Oh, dear. She should not have said that word either.

'I am no spy, my lady. I do not believe in subterfuge.'

Disappointed, but undaunted, Frederica asked, 'Do you invariably wear your British uniform while collecting information in France?'

Samuel snorted, but did not say anything.

Grant set his cup down on his saucer with a clatter. Frederica feared he might shatter them both. The china was too dainty for such handling. Her mother would have given the man, spy or no, a sharp reprimand.

'Of course. I am a man of honour.'

He also appeared to be a man who thought quite a lot about himself. This brought a small smile to her lips, but she quelled it. 'But is it not dangerous to proclaim your allegiance by your clothing?'

'This is no place for a lady. But I will have you know that I have never condescended to sneaking about in civilian clothing. And when I was captured during the Peninsular War, my companion who wore plain clothes was shot, whereas I was brought to the general and treated according to my rank.'

Samuel cleared his throat. 'Have a care, Grant, on how you speak to a young woman that also happens to be a lady and the daughter of a duke. Lady Frederica is here at General Lord Wellington's request.'

Frederica handed the intelligence officer a tray of scones. 'I am glad that you were spared, Lieutenant-Colonel.'

Grant grunted at this, but dropped his scone on the table and rifled through his satchel. He handed Samuel a stack of grubby papers. Standing, the spy drained his cup of tea and took his half-eaten scone in his hand. He saluted with it. 'Be here next week. Same time, Colonel Lord Pelford.'

'Very good,' Samuel said, but did not bother to stand as their brusque guest left the small parlour with a slam of the door.

Frederica watched him straighten the papers before placing them in a satchel that he wore around his neck and shoulder. She eyed Samuel closely. His movements were controlled and he did not seem at all alarmed that they were carrying intelligence documents. He had always been terribly brave. It used to annoy her. Samuel never once refused one of her brothers' dares. Even if he did break his foot in that dark cave.

His gaze met hers. 'Sorry about Grant. I have met him a few times before and the fellow is insufferable. He should have treated you with more respect.'

'When you proposed, I asked about your war experiences and you were equally disdainful.'

She watched as he pulled at his cravat.

Samuel's brow furrowed and he shook his head. 'I don't remember.'

'I do,' she said, swallowing and holding up her fingers as she quoted, *'"They are not fit for a woman's ears".'*

Frederica expected him to be embarrassed, not to laugh. But he did and loudly. The sound did something to her inner organs.

He grinned at her. 'I am surprised you didn't box my ears on the spot.'

Her fingers touched her parted lips. 'I wanted to.'

Taking a deep breath, he sobered. 'Forgive me, I was angry and out of sorts that day. I only remember feeling as if I had no choice and resenting it. I know that your ears and the rest of your very beautiful body are more than capable of anything that you set your mind to.'

She could only blink at him. Frederica felt surprised by his apology and his compliment. She had not expected either from him. Moving her hand to her throat, she felt the quick stutter of her pulse and the fluttery feeling in her stomach. 'And do you still resent me?'

He licked his thick lips, making her wish to kiss them. 'I never resented you. I resented that my father's debts did not allow me to make my own choice.'

Sipping her tea, Frederica realised that her cup had gone cold. She set it down on the saucer with a little clatter. She thought of Lady Caro and the other women who had flirted with Samuel at the parties and balls. 'Who would you have chosen?'

As soon as those words left her mouth, she regretted

them. Her heartbeat thundered in her ears. She did not want to hear about a dainty and well-behaved, but less wealthy, young lady that he preferred to her.

'I do not know.'

His answer was better than she could have hoped for, but still disappointing. She knew it was irrational, but she'd wanted him to say her. She wished to be his choice. Frederica got to her feet, her body stiff from her earlier ride, but she could not show Samuel any of her weaknesses. He knew too many of them already.

'Come on, sloth,' she said in a falsely chipper voice. 'We've got a long ride back home and poor Harper can only cover for me for so long.'

They returned to the taproom, where Samuel dropped several coins into the small man's hands. They left the inn, and the innkeeper assured them that he had fed and watered the horses and that they were ready for the trip home. Samuel threw the lad a coin and then assisted her into the side-saddle of her horse. His hands on her waist made her feel strangely breathless. And for once, she actually needed the help. Her leg muscles cramped something awful.

She stroked the neck of her horse and spoke soothingly to it. 'There there, girl. We are almost done.'

If only she could assure her own body of the same thing.

Samuel mounted his mare with ease and they took a more leisurely pace back towards Brussels, only passing a few carriages and wagons. Frederica reined in, placing her right hand over her eyes to get a better view of the area—mostly farms, a few stray trees, and a small blue lake. Her eyes alighted on a black stallion with a slim rider that galloped furiously towards them. Instinctively she gripped the reins of her horse tighter, but then she relaxed them when she saw the face of Captain Mark Wallace.

He rode up beside her and took off his tall hat. 'Good afternoon, Lady Frederica, Colonel Lord Pelford. Off for a bit of exercise?'

She grinned, sighing in relief. 'Yes. And what a superb specimen! Such shoulders and so perfectly black.'

Mark touched his chest. 'Alas, for a moment I was hoping you were talking about my humble self and not my cousin's horse.'

'I hope you haven't stolen it,' Samuel said in a gruff tone.

'No indeed,' he assured them with a confident smile. 'The Duke of Wellington is keeping all of his staff, including my cousin Alexander, so busy training the new recruits that I thought to do him a favour by exercising his horse.'

Frederica raised her eyebrows. 'Is Alexander aware of your kind favour to his beautiful horse?'

Mark winked at her. 'As of yet, no.'

'Perhaps I can ask the general to find something for you to do, Captain,' Samuel said stiffly. 'If you have so much spare time on your hands.'

Frederica's grin widened until it hurt. Despite not choosing her, Samuel seemed quite territorial over his bride-to-be.

'But what of my poor cousin's horse? Someone must take care of him.'

She laughed merrily. 'We are on our way home, Mark. Should you like to accompany us?'

'With pleasure.'

Samuel groaned as Mark brought his horse parallel

to hers and they cantered together to Brussels. He told her blithely about his family's castle in Scotland, his perfect elder brother, James, and cut several jokes at his own expense. He begged to go riding with her again, before bidding her a merry farewell at her door. Samuel was unable to get a word in edgewise. He just scowled at them both. Nor did he bother to tell her goodbye.

Harper opened the front door of the rented house and Frederica saw her mother descending the stairs in a cotton day dress with a little red flower print.

Mama yawned. 'Good heavens! Have you gone riding all afternoon? You should take a short rest before the party tonight. I do not want you looking fagged.'

'Yes, Mama,' Frederica said dutifully and gratefully went upstairs to her room.

Chapter Nine

A few days later, Samuel saw Frederica jumping a high fence on her horse, as if she knew the Belgian countryside as well as her own castle. She was always heedless and fearless like that. Samuel took the same fence on his own horse. Urging his mount to a gallop to catch up with her, he overtook her groom first and then reached her. At least Harper had not let her go out alone. Frederica had a way of twisting people around her little finger.

'What do you think you are doing?' he demanded in a loud voice.

Not at all perturbed, she beamed back at him. 'Oh, hello, Samuel. And I thought it was rather obvious— I am riding.'

Samuel shook his head, a stiffness in his jaw. 'I know that you are riding, but what are you doing jumping unknown fences in a foreign country?'

Frederica slowed her horse down to a trot and glanced over her shoulder at him coquettishly. 'I ride every morning for exercise. I do not know about you, but the ride to Genappe left me quite sore in the most unmentionable places.'

His eyes descended to her curvy body for a moment before he forced them back up to her face. Despite not choosing her for his wife, he wanted Frederica more than was decent. Few women could boast her perfectly balanced and generous curves. And like a courtesan, she seemed to know how to display her figure to the most advantage. In addition, she loved embarrassing him and he too easily fell into her traps. She'd wanted him to stare at her figure and he did.

Pressing his fist to his mouth, he said, 'What if you fell and broke your neck?'

She shrugged her shoulders and raised her eyebrows. 'Then you wouldn't have to marry me after all.'

The thought of not marrying her annoyed him even more for some reason. He clenched the reins tighter. 'You should be more careful. There are all sorts of unsavoury characters about.'

'Like yourself?'

Samuel grimaced. After all these years, Frederica's words still managed to needle him. 'You didn't find me so unsavoury the other day when we kissed.'

She raised one eyebrow. 'Which one were you again?'

He opened his mouth, but then closed it.

Frederica let out a peal of laughter. 'You've always been too easy to tease! Shall we have a race?'

'Very well.'

Glancing back at her groom, she said, 'Jim, you may go home and tell Harper that I am in Lord Pelford's company.'

He doffed his hat to her. 'Very good, my lady.'

Turning back to Samuel, she pointed to a white farmhouse in the distance. 'The first one to jump the fence wins. On your mark, get set, go!'

He watched her spur her horse onward at a spanking pace. Samuel had a little more experience over the terrain and wanted to save his horse's energy for the final gallop. Frederica led the entire race, over the fields, and past a road. Leaning forward, he squeezed his horse's flank with his boots. His mare responded by increasing her speed and flying over the fence, a length ahead of Frederica's grey. Samuel walked his horse a few more yards before turning back to her. The race had brought colour into her cheeks and she looked beautiful.

Frederica grinned at him. She angled her horse next to his and bumped his shoulder with her own.

'Oh, good race, Samuel.'

For all her faults, she was never a sore loser.

'Thank you.'

'I do not know about you, but I am famished! Shall we buy some bread and cheese from the farmer and have a picnic?'

'I need to get back to my duties,' he said gravely.

Frederica laughed in his face. No soldier would have dared to do such a thing. 'I almost believed you for half a moment. You do take yourself rather seriously, don't you? Is that why you do not discuss politics with women?'

Samuel shook his head. 'Must you dredge that up again? I only said that to avoid an argument with you. I am sure if I tell you that I am a Whig, you will proclaim yourself a Tory. Or vice versa.'

'I *am* a Tory and please do *not* try to stop arguing with me. I love quarrelling with you. You have always been such a worthy foe.'

She slid off her horse, tied it to the fence, and walked

off merrily to the barn behind the farmhouse. Huffing, he followed her, half hoping that the owners would rebuff her request. The Belgian farmer was in his late forties, with a scraggly beard that reached his waist, and after a few words exchanged in French, he treated Frederica like his daughter. He ushered them into the house, where a woman wrapped them a loaf of bread, a wedge of cheese, and a carafe of milk. Frederica thanked the woman profusely and paid her with a gold coin. He could not help but be impressed by Frederica's fluency and accent. She sounded like a local and not an aristocratic one.

Frederica held up her newly purchased wares and gave him another smile. The farmer handed him a blanket and told Samuel to be sure to return it.

'I will keep him in line and make sure he does,' she said in French, winking.

Both the farmer and his wife laughed.

Frederica led the way from the farmhouse to a large tree on a slight hill. 'This is the perfect place for a picnic.'

Samuel laid out the blanket, and before he could assist her, Frederica lay down on it and stretched out her arms. 'I am exhausted. I did not see you at the Nottinghams' party last night, but there were plenty of officers there. We frolicked until the early hours of this morning.'

'I am sure you danced with them all.'

She shaded her eyes with one hand. 'Oh, I did!'

Sitting down beside her, he leaned against his elbow. Samuel could not remember the last time they had simply sat together, relaxing. Then he felt her fingers crawl up his side and tickle him just below the arm at his most sensitive spot. He laughed and yelped, trying to grab her hands. But all Stringham girls were experts at torturing boys and she evaded his grasp, causing him to laugh even harder until he could barely breathe. Even then she did not show him mercy, but straddled across his lap and began to tickle his other side.

'You're still ticklish here!'

'Stop! Stop!' he managed between laughs.

Surprisingly, she did. Frederica's eyes widened as she realised that she was all but sitting on his lap. A becoming blush stole into her cheeks, but she did not retreat. He didn't think she knew how to. Instead, she leaned forward and pressed her lips to his. Again, Samuel could not breathe. Her mouth slid over his insistently, until he opened his own and deepened the kiss. Despite already being on the ground, he felt like he was falling. Hard. Fast. And out of control. That was how Frederica always made him feel, but for once he did not fight it. He surrendered. There was no feeling in the world to compare it to. No thrill was equal to this pleasure.

Then just as abruptly as she started it, she ended the kiss. Frederica jumped off him and opened the picnic basket as if she had not been kissing him moments before. She tore off a piece of bread and handed it to him. 'Our second course, Belgian bread.'

He sat back up. 'What was our first?'

She grinned at him, her eyes dancing. 'English lips. Ever so much better than cow tongue.'

He laughed. He loved her wit. Taking a bite, Samuel discovered that the bread was soft and delicious. He tried to concentrate on the flavour and not the fact that Frederica had been on top of him moments before.

She certainly knew how to torment a man, but she always had.

Samuel took a drink of milk from the carafe—there were no glasses. 'Tell me more about yourself. What are your interests? What do you like to do? I feel as if I know everything and nothing.'

Frederica took the jug from his hand and pressed her lips where his had been only moments before. 'What a good line! Have you used it on many ladies?'

Squeezing his eyes shut, Samuel should have known better than to try and converse like an adult with her. 'You are impossible!'

She let out a high trill of laughter. 'Now that is a phrase I do recognise, for you have said it about my poor self at least a hundred times.'

Ripping off a piece of cheese, Samuel ate silently. He was not about to rise to her bait again.

Frederica continued merrily, 'I discovered Mr Foxworth, the latest London poet, going around to different young ladies and comparing them to Miss Elizabeth Bennet from *Pride and Prejudice*. And I can assure you that line worked wonderfully well on myself and many a lady. It was a trifle disappointing to both my heart and my pride that he had not truly meant it.'

The poet's description was not entirely inaccurate, his betrothed was certainly a headstrong girl.

She took a few bites of bread before speaking again. 'Have you read *Pride and Prejudice*?'

As a matter of fact, his mother had sent him a copy in Spain. He had read it out to his fellow officers and they all enjoyed it greatly. 'Yes.'

'I am going to need more than monosyllabic responses if we are going to get to know one another better as adults.'

'Is that what we are doing?'

Frederica waved her chunk of bread at him. 'You asked to know more about me. I love to read. I have just finished reading all the novels by Maria Edgeworth, but Miss Austen's novels are my favourite. *Pride and Prejudice* is a particular treat because there are five sisters in it. And I do think that my sister Mantheria would make a most excellent Jane. And Elizabeth's wit and beautiful singing was just like my late sister, Elizabeth. I miss her every day.'

Her elder sisters were twins, but Elizabeth had died when she was only ten years old. She had been a bright young girl who sang more than she spoke. Samuel had wept when Elizabeth and Charles had died from scarlet fever. Charles had been his dearest friend and so young, only in his first year of school.

'Unfortunately, as the third that would make me Mary,' Frederica continued, counting on her fingers, 'and I cannot help but see some similarities between us.'

'You are anything but plain,' Samuel scoffed.

She smiled at him, but there was a wistfulness in it. 'That is nice of you to say. But Mary plays the pianoforte, like myself, and she tries so hard to be something more, only to be a figure of fun. A caricature of a young woman.'

He had no response. He did not know how a bright and talented young woman could become something more. The most that she could hope for was to be known as a brilliant society hostess and possibly help write her husband's parliamentary speeches. There was no place in politics, business, education, or even the arts for a woman of high birth to succeed. Even though Frederica played the pianoforte with the flare and feeling of a professional, it would never be more than a talent to 'exhibit' at a party.

After a few moments of painful silence, he said, 'Does Becca still draw caricatures? I recall her being very talented at them. Or has she relinquished rodents for suitors and soldiers? Like Kitty and Lydia Bennet?'

Dropping her head, she laughed. 'No. Alas, no. You are right. My two younger sisters are nothing like Kitty and Lydia. Helen and Becca are still more in love with mice and snakes than they are with men. And I do not think Helen could flirt even if her life depended on it.'

He snorted. 'Then it is a good thing that she is always carrying a snake. Perhaps it could save her.'

Frederica wrinkled her nose as she smiled winsomely. 'I am sure she and Becca are finding all sorts of reptiles in Greece. How I wish I was there with them.'

'And not here with me?' The words were out of his mouth before he could stop himself.

Picking up his hand with both of hers, she squeezed it. 'Oh, I am having a lovely time here with you. It is only that sometimes as the middle sister, I feel a little left out. Like poor Mary Bennet. Becca and Helen are closer to each other than they are to me. And Mantheria has always been a bit aloof emotionally since Elizabeth died. She has never tried to make me her confidant. Even when I travelled with them to Italy, she kept everyone at a very polite and correct distance. She is still playing the role of the perfect daughter and duchess. It must be exhausting.'

Samuel understood how she felt. Ever since Charles

died, he had not known where he fit with the Stringham sons. Wick and Matthew were a pair and he trailed behind them. Not that the Stringham brothers had been anything but good to him. He was never bullied at Eton because of Wick, and if he ever needed help with his studies, Matthew had been kind enough to tutor him. But it was not the same being the third person—the one on the outside of the pair.

'They all love you.'

'I know,' she said, bringing his hand to her cheek and rubbing it against her smooth skin.

'I felt the same way when Charles died,' he said in a quiet voice. 'My brother, Jeremy, is so much younger than me, and Charles was like a brother to me. And I resented when you tried to fill his place when we were children.'

A tear slid down her curved cheek as her lips smiled. 'No one could ever fill Charles's place. He was nothing but light.'

Nodding, he swallowed heavily. 'I do not think that I have been very good at letting people close to me since then. I have many friends but, like you, no confidants. And sometimes I think it is easier not to care as much, especially in the army. You bury your friends and must continue on without them.'

'Since you know *everything and nothing* about me,' she whispered, 'could you let me become a close friend? I promise that I will keep your secrets.'

The words had not been a studied line. No other flirtations would ever be like speaking to Frederica. The other women played by the rules and Frederica made her own. They had been childhood enemies, but now could they be friends? Should he trust her with the burdens of his soul? How his mother had leaned on him at such an early age that it was crushing? Could he tell her the truth about his father's life and death? The real reason that he had joined the army. But shame filled his throat and the words would not come.

'When I know more of your nothings, I can tell you my everythings,' he said lightly, steering their conversation away from the deeply personal.

Releasing his hands, her expression became guarded and civil. 'I also devour every Gothic romance I can get my fingers on. I think I have read almost every book in the lending library. Stories help alleviate the boredom of the Season.'

Society and the Season were safe topics. Impersonal ones. He raised one eyebrow. 'You do not enjoy the London Season?'

Frederica took a drink of milk, before shrugging one beautiful shoulder. 'I do not mind it, per se. It is just for once I would like to do something that truly matters. Not simply spend the bulk of my time thinking about my wardrobe and whether or not I will dance every set… Mama used to read out your name in Wellington's dispatches about the important things you were doing. As you know, Papa does not care about politics or wars, but he would always ask her to read it again. He was ever so pleased to hear of your successes. It irritated me to no end.'

A slow smile built upon his lips. She had managed to make the conversation personal again. 'Your father is a good man.'

Leaning forward, she kissed his cheek. 'And he thinks that you will be a great one.'

Touching his face where her lips had briefly resided, Samuel felt himself blushing. Lord Hampford had been his mentor growing up and he could think of no greater compliment. He only wished his own father would have thought of him so highly. That Papa would have been the sort of man that he could look up to and not the cause of his family's shame.

Chapter Ten

Once Frederica's fingers found their places on the keys of the pianoforte, the guests, and the room around her, faded into the background. It was just her and Beethoven having a most marvellous battle for musical predominance. Chopin was too subtle for her taste and Bach too orderly. But Beethoven knew how to wring every bit of feeling out of each note. She loved his minor chords and dissonant cadences. She would never tire of playing his music. Of being transported away to somewhere entirely new.

With one last crescendo, she finished the piece with a flare. Frederica lifted her eyes to glance back at the crowd. It was mostly members of the *ton* with a few foreigners of the highest rank in the mix. Her mother was a notable hostess and even being in a different country did not stop her from being selective in her invitations and expansive in her wine list.

Standing up, Frederica feigned as if she were leaving her place at the pianoforte, knowing full well that she would be asked to play another piece for the company. It was, however, extremely gratifying when none other than General Lord Wellington begged her to favour them with one more. Sitting back down, she pressed the keys loudly to begin Beethoven's 'Piano Sonata 23'. If anyone had fallen asleep, they would be awake now. Her fingers moved quickly on the keys, faster than even her mind could keep up with the notes. Oh, how she loved becoming one with the instrument.

She played the complicated piece until the tips of her fingers were sore. The sound of clapping brought her back to reality with a most unpleasant thud. She slid back on her long dinner gloves, bowing and smiling as she accepted compliments. Georgy took her spot at the pianoforte and began to sing and play a sweet, uncomplicated tune. She had a lovely voice and her fingering was good. Frederica could not help but realise that the audience enjoyed Georgy's simpler performance more than her own. She clapped louder than the rest when her friend finished and was happy that Georgy was asked by Wellington as well to favour them with another piece.

A small, ugly part of herself had to admit that she wished that she was the only person to be asked by the general for a second song. And that the guests would have realised that her performance was equal to a professional male musician. It was not merely a pretty accomplishment to display, Frederica was truly talented and worked extremely hard at practising. Shaking her head, she tried to rid herself of such petty thoughts. They were beneath the person she wanted to be.

'You were extraordinary,' Samuel whispered from behind her. Frederica's knees felt like jelly as he placed a hand on her waist and she could feel his warm breath on her ear. Butterflies danced in her belly. It was terribly annoying that he had this effect on her.

Turning, he kept his hand on her waist. They were standing at the back of the room and everyone else was politely listening to Georgy finish her second song. It was a Scottish air with a playful lilt.

'I didn't notice your arrival.'

It was not the wittiest sentence she had ever uttered, but it filled the silence and the space between them. Their noses were close enough to brush against each other and the bottom of her gown draped over his boots.

'You were well occupied,' he whispered. 'No one could fail to notice you in a room.'

Frederica's eyes lowered to his lips. They were wet, as if he had recently licked them. She would have liked to lick them as well, but she could hardly do that in the middle of her mother's soirée. 'Are you trying to flatter me?'

Samuel brushed his mouth against her cheek in the lightest of touches. 'Possibly. Is it working?'

All too well.

'I missed you today.'

The words were out of her mouth before she could stop them. She could not allow Samuel to know how much she wanted him. She had learned that lesson at the age of eleven: the more she pursued him, the faster Samuel fled. No, she had to make him come to her. Keep him on his toes. 'Fortunately, Mark was around to keep me company. He even let me take a turn riding on Alexander's stallion.'

His hand dropped from her waist and she missed the warmth of his touch and the tender look in his eyes. Lifting her chin, she stood beside him as Georgy finished her song and Lady Anthea took her turn.

Their shoulders occasionally brushed each other,

but the gulf between them felt as large as the English Channel. Perhaps it always would be. Samuel had not chosen her. It was different than when they were children and she'd had to fight for his attention, following him around like a loyal dog. All the terrible tricks and mean words had been her way of getting him to notice her. It was negative attention, but at least he could not pretend as if she didn't exist. Frederica had thought he didn't like her because she was always dirty, bedraggled, and in trouble. At fourteen, she had still been very naughty, but had become more clever about it. Her clothes and hair were tidy, and her womanly shape had already begun to show. Yet, still Samuel had avoided and ignored her more than ever before.

Putting a bear cub in his room had been the final straw, Frederica had made certain that he could not pretend that she was not there any more. Alas, being mauled by claws and requiring stitches did not endear her to him. Samuel hated her more than ever and a few months later he'd joined the army. He did not write to her even once. Or even to her family. She had severed the connection by her unseemly behaviour. Her desperate attempts to get him to see her.

Her arm brushed his, but Frederica was still not certain that Samuel could see her. Or if he wanted to. She knew he noticed her figure, but was he simply making the best of a bad situation? Did he kiss her because she was convenient, or because he felt something for her? And would he ever see her as a friend? A confidant?

It was beyond silly, but after all these years, she wanted him to choose her. Pursue her.

He was so close. But so far from her.

The dichotomy of proximity and distance pinched

at her soul. How could she endure a life of having him near, but not holding his heart? Somehow, she doubted that every bottle of perfume and bar of red scented soap at Duchess & Co. could make up for the lack of love in her personal life. But what could she do, other than what she was doing? Making him work for her kisses and try for her touches. And maybe, just maybe, he might grow to care for her.

Lady Anthea finished her second piece and everyone clapped. The older gentlemen made a swift retreat to the card room with some of the matrons. The chaperones, eligible young ladies, and unattached soldiers stayed in the main room and mingled. Frederica and Samuel stood silently by each other.

'Did your mother send you *Mansfield Park* too?' she asked, desperate to fill the quiet between them.

Nodding, one side of his mouth quirked up into a smile. 'She did.'

'It was my copy, or rather, I sent her both *Pride and Prejudice* and *Mansfield Park*. She must have posted them on to you. Did you read *Mansfield*, as well?'

Samuel swallowed. 'I read it out loud to my soldiers, but we did not enjoy it nearly as much as *Pride and Prejudice*.'

Shifting her weight to one side, she leaned slightly against him. 'I agree. Miss Fanny Price is a very dull character. She is entirely too good. It would have been a much better book if Miss Mary Crawford had been the heroine. She was clever and funny and just the right amount of naughty. Alas, wicked girls are not given happy endings.'

'No indeed. And good girls are given marriages based on their moral behaviour. Miss Elizabeth married Darcy with ten thousand pounds a year and Miss Jane, although good, only got five thousand pounds with Mr Bingley.'

How clever he was!

Frederica grinned, saying, 'And Lydia got Wickham with only his profession to maintain them.'

'And your Miss Mary Crawford received no marriage proposal at all.'

Sighing, Frederica shook her head. 'Precisely. 'Tis most unfair. A man does not have to be virtuous to get a happy ending in a book. Take Tom Jones for example. He was more promiscuous than a tart at Haymarket and he still got Sophie and a fortune in the end.'

Samuel laughed loudly, as if he was genuinely amused by her observations. A few people glanced their way and Frederica felt her colour rising.

'I am surprised, although I know that I should not be, that you have read *Tom Jones*. It is not considered proper for young, unmarried ladies.'

'My parents have never kept any knowledge or books from us,' she said, touching one of her burning cheeks with her gloved hand. 'Good or bad.'

'The problem with most books is that no person is wholly good or bad. We are all a mixture of parts. Take General Lord Wellington for example, he is an excellent military leader, but a terrible husband.'

'The same could be said of the Prince Regent,' Frederica added. She had always felt sorry for his wife, whom he openly despised. His parents should not have forced him to marry his first cousin to pay off his debts. The only good thing to come out of their marriage was their daughter Princess Charlotte, who would one day become queen.

'And I do believe that wicked young ladies deserve happy endings,' Samuel said with a wink. 'But for Miss Mary Crawford, her happy ending would be to elope with the heir, Tom Bertram. Edmund was a dull dog after all. She was much too entertaining to spend her life as a vicar's wife.'

She laughed so hard that she snorted.

Frederica touched his arm. 'You are right! Miss Crawford deserved at least an eldest son.'

Picking up her hand, he tucked it in his arm. 'Shall we go and find the refreshments? I have yet to have my dinner and if we stand here much longer, I might be forced to eat you.'

Frederica could not hold in her giggle. Samuel was hardest not to like when he was witty. 'I suppose so, however, I am not afraid of your bite.'

His eyelids lowered and he whispered, 'I'll remind you of that the next time we are alone.'

'Please do,' she said primly, even though a proper young lady would never say such a thing.

She guided him past the refreshment tables down the stairs and to the kitchens. The light desserts on display would not satisfy a man of his size. In French, she asked the chef to prepare a plate for Samuel. Then they shocked both the English and Belgian servants by sitting at the kitchen table. Samuel ate his chicken like a man who had not tasted food in a week.

'It is a good thing that I didn't know how voracious your appetite is,' Frederica said, raising her eyebrows. 'When I offered to let you bite me, I was thinking of little nibbles.'

A blush stole into his cheeks, but Samuel smiled

at her. 'I have had nothing to eat since this morning. I have been too busy.'

Leaning closer to him, she asked, 'May I ask how?'

She steeled herself for his rebuff as he shook his head slowly.

Samuel cleared his throat, dabbing his mouth with a napkin. 'There is too much to do and not enough soldiers to do it. The dispatches we retrieved from Grant say that Napoleon will go on the offensive to avoid a four-front war. His first target will be us and our allies the Prussians.'

She touched her neck. 'What size is the French army?'

Biting his lower lip, Samuel sighed. 'Currently over two hundred thousand and they are all volunteers—veterans from Napoleon's previous wars.'

'And the British forces?'

'Wellington has called it *"an infamous army, very weak and ill-equipped, and a very inexperienced staff"*.'

Frederica bristled at this, offended on Samuel's behalf. Reaching across the table, she placed her hand on his arm. 'Surely, he does not mean that you are inexperienced. You were also his aide-de-camp in the Peninsular War.'

Covering her hand with his own, Samuel sighed again. 'Thank you, Frederica. When he said it, Wellington did not mean me, Gordon, or Fitzroy, nor his returning staff from the Peninsula, but rather Sir Hudson Lowe. Horse Guards made him chief staff officer without consulting the general. Wellington has written home to complain, but there may not be time before the battle to replace him.'

Frederica did not precisely know how a general's staff worked and it did not help that her mind was equally focused on the pleasant weight and pressure of Samuel's hand upon hers. Even more so now that he was finally confiding in her. She could not let this moment pass. Cudgelling her wits, she managed to ask, 'Is Lowe's incompetence keeping you busy?'

'We are in a very bad way,' he admitted, rubbing his thumb over her fingers. 'We have not one quarter of the ammunition which we ought to have, on account of the deficiency of our drivers and carriages. Our soldiers are inexperienced and ill-equipped. I feel as if I spend from sunup to sundown putting out fires instead of preparing for the upcoming battle.'

Her stomach hardened. Had her presence in Brussels made his life more difficult? She watched him finish off his plate and asked if he would like more.

Samuel gave her a tired smile. 'No, thank you. The general expects us to attend parties and keep up appearances. It was much easier in the Peninsula when we did not have the *ton* watching our progress like a scene in a play.'

'Do you wish I was not here?'

He stood up slowly, like a man twice his age. He must be exhausted. 'I should wish you safely in England, but I am selfishly glad you are here. There is no one else that I'd rather spy with.'

Frederica linked her arm with his. 'You mean intelligence officer with.'

'Call me a spy and I will kiss you,' he said, repeating her words from that fateful morning.

Glancing around the kitchen, there were servants coming in and out. There was no place to be private.

'Scared?' he taunted softly.

Drat, Samuel! He knew that she would never back down from a challenge. Especially not one from him.

Bold as brass, she lifted her chin. 'My Lord Spy.'

With one hand, he cupped her face and angled his mouth towards hers. His kiss was light and sweet, tasting of red wine and decadence. His teeth gently tugged on her lower lip as he broke the kiss. He did bite her after all and she loved it.

'And I do not think that you are a wicked girl,' he said, caressing her cheek. 'I think that you are a different one.'

She gave him a sad smile. 'To the *ton* they are the same thing.'

Samuel twirled one of her curls on his finger. 'You will have such a happy ending that all the books you have read before will pale in comparison.'

Her gaze met his. For once, he had left her speechless. Her heart was pounding like a cannon in her chest and her pulse was racing as if she were going into battle.

'There you are,' Mama said from behind them. 'I have been looking all over for you, Frederica. Your presence has been missed.'

Lady Hampford's expression appeared stern at first, but Frederica knew that she was pleased to see them together. She gave Samuel a knowing smile.

Stepping back from Samuel, Frederica went to her mother. 'Sorry, Mama. Samuel missed dinner and he was positively famished. He nearly ate the curtains.'

'And the chairs,' he added helpfully.

Mama did not appear at all convinced by their flummery. 'I am glad Samuel was not forced to such dire straits. This house has been let after all. The younger members of our party appear a little dull. I thought that you two could begin the dancing.'

Frederica grinned. 'But who will play the piano-forte?'

'You are not the only one who is proficient,' Mama said in her most duchess-like voice. Her mother did not practise often, but she did play well.

Frederica grabbed Samuel's hand and dragged him back up the stairs to dance with her.

Chapter Eleven

Samuel wasn't riding the next afternoon in hopes of running into Frederica.

No.

Of course not.

Why would he want to do that, when he had danced with her three times the night before? The Duchess of Hampford had indeed been a proficient musician and played for nearly two hours while the younger couples danced jigs. Alas, she seemed not to know any waltzes; however, she overlooked Samuel squiring Frederica for a third dance. Only two was considered proper.

He certainly had not woken up early to complete his lists of tasks for the general so that he would be free for most of the afternoon. His horse clearly needed the exercise and Samuel had unaccountably developed an interest in locally made cheeses. He had discovered that no two farms' wares tasted alike. Something he would not have known if Frederica hadn't insisted on visiting a new farm around Brussels each day. With or without him.

And perhaps he had also grown accustomed to a certain young lady's enthusiastic kisses. They no longer felt like falling, but flying. Each kiss sending him closer to the hot sun. Until like Icarus, his wings would melt.

'Yoo-hoo! Samuel!'

He turned to see Frederica and her groom riding towards him at speed. She probably never allowed her poor horse to walk. No. Frederica ran towards life with an exuberance that left uproar in her wake.

'I found us a new farm.'

Samuel reined his horse around to meet hers. 'And cheese?'

She smiled at him and something inside of him broke and was remade. 'The most delicious cheese.'

'Shall we race there?'

Shaking her head, Frederica said, 'No. No. I am tired of losing to your mare. But perhaps we can have a shooting contest when we get there. Jim brought empty bottles for us.'

Sure enough, Frederica's groom had a bag slung around his shoulders and Samuel could hear the clinking of bottles. 'I don't think that shooting in a war zone is wise.'

She leaned over and rubbed his horse's nose. 'What is wise, is rarely fun.'

Samuel half wished that she would rub his nose. What an absurd thought! 'Come, I'll let you lead the way this time.'

Throwing him an arched look over her shoulder, Frederica grinned and cantered towards a large red barn. Instead of stopping, she passed it and rode on until they came to a blanket with a picnic basket underneath a tree, near a wooden fence. She had been waiting for him, and for once, he didn't mind being her prey.

Dismounting, he tied the reins of his horse to the fence. 'What would you have done if you hadn't met me?'

She pushed back her bonnet and let her wild, curly brown hair fall in tresses down her back. 'Found another handsome officer to share my picnic with me.'

He would not rise like a fish to her bait this time. 'You find me handsome.'

Finishing her knot, she grinned at him. 'Very. Which is most fortunate, because we are being forced to marry by our *wicked* mothers.'

His mother's illness was not her fault. 'My mother isn't wicked.'

No. His poor mama carried the burden of her husband's profligacies. And if she had leaned too heavily on him when he was younger, who else did she have? When she first became sick, Jeremy had been toddling about in short coats. Even at a young age, Samuel had wanted to help her. To be someone that she could depend on. And if Mama sometimes cried to get her way, he could not fault her. All the blame rested with his father, who was six feet under.

Frederica giggled, placing her hands on her face. 'My mother is delightfully wicked and I would not want her any other way. She could outbargain the devil himself.'

Lacing her arm with his, she pulled him to the blanket and asked her groom to go to the nearby field to set up the bottles for their shooting match. Alone they ate their picnic and Samuel could not help but yawn several times. In response, Frederica grabbed his head and pulled it down into her lap, stroking his hair. Samuel felt like a contented cat. He had no desire to leave her lap, nor for her to stop touching his curls. She even took off her gloves and he felt her soft skin against his. Closing his eyes, he could have purred.

'Poor Samuel, you look so tired.'

He nodded, unwilling to open his eyes or his mouth.

Frederica continued to stroke his hair. 'I wish that I could help you more.'

Samuel only made a sound in response—a mix between a moan and a sigh. Then he felt her lean down and nip at his ear. His eyes popped open in surprise and he turned his head.

Frederica was above him, her head haloed in light, smiling. 'Do you mind terribly that you have to marry me?'

He blinked. Truthfully, he did not mind at all. In fact, he could barely wait to say his vows and make her his in every possible way. But he was not stupid enough to tell her that. She would only tease him more. 'I can think of worse fates.'

She wrinkled her nose. 'Truly?'

'No.'

Frederica leaned down and pressed her lips lightly against his, tantalisingly brushing them over and over his mouth. He reached his hand up to cup her face and pull her down to him. His tongue slipping between her lips as she gasped. He tasted her moan more than heard it as his tongue stroked hers and teased the sensitive spots in her mouth. Not breaking the kiss, she twisted until her body was lying next to his. Her hands moved to his hair and her fingers raked through his curls. Samuel could not help but deepen the kiss, rolling his chest on top of her soft one. Her curvaceous figure always set him on fire. Pausing for breath, he made a trail of kisses to her neck and then her ear. He licked the lobe and then nipped it, like she had his.

She yelped and wiggled out of his hold. His head hit the ground on the blanket as if waking up from a delightful dream to reality.

Frederica got to her feet, brushing out the wrinkles on her skirt. Her hair mussed and her cheeks flushed. She looked as if she had been properly kissed. 'I only kiss young men who wish to marry me.'

Samuel sat up, running his hands through his own messy hair. Perhaps it was for the best that their embrace ended when it did. Their kisses were growing more frantic and his control was almost gone. He would not be promiscuous like his father, even if Frederica had him hot under the collar all the time. 'And what do you do with young men who don't wish to marry you?'

She pulled a pistol out of her reticule and blew on the barrel. 'Shoot them… Shall we have our match? Jim is waiting discreetly away from us. He's such a dear.'

Frederica offered him her hand and Samuel let her help him to his feet. He went to his mare and took the pistol out of his pack. He would need a weapon he felt familiar with if he wanted to give her a proper match. At Hampford Castle, not even her father or brothers could beat her in a shoot-off.

'If I recall, you're a rather good shot.'

She beamed back at him. 'I am the best.'

'We shall see.'

They walked thirty paces from the fence. Samuel allowed Frederica to shoot first. She barely aimed her weapon before firing it. A green bottle exploded off the fence.

Frederica grinned, pointing her smoking gun at him. 'Your turn.'

Samuel cocked his pistol back and took a few moments to aim, before squeezing the trigger. His shot hit the top of a clear bottle, but it was not central enough to shatter the entire glass. As a boy, he had hated losing to her. But as a man, he could appreciate her rare skill. 'Your point.'

She shot five more times. Each time she hit her mark. Samuel had never seen Frederica's equal with the pistol in any officer in Wellington's army. He was not a bad shot and hit his mark three times, but she never missed a bottle. Each time she aimed, the glass shattered. Frederica beat him handily and her groom, Jim, clapped, hooted, and hollered. The young man was clearly on her side.

'Good match,' Samuel said, giving her mild praise. Nothing annoyed her more. 'You are a fair shot.'

He returned to the picnic blanket and picked up his hat. A bullet whistled past him and he dropped it. Turning, he saw that Frederica had shot his hat out of his hand. He picked up his hat and put his finger through the hole. 'You could have killed me!'

'Don't be a ninny, Samuel,' she said, her hands on her hips. 'I have no intention of murdering you until after I have married you and provided an heir. How else would I be able to keep Farleigh Palace and all your ducal titles?'

Clamping his lips closed, he was determined not to smile at her words or her murderous wit.

Frederica threw back her head, laughing. 'Come on, Samuel, let yourself laugh. That was hilarious.'

His lips twisted up into a small smile. 'Macabre at best.'

She put her pistol back into her reticule. 'Perhaps I am better than *a fair shot*, would you say?'

'Perhaps.'

'Come on then, I have another surprise for you,' she said as her groom helped her mount her horse. 'I have arranged with the servants to give us a formal tour of the gardens and orchard at Château d'Hougoumont. It is quite lovely.'

He mounted his own horse and followed her to a large farmhouse with a garden enclosed behind stone walls and hidden from the road by trees. It looked like a small fortress. Frederica hailed a gardener, who took them through the wooden gate into a new world of flowers and flora. The garden was well-ordered in rows, but had a sense of whimsy. When they reached the orchard, Samuel paid the gardener and groom to go away. He pressed Frederica up against a flowering cherry tree and kissed her until he could no longer think.

Chapter Twelve

The ride to The King of Spain Inn in Genappe did not seem as long the second time. Nor was Frederica so stiff that she could barely walk when she got there. Still, she allowed Samuel to help her down from her horse. And if she pressed her body against his by accident as she slid down, who could blame a poor defenceless young woman getting off a horse? She smirked even if she could not tell if he was groaning in annoyance or moaning in appreciation. The sound he made caused a fluttering in her chest that was almost painful.

The innkeeper recognised them on sight and gave her one of his extremely low bows. He quickly wiped his hands on his apron and led her to the private parlour. 'Tea for two?'

'*Trois,*' Samuel corrected as the man led them back to the private parlour.

Frederica flashed him a wide smile and winked at him. The innkeeper's red face turned even redder and he nodded vigorously. The next person to open the door was a waiter with a broken nose who introduced himself as Peters. He placed the tea service on the table and asked if they would like anything else.

'No, that is all. Thank you, Peters.'

She and Samuel had drunk two cups of tea before Grant arrived. His wide-brimmed hat shadowed his eyes, but his thick lips were pursed. He still donned his scarlet uniform coat, but it looked a little worse for wear. The cuffs were fraying and the fabric would have been all the better with a thorough washing.

'Ah, Lieutenant-Colonel Grant. We had almost given up on you,' Frederica said, pouring him a cup of tea and placing it on the table near his chair. 'I am afraid the tea may be a little cold.'

''Tis no matter,' Grant said sharply.

'My lady,' Samuel added tersely.

The intelligence officer's cheeks flushed a bright red as he added a reluctant 'My lady'.

The Scot clearly did not like her. Or perhaps, it was just that he did not approve of a woman assisting in intelligence work. If that were the case, then Frederica did not think very highly of *his* intelligence.

Samuel cast her an apologetic look and the fluttering pain in her chest returned. He had never stood up for her before and now he was defending her like a knight in shining armour. Somehow, she seemed to have grown on him. Her lips curved up in a smile as she pictured her little sisters comparing their relationship to a fungus. They would probably compare her to the carnivorous American plant: the Venus flytrap. And like that plant, once she had Samuel in her tendrils, she had no intention of ever letting him go. His assurance, which had once felt insufferable, she now found terribly attractive. She'd never doubted that he was a loyal son and brother, and a noble friend. If he cared for her, there was nothing that he would not sacrifice for her good. She could not think of a worthier man whose heart she'd like to hold. But she couldn't reveal her feelings for him yet. She needed to be sure that he returned her affections first.

'Anything to report, Lieutenant-Colonel?' Samuel asked.

Grant drained the rest of the tea from his cup before pulling out a wrinkled, sealed envelope from his coat. He handed it to Samuel, not sparing Frederica a glance. 'Same time. Same place. Friday.'

Samuel nodded, tucking the dispatch into his plain black coat. 'Very good, Grant. Good day.'

The Scot stood and saluted Samuel before leaving the room in the same abrupt manner that he had entered it.

Frederica delicately sipped her cold tea. 'I am afraid that Grant is not fond of me. I am not saying that it is undeserved, but usually that level of disdain is reserved for people who know me better.'

She watched Samuel rake his fingers through his hair.

He shook his head back and forth slowly. 'I do not think it is personal, Frederica. But rather, he knows how dangerous it is for you and he does not approve of me bringing you here. I do not blame his curtness.'

Lowering her head, she swallowed hard. 'Do you blame yourself?'

Samuel rubbed the back of his neck. 'Yes. No. I do not know. Wellington himself asked me to bring you with me and I could have told him no, but I did not.'

Frederica winced. 'Then you too wish that I was not here?'

His gaze met hers and it pierced into her very soul. 'No, I thought it was a good plan.'

Somehow his words made her feel worse. As if her ribs were growing tighter, making it impossible to breathe. She turned her head, breaking eye contact with him.

'And foolishly,' he continued, 'I wished to spend more time with you and I did not seriously consider the danger I was putting you in.'

Her chin jerked back up.

'You wanted to spend time with me?' She said it slowly, as if each word was a question.

'Well, we are about to be married.'

She hunched her shoulders and said in a small voice, 'A marriage that you do not want.'

Samuel's jaw was set in a tight line. 'Rather, a marriage that I did not choose.'

Frederica did not know what to think or how to feel. She had loved and hated Samuel for as long as she could remember. He infuriated her like no one else could. He also brought out her very worst side. The one that never failed to get her into trouble. But she'd still longed for his attention. His smiles.

'Perhaps you are hoping that I will be killed and then I will never be your wife.' She knew as soon as the words left her lips that they were petty and untrue. But she wanted to hurt him as he had pained her with his indifference. 'Then you can keep my mother's money and live happily ever after.'

With a perfect wife of his own choosing. Who was pretty and not petty or impertinent. Or wicked. Who followed the rules and allowed the man to lead while dancing.

Samuel clenched his fist and brought it to his face. 'It is far more likely that I will die in the following weeks.'

'You survived the Peninsular War,' she said in a small, gruff voice.

He shrugged his broad shoulders. 'It only takes one stray bullet and then *you* will not have to marry me.'

She tried to swallow, but there was a lump in her throat. Standing up, she surprised Samuel by sitting on his lap and putting her arms around his neck. 'Promise me that you will be very careful?'

His arms wrapped around her waist. His face close to hers. 'Are you saying that you wish to marry *me*?'

Leaning forward, Frederica kissed his nose. 'I wish to be a duchess. You happen to be a delightful addition to the title.'

'A side benefit?'

Kissing his cheek and neck, she murmured her agreement. She loved how his skin tasted. The friction of brushing her lips over the stubble of his cheeks. But nothing could compare with his mouth upon hers and his tongue tangling with hers for dominance. Neither of them would concede without a fight in this sensual war. Taking a quick breath before diving back in with another lip-bruising kiss, Frederica thought that perhaps she was winning this battle. Her fingers were in his hair, their bodies close together, and she knew in this moment that she could not bear to lose him. That any hate she felt for him in the past was overwhelmed by love. Samuel was her opposite. Her antagonist. But she would have chosen no other man to stand at her side. He was her equal. Her everything.

Samuel nipped at both her upper and lower lips. The sting of his bites gave both pain and pleasure.

Peters entered the room to take the tea tray and she jumped off Samuel's lap. Turning away from both men, she attempted to straighten her dress and her hair. Her neck and face hotter than the noonday sun.

She heard Samuel thank the waiter and the door close before she spun to face him.

Samuel's lips were red and a little swollen from her kisses. 'Clearly, that servant doesn't know the meaning of a *private* parlour.'

A giggle escaped her lips.

He took a step closer to her. 'And we were so comfortably situated too.'

She held out her hands to him and Samuel's larger ones encompassed hers. 'I still need your promise that you will be careful.'

Samuel brought her right hand to his lips and kissed it, then lifted the other and repeated the action. 'I will be as careful as a cat.'

'My father is a naturalist. I know that cats do not have nine lives,' Frederica protested. 'For once, do be serious. Promise me that you will do everything in your power to come back to me.'

'I promise,' he whispered, and the words felt more solemn and holy than vows spoken in a church.

Frederica felt too overcome to speak, so instead she flung herself into his arms and held him tightly. Wishing that she was brave enough to tell him how she truly felt. Hoping that somehow, he knew.

Chapter Thirteen

Samuel delivered the wrinkled dispatch directly into Wellington's hands. He was slightly curious to know what it contained, but knew better than to ask. The general would tell him what he wished for him to know.

Retrieving the dispatch was becoming more perilous, Samuel thought as he took a drink of water. The waiter, Peters, had entered the private parlour without knocking. Even the greenest of servants knew that they were supposed to wait before coming into a room. The Frenchman had a broken nose and the build of a bruiser. Samuel was pretty sure that the man had once been a soldier and that he was one still, or at least reporting their movements back to the French army. For all he knew, the innkeeper was also an informant.

He should not allow Frederica to continue accompanying him to The King of Spain Inn. Grant was right. It was not safe. But refusing Frederica something only made her want it more. She might even try to go without him. No, the best and only course of action was to go with her and remain alert. And he would need to tell Grant about his suspicions.

Frederica.

Samuel could not recall her becoming maudlin before. Yet, he was certain at the inn that she had been holding back tears and she made him promise to come back to her. From another young woman those words might have been the sentiment of a friend. From Frederica, they were practically a declaration of love. Who would have thought it?

What was even more surprising was that he was eager to marry her and not only to enjoy his husbandly privileges. Although, he would be lying to himself if he did not admit how eager he was to bed her. She had him running hotter than a buck in mating season most of the time. But it was more than desire. He enjoyed her witty tongue and not just for kissing. Her mind was rare and sharp. She would make a wonderful companion and an even better confidant. He could see them building a life together. Theirs would be a marriage of equals. Frederica's gifts and talents would complement his. Their children would grow up in a close and adventurous family, like the Stringhams, whom he had always been so envious of. He could see Frederica slowly transforming Farleigh Palace from a stately building into a warm home. Samuel would become the father that he had always wanted. One like the Duke of Hampford, who taught his children how to ride and swim and shoot. A father who hugged and loved his children. Who made them feel special.

If he survived the war.

Samuel had made her a promise that he could not keep. One that no soldier could. He only prayed that he would be lucky again. His mind whirled with painful memories. Fitzsimmons had not been so fortunate—

a sword through his chest. Neither had McGovern— a bullet to his head. Officers, soldiers, even drummer boys were lost in every battle. He could not depend on his former luck. No. He needed to share his confidences with her now. Before the battle. And he needed to write three letters in case he never returned home. He could not leave these words unshared. The first to his mother. The second to Jeremy. And the last to Frederica.

Taking out a sheet of hot press paper, he dipped the pen in the ink bottle.

Dearest Mama,
If you are receiving this, I am not coming home. Please know how much I love you and please forgive me for not returning sooner and helping you with the burden that you have had to carry on your own. I am sorry that I ran away, from home, from Father, and from our family.

He lifted the nib of the pen to his lips. Samuel had left home at seventeen, still a youth. But seven years in the army had made him a man. And now his brother was fifteen, nearly the same age. He hoped that he would be there to guide Jeremy. To help him when he overran his allowance or prevent him from being taken advantage of by the gulls and captain-sharps of society. To prepare him for a profession or a life in Parliament. One letter would not be nearly enough to convey all that he had learned to his brother.

'Skimping out on working, I see,' Slender Billy said, leaning on the door-frame.

Samuel set down the pen. 'Writing my goodbyes. I never got around to doing them before.'

The prince slunk into the room with the ease of a royal and sat on the edge of the desk. He lifted his fingers up and spoke in a mock, deep voice. 'I really believe that I have got not only the worst troops, but the worst-equipped army, with the worst staff that was ever brought together.'

Sighing, Samuel said, 'I see that you have been talking to Wellington. He is not pleased with any of the arrangements or appointments from the Horse Guards. Nor the promotions made by the Duke of York.'

Slender Billy folded his arms. 'I told you that you should have joined my staff. I have the best troops, the best equipment, and the best staff that has ever been brought together.'

A smile played on his lips, but Samuel tried to squash it. 'Is it better to be overly positive or pessimistically negative about one's chances?'

'Confidence is worth a cavalry in my opinion.'

'In your case, I should say it is worth three companies of cavalry.'

Billy laughed and gave Samuel a playful push on the arm. 'Shall we go out and dance, drink, and be merry before we die?'

Samuel got to his feet. 'Why not?'

Chapter Fourteen

Thanks to her rides with Samuel, Frederica knew every road that led into the great city of Brussels and all the good nooks and crannies for stolen kisses. This morning she did not see Samuel but Captain Mark Wallace, riding towards her on his cousin's black stallion. She waved to him, smiling.

Mark took off his hat, grinning back at her. 'Might I take the place of your fiancé this morning?'

She touched her hat. 'The position of fiancé is already taken, but you're welcome to be my groom.'

He bowed, still sitting on his horse. 'My dearest wish is to serve you.'

Frederica turned to Jim, thanking him, and sending him home. Then she pulled the reins of her horse to angle her mare next to his stallion. 'Shall we race?'

Mark pointed to a fence a couple of hundred yards away. 'First to the fence?'

'First over the fence,' she said, kicking her heels into the horse's flank and yelling, 'Giddyap.'

Frederica did not turn her head to see if he was following. She knew he was. Her grey was a beautiful animal, but it was not in the same class as Sir Alexander's stallion. If she had any hope of winning, she could not lose focus for a moment. She heard the other horse's footfalls behind her. Spurring on her own mount, she let her head fall back and wind rush over her face. It was moments like this where she felt truly free.

Weightless.

'Come on,' she urged her grey as they approached the fence.

Mark soared past her and over the fence, as if it were no more than a small stone in the road.

Her winded grey took the fence, but it was not a victory. 'I suppose you won.'

He grinned at her again. Mark was truly handsome, but he was not Samuel. 'Even after you cheated.'

'If you're not cheating, you're not trying.'

Mark laughed, a merry sound. 'Shall we return to the city?'

She nodded and they cantered together across a green field. Frederica pulled up on her reins when she saw Samuel. Her body was all shivers and tingles at the sight of him.

Mark checked the stallion as well and touched his hand with his chest. 'He's come to steal you away.'

'If you knew me better, you would want me to be stolen,' Frederica told him primly.

Laughing, he bowed his head to her and then to Samuel before riding away. Her betrothed looked furious. His full lips in a tight line. His broad shoulders back and tensed as if he was preparing for a fight. He was a stocky young man and Frederica was certain that Samuel could brawl with the best of them. Her brother Wick had taught him how to throw a nasty left hook.

'What were you doing with Wallace?'

She gave him an arched look. 'What do you think we were doing?'

He grimaced. 'Riding.'

'Nothing that naughty,' she said, shaking her head. 'We were racing.'

Samuel nodded, his expression still murderous. He did not seem to appreciate her euphemistic jest. 'And did you already find bread and cheese for your midday meal?'

'Not yet,' she said, pointing to a farmhouse near the road to Genappe. 'And we have yet to try the fare of La Haye Sainte.'

'Far be it from me, to keep you from your cheese.'

She clicked her tongue and urged her mare to a walk on the road. 'This farmhouse is not nearly as large, nor as grand, as Hougoumont.'

'I daresay the gardens aren't as secluded either,' he said dryly.

It was her turn to blush. Unwittingly, her fingers stole to her lips. Samuel had kissed her so thoroughly that day that she had forgotten where she was. He had pressed his hard body against hers and she had melted into his arms. And for the first time in any kiss or embrace, she had lost all control of herself. Of her feelings. Her heart.

When they reached the white farmhouse, Samuel assisted her off her horse and tied their animals to a fence. They walked around the picturesque farm and Frederica wondered if it would be the same after the battle. There was a sort of frantic energy in the air. Like the breath of wind before a mighty gale. Would it ravage this peaceful little farm and all those around it?

After the tour, she purchased some bread and cheese

from a farm worker. Samuel offered to pay, but she liked handling the money herself.

She broke off a chunk of bread and handed it to him. 'Shall we eat like heathens?'

Samuel had already taken a large bite and he said with a full mouth, 'Yeth.'

Frederica let out a trill of laughter and broke off a piece for herself. She liked that he had a large appetite like her. The bread was warm and flavourful and she chewed it slowly. She saw that Samuel had already swallowed his entire piece, so she tore off a large chunk of cheese and gave it to him. Tasting the delicious cheese slowly, she looked about her. She memorised the number of buildings inside the farmhouse enclosure, the doors to the courtyard, and the height of the walls.

Samuel looked at her quizzingly. 'I should dearly love to know what you are thinking.'

Turning back to him, she asked, 'Do you think the fighting will reach here? I was pondering if the walls and courtyard would give enough protection or if they would be a trap to be stuck in.'

He did not answer her immediately, but she didn't mind. He appeared to be considering her opinion and his answer like he had that night in the kitchen.

At last, he said, 'There is a high probability that there will be fighting at this farm and all the others round about it. In the coming days, there will be four armies and hundreds of thousands of men.'

She held up four fingers. 'The English, the French, the Dutch, and the—'

'Prussians,' Samuel said, taking her hand, 'who are our allies, but it is difficult for armies from different countries to fight together. It would not surprise me if lives were lost between ourselves. Lines get blurred. Guns and cannons fill the air with smoke. Officers get shot. Screams make orders hard to be heard and difficult to follow. It is impossible to keep track of every soldier during a battle.'

He caressed the top of her hand with his thumb, holding it in his lap.

'Are battles terrible?'

Samuel was silent and Frederica feared that he would snub her again, or shut her out of his deepest thoughts. He brought his free hand and set it on top of their joined ones.

'When I first enlisted,' he said slowly, 'I was too young and foolish to realise how awful they were. All the sounds and bullets were thrilling for a young man. I thought I was invincible and I fought like it. I even rose quickly in the ranks because I was foolhardy and fearless. But it does not take long for even the most daring of young soldiers to realise that many of his friends are dead. And that his bullets and his sword have dealt death to his enemies' family and friends. In those moments, precious and terrible, you realise the value of life, but you are forced to take it. Killing another person changes you. Murdering many people even more so. And it must, for we are breaking nature's laws.'

She had never thought about it that way. Like so many others, she had been blinded by the spectacle of fancy uniforms and the army parades.

Frederica squeezed his hand. 'You are not a murderer. You are a soldier, defending your country and other countries from cruel tyrants like the Emperor Napoleon. Any creature alive would defend its own. That is the true way of nature.'

He shook his head, regret lining his eyes and mouth. 'That is what the newspapers print and I hope that it is true, but that does not change the fact that I have taken countless lives. And I do not know their names or their situations, the most I can remember is their faces when they haunt my dreams. I wonder who they have left behind and if their sacrifice has any meaning at all. But mostly, if my life and sacrifice would have a purpose.'

Frederica moved her hands to cup his face, his square jaw a little scratchy on her palms. She loved the friction between them. Her eyes met his. 'Your sacrifice has meaning, Samuel. And your actions have made a positive difference in the world. You are a good person and a good soldier.'

Samuel closed his eyes and rubbed his cheeks against her hands. 'I did not join the army to get away from an unwanted marriage, Frederica. I joined it to get away from my father.'

Gasping, she dropped her hands, but he caught them in his larger, warm ones. He was not retreating behind his wall. He was opening himself to her for the first time. Showing his vulnerabilities and scars. If only she could be as brave.

He kissed the back of her hands. 'I should have told you that when you asked me before.'

Her mouth fell open and one word came out: 'Why?'

Dropping his gaze, he no longer met her eyes. 'I had not finished at Eton, when I stopped at my parents' home in London and found my father with a duo of Cyprians there. He offered to share one with me. I was shocked and ashamed. And then I saw the telltale sores on my father's hands. He contracted the French pox soon after Jeremy was born… How much do you know of the disease?'

Frederica could only shake her head.

'When one is first infected, sores form around their mouth and personal areas. They only last a few weeks and heal on their own, but it is just the beginning. Rashes, sores, and fever come next. Then it all goes away. Our family physician called this the latent stage. The illness has no symptoms for ten to thirty years, and then it returns for the tertiary stage, which affects your heart, blood, nerves, and brain.

'That night I entered our London home, I saw that the sores had returned to my father's mouth and hands. Yet he was still whoring around town, no doubt carelessly infecting others. I now understood why my mother kept rooms on the other side of the palace from my father. I left the house immediately and went straight to enlist as a common soldier. And I would have, if I had not run into Sir Alexander Gordon. He convinced me to purchase a proper commission and not a fortnight later, I was off on a boat to fight in the Peninsular War. I never completed my studies. Neither did I say goodbye to my mother or Jeremy. I just wrote a brief letter telling Mama that Father's pox had returned.'

'I knew about your father's illness,' she admitted in a low voice. 'It was my mother's idea that your mother tell people that the duke had had a stroke. His decline was slow and painful.'

He lowered his eyes, shaking his head. 'Not painful enough for what he did. I should have known your mother would have told you. I suppose you deserved to know what sort of family you were marrying into.'

Frederica rolled onto her knees and threw her arms

around her childhood nemesis's neck. Leaning her cheek against his, she shook her head. 'Neither of our mothers told me. I have always been a champion eavesdropper and I taught my little sisters all my tricks. But do not worry, I have never spoken of it to another soul. Nor will I ever betray your confidence.'

'Does it change how you think about me?'

She blinked. 'Your father's choices?'

He nodded his scratchy cheek against her smooth one.

'Of course not, silly,' she said, pressing a kiss against his cheekbone. 'You have always been a very different sort of man. There is no comparison between you, even if you have your father's build and colour of hair. Besides, if you were unfaithful to me, I would not live on the other side of the house or hide in the country, I would simply shoot you.'

Samuel let out a watery chuckle. 'I do not doubt it.' She felt his arms move around her waist and he gripped her tightly. 'Even now, I could not bear to tell my little brother the truth. I did not want him to have to carry the family shame.'

She squeezed him tighter. 'It is not your shame, nor Jeremy's, and you do not have to carry it.'

He buried his head into her neck, moving his head back and forth. 'I should have been there for my mother. I should have helped her. Instead, I ran away.'

She caressed his soft curls with her fingers. He seemed so vulnerable and she wanted to comfort him. 'You were little more than a child and your mother is a very capable woman. She managed to keep your father's condition and confinement a secret from all the *ton*. Your father's mistakes are not your responsibility.'

But as she spoke those words, she realised that they

were not true. The only reason that Samuel was marrying her was because of his father's choices. His debts. Samuel had not chosen her, but she had chosen him. Or at least, she had chosen to accept the bargain with her mother to marry him in exchange for the perfume business. Her hands dropped and she slowly backed away from him. She could not release him from his promise to marry her. It would break her heart to do so.

Frederica got to her feet, her knees a little shaky. 'I am feeling a bit thirsty.'

'Shall I ask that fellow for some water?' Samuel asked, standing beside her. His expression blank, retreating behind his wall of implacability.

'Oh, no,' she said with a forced smile, tucking an errant curl behind her ear. 'I am thirsty for something a little stronger. I believe there is an inn, not too far down the road. Shall we mount up and go find it?'

Samuel held out his arm and they walked back to where the horses were tethered. They led their animals to a trough and allowed them to drink their fill, before Samuel assisted her into the side-saddle. He mounted the magnificent horse, and they rode to a small inn called La Belle Alliance. The paint on the exterior of the building was chipping, and there was no private parlour. Frederica waited in the saddle while Samuel went inside and purchased two tankards of ale. He handed one to Frederica, and she sipped it cautiously. It burned down her throat and she coughed as black spots filled her eyes.

He took several large gulps and laughed at her. 'Not had much experience with tap drinks?'

Taking another sip, she made a face. 'I do not think I have missed much.'

Samuel held out his hand to take the tankard and drained it. 'I shall see if the rascally barman has any milk.'

He returned with a glass of milk.

Frederica took a hesitant sip. It was a little tepid, but otherwise tasted familiar. 'This is much more to my liking.'

She finished the glass and he kindly took it back inside the inn. They set off for Brussels in silence. Samuel had shared his most intimate secrets with her. His shame. And she had been unable to comfort or absolve him. She could not even kiss him, even though she'd wanted to. She was just another burden that he did not want. That he did not choose.

When they reached her house, Samuel helped her dismount her horse and handed the reins to Jim, who stood waiting.

'Shall I see you tomorrow night at the King and Queen of the Netherlands's fête?'

She cocked her head to one side. 'To be sure.'

'May I have your first waltz?'

'I am afraid Captain Wallace has already claimed that dance, but you may certainly have the second.'

'Why do you dance with that Scottish fellow so much?'

'We are discussing military secrets, of course,' Frederica said with a laugh and walked into her house on Rue de Lombard.

It was obvious from the expression on Samuel's face that he did not believe her. Jealousy looked rather good on him.

If only honesty became her.

Chapter Fifteen

Frederica had attended many parties with her mother
since arriving in Brussels, but none that impressed her
as much as the King and Queen of the Netherlands's
fête. It was truly a splendid affair. The rooms were
filled with men in a colourful array of fancy dress uniforms. Countless chandeliers hung from the ceilings
and their candles burned brightly. She was introduced to
the King and Queen of the Netherlands and danced the
first country dance with the Prince of Orange. A slender but handsome young man with receding chestnut
hair and a winning smile. Unlike Samuel in every way.

'It is a great honour to dance with you again, Your
Highness,' Frederica said as they made their first turn
of the set.

'No, no, Lady Frederica. I have been most eager to
get to know Samuel's fiancée better and could not resist the opportunity to spare myself a dance with one
of the old high-ranking frights.'

Raising her eyebrows, Frederica giggled. 'A prince's
lot is a hard one.'

Prince William smiled broadly at her and agreed

readily, 'One is always forced to dance with and talk with people whom one would least wish to.'

She shook her head. 'That terrible fate is not reserved only for princes.'

· They parted in the dance and circled back to each other. The prince was an elegant dancer. He took her hand and led her in a promenade. 'Well, truthfully, I only dance with a few of them, and then escape to my English friends in the card room.'

Frederica opened her mouth in pretend shock, bringing her free gloved hand to her chin. 'For shame! How long have you known Samuel?'

'Since Eton. Smashing good fellow. No better soldier in the entire Allied forces. I only wish he were my ADC instead of Wellington's, but the duke would not dream of parting with him. Ah, there he is.'

Samuel walked into the room and Frederica was not the only one whose eyes were upon the handsome, broad young soldier. Lady Caro broke from her circle of admirers to greet him at the door. She must have chosen him to be her newest victim now that Lord Byron had spurned her. Frederica had disliked the dashing matron before; now she positively hated everything about her. From her painted toenails to her dampened chemise meant to show every line and curve of her figure.

The music ended and Frederica thanked Prince William for their country dance and then he escorted her to the side of the dance floor where her mother was standing. Her hand was immediately claimed by Georgy's brother, Charles Lennox, the Earl of March. He was a tall, agreeable-looking young man with brown curly hair and matching eyes. He was also a superb dancer, something that she would have appreciated at any other ball but this one. She wanted Samuel by *her* side, laughing at *her* wit, and touching *her* arm.

Over his shoulder, she saw Samuel and Caro join the dancers. For half a moment, Frederica contemplated calling Lady Caro out for a duel. Her mother had once told her a story about how Lady Almeria Braddock took offence at a comment Mrs Elphinstone made about her age and they had a duel in Hyde Park. Both ladies missed their marks with pistols, so they moved on to swords. Mrs Elphinstone was wounded in the arm and promised to write an apology. Swords or pistols, Frederica was more than willing to give Lady Caro a flesh wound. Frederica would not miss with her pistol. Nor would she apologise.

'I feel as if I know you already, Lady Frederica,' Lord March said. 'Georgy talks about you so often.'

She gave him a simpering smile. 'All good things, I hope.'

'The very best and I hear that you are to be congratulated on your engagement to Colonel Lord Pelford. Samuel's a splendid fellow. I only wish Georgy could find such another.'

Frederica felt her body temperature rise. 'Perhaps you should be congratulating him on his engagement to *me*.'

Wiggling his eyebrows, Lord March let out a bark of laughter. 'The reports did not do you justice, my lady.'

Unless the rumours were from Georgy, Frederica was certain that they were not favourable to her at all. Spinning, she decided to change the subject. 'Is it true that you have a bullet inside of you?'

Charles pointed to his puffed-out chest. 'Right here.

Shot at the Battle of Orthez in 1814. It was never re-
moved.'

'Does it pain you at all?'

'Not a bit. I do not notice it at all.'

After Charles, she danced with Mark. But not even
his wit could make her smile. Frederica tried to stop
her eyes from searching the room for Samuel. Unfortunately, she found him with Lady Caro clung to his
arm like she was drowning in the sea.

When the dance ended, Mark escorted her to Georgy's
side instead of her mother's. Georgy shooed her cousin
away and linked arms with Frederica. They walked
around the edge of the ballroom together. Frederica resisted the urge to rub her sleepy eyes. All the late nights
and early mornings were catching up with her. She could
barely keep her eyelids open.

Georgy whispered in her ear, 'Take care how you
flirt with Cousin Mark and my brother, or you shall
lose your Lord Pelford to Lady Caro.'

'She is already married and a notorious flirt. Besides, he must be several years younger than her,' Frederica countered. Unlike Samuel, jealousy was not a
colour that favoured her.

'You're right and I have heard it rumoured that she
is still obsessed with that limping poet who was all
the rage.'

'Lord Byron. Mama does not approve of him at all,'
Frederica said. 'But he might be respectable now that
he married Miss Annabella Milbanke, Lady Caro's
cousin. Now that is poetic revenge.'

Georgy squeezed her arm. 'I do not care about Lord
Byron. I think you are a great fool if you do not stop
Lady Caro from adding him to her string of conquests.'

'What do you suggest I do?'

'Smile at him. Talk with him. Flirt with him. He is your fiancé after all,' Georgy said, steering her to Samuel, who was still standing by the infamous Lady Caro.

'I'd much rather kiss him,' Frederica muttered truthfully.

Samuel arrived late to the King and Queen of the Netherlands's fête. He paid his respects to the current monarchs, then entered the ballroom, where he looked for Frederica. He saw her dancing with Billy, the Prince of Orange. Her hazel eyes flashed with mischief and her cheeks were flushed with excitement. He had not seen her since yesterday and he realised how much he had missed her in that short time. He'd started to walk towards her when he felt a slender hand on his arm. Turning, he saw the petite, pretty, and painted face of Lady Caro.

'Oh, hello, Lady Caro. How do you do?'

'Not well at all,' she purred, placing a hand on his arm like a claw. 'For I have yet to dance with you.'

'Shall we?' Samuel said, leading Lady Caro to the dance floor.

They circled around the room together and she told him of the latest gossip. Lady Caro had a gift for mimicry and he laughed merrily as she parodied their various acquaintances. After the dance was over, she insisted on a second with him. Samuel could hardly refuse her without offence. When the second set was over, he led her by the hand to the side where his friend Sir Alexander Gordon and his new wife were standing. Lady Caro squeezed Samuel's hand before releasing it.

She stayed next to his side as if they were tied together by a string, instead of merely acquaintances.

Alexander was a tall man with thick brownish-red hair and a welcoming smile. He was also an ADC to Wellington and a good man, except for the fact that he let his cousin ride his stallion with Frederica.

His friend bowed. 'Pelford, Lady Caro, allow me to introduce my bride, Lady Gordon.'

Samuel bowed to a short young lady with flaxen hair and brilliant blue eyes. She was pretty in the English style and had the glow of a new bride. 'It is an honour.'

'A pleasure,' Lady Caro purred in a bored voice.

The new Lady Gordon ignored the other woman and turned to face Samuel. 'Alexander has told me all about you and your practical jokes, Duke.'

Ones he had learned from the Stringhams.

Lady Caro cackled and hit his arm with her fan flirtatiously. 'You never told me you were a jokesmith. For shame!'

Samuel was about to step away from Caro and her claws, when he felt a tap on his shoulder. He turned to see the beautiful face of Frederica, her countenance a bit pale.

'I am sorry. I did not mean to startle you,' she said, her neck turning a blotchy red and her cheeks pinker than usual as she smiled at him.

'No, no,' Samuel said, taking her hand in his. 'I was hoping to find you. May I escort you to the terrace? I believe there is to be a fireworks show there.'

He ought to have introduced her to Sir Alexander, Lady Louisa, and Lady Caro, but he forgot his surroundings when she smiled at him. Before he knew it, he was leading her to the terrace to watch the fireworks display. He cursed inwardly that it was so crowded, he would dearly have liked to have kissed her again. He led her to the edge of the crowded terrace and they looked at the crescent moon.

But as soon as the fireworks began, she moved closer to him. Pressing her curves against his side. 'I have decided that I do not like sharing.'

'What are you talking about?' His words were muffled as red fireworks exploded above their heads.

She cupped her hands around his ear. 'You. I do not like sharing *you*.'

He opened his mouth and waited to speak, for another barrage of fireworks was going off at the same time. The sky glittered with gold, but nothing shined brighter than Frederica in her finery.

'Am I not allowed to dance with other women?'

Frederica shook her head. Her curls brushed his cheek tantalisingly.

'Or speak to them?'

'If they try to talk to you, simply run in the opposite direction,' she said primly, but her eyes were dancing with mischief.

Samuel had his own bone to pick with her. 'I shall run from all the ladies, if you promise to do the same from all the men. No more rides with Captain Wallace.'

Her mouth opened. 'But he is just a friend.'

'So is Lady Caro,' he countered.

She gritted her teeth and he tried not to smirk. 'Fine. I shall flee whenever I see him.'

Lifting his hand, he brushed a curl back from her face. It was dark, but the light from the fireworks illuminated her beautiful countenance. 'I never thought to see you jealous.'

'Is jealousy a hideous colour on me?'

He pressed a light kiss to her cheek. 'Quite fetching actually. Perhaps we might find a suitable corner and make our own fireworks show?'

Samuel loved the way Frederica's smile began in her eyes and slowly spread to the rest of her face, finally to her mouth and her beautiful sharp white teeth. She had bitten him before and not only while kissing.

'Yes!'

Putting his hand on her waist, he steered her through the crowd and they were about to make their escape into the gardens, when the Duchess of Hampford appeared in front of them.

He dropped his hand and swore underneath his breath.

Frederica startled and he steadied her with both arms. 'Mama, how…how lovely it is to see you.'

Lady Hampford linked arms with her daughter. 'You know how I enjoy fireworks. Let us watch them together.'

Before Samuel could make his escape, the Duchess had taken his arm into her tight grip. She guided them both back to the middle of the crowd like naughty children. He tried to catch Frederica's eye, but her mother stood directly between them and the Duchess was a very tall woman. And a shrewd one. Samuel was certain that she knew exactly what he and Frederica had been planning to do.

After the fireworks, Lady Hampford dragged them both inside to the dance floor and did not release her hold until the musicians began to play a waltz. 'Ah, should you two like to dance?'

Frederica melted into his arms like she belonged

there. Samuel spun them around together slowly; Frederica's head was practically on his shoulder.

She yawned. 'I am sorry. I am still a little tired from this morning. I woke up early and waited for you, but you never came.'

Samuel did not wish to know if his betrothed had found someone else to keep her company. What mattered is that she wanted him. It was long odds, but he would even wager that she loved him.

'Go to bed early tonight,' he whispered in her ear, 'and we will go riding in the morning. I will come to your house and collect you.'

'Like a package?' she asked with another yawn.

He brushed a light kiss against her sleepy forehead. 'Just like a package.'

After the dance, he returned his tired companion to Lady Hampford and suggested mildly that they might wish to retire early.

Lady Hampford agreed readily and Frederica yawned behind her glove. He walked with them to the entry, where they put on their wraps and called for their carriage.

'I trust we shall see you at Wellington's ball?' Lady Hampford asked in the tone of a command.

'Yes, Duchess,' Samuel said with a slight bow of his head. 'I shall hope for the pleasure of dancing with Lady Frederica.'

Frederica yawned again. 'I will try to stay awake next time.'

Lady Hampford offered her hand. 'Until then.'

Samuel bowed over it and then took Frederica's arm. 'Tomorrow morning, we need to visit the King. Nine o'clock, sharp.'

Her eyes widened and she nodded. Frederica had understood his covert message. He handed her up into the carriage. He thought that she would be asleep in minutes.

Returning to the fête, he saw Slender Billy walking crookedly towards him. It would appear that his old friend had already hit the bottle a little too much that evening. 'Was one of your dreary death letters to her?'

'Not now,' Samuel said, holding up his hands. 'I am afraid that I am in no mood for jokes.'

The prince smiled with only one side of his face. 'I shall not joke with you then. I just thought I would give you a friendly word of advice.'

'Yes?' he said impatiently. Advice from a drunk friend was rarely helpful.

'N-not that I am any great hand at women,' Billy said in a slurred voice. 'The whole world knows of my broken engagement with Princess Ch-Charlotte. I just think that if you are going to marry the girl anyway and you happen to be fond of her, you might do worse than to tell her. Don't make her wait until you are dead to read it in a cold letter.'

Samuel bristled. His relationship with Frederica was like handling a hot coal. One had to be careful or they would get burned. He was certain of his feelings and nearly sure of hers. But like any rider, he did not want to rush his fences. He wanted to wait until the perfect time to tell her. Not some rushed-up job that she might attribute to fear of his impending death.

He laughed. 'Come on, Slender Billy. I think we both could use a drink.'

'Several!' His Royal Highness replied cheerfully.

Chapter Sixteen

Frederica slept poorly. Jealousy burned like poison through her veins. She had dreamed about Lady Caro all night long, except the petite lady had shot her instead of the other way around. Dragging herself out of bed at eight o'clock, she rang for her lady's maid to help her into her riding clothes. Last night her wits had been sleepy and it had taken her a few moments to realise the 'King' that Samuel wished to visit was The King of Spain Inn. She certainly would not mind a visit to a certain *private* parlour.

Watching Jim saddle her horse, Frederica blushed at her words the night before. She had demanded that Samuel not even look at or dance with another woman. While she was a much bigger flirt. The irony was not lost on her. Yet he had not refused her request. He had merely asked her to do the same. Could Samuel actually have feelings for her? Beyond the affection of their childhood memories and family connections? He did not choose her, but could he grow to love her as a man loved a woman? That he was attracted to her, she knew. But she wanted a love as enduring and as rare as the one her parents shared. They were like a team of oxen, equally yoked. They always moved forward together. Not that her parents were at all the same. Papa was an absent-minded naturalist and Mama was a sharp-minded businesswoman, yet their different gifts complemented each other. They supported one another.

How could she create a similar relationship with Samuel?

Smiling wryly, Frederica remembered the story of her mother giving Papa a contract of what she wanted and what he needed. They had not followed it precisely in their marriage, timing and children affected it, but eventually both Papa and Mama had fulfilled all their dreams and ambitions.

Together.

She should tell Samuel about her red scented soaps and her half ownership of the company. And she needed to ask him what he wanted from life. Did he intend to sell out of the army? Become a leader in Parliament? Watch over his estates? She was ashamed to admit to herself that she knew nothing of Samuel's dreams.

Cupping her hands, Jim helped Frederica onto her horse. He led the animal out of the stable by the bridle and into the street just as Samuel arrived on his mare.

Jim tipped his hat to Samuel and then patted the saddlebag. 'I packed your loaded pistol and extra shot. Be careful with it and be careful, my lady.'

Frederica smiled. He was a dear friend. 'Thank you, Jim.'

Clicking her tongue, she urged her horse forward and took her place by Samuel's side.

'Perhaps you should stay home today.'

His words surprised her into pulling up on the reins of her horse. 'Whatever for?'

She saw him swallow, not quite meeting her eyes. 'I think the waiter, Peters, is a French informer. Perhaps even a former member of Napoleon's army. He has the look and the build and his behaviour was not normal. It is dangerous for you to return to Genappe.'

'But not for you?'

Samuel shook his head. 'For both of us. But I would never willingly put you into danger.'

Frederica snorted. She was no simpering miss. If Samuel was going then so would she. 'Jim loaded my pistol and I'll keep it at the ready. Besides, two people are safer than one and perhaps the waiter has not guessed our real purpose.'

They rode silently together through town. There were not many fashionable people about at that time in the morning. The streets were filled with sellers and sweepers. Passing through the last street, they cantered across the field.

Frederica felt like a ball of nervous energy and the quicker pace helped calm her nerves. They rode about five miles, before they slowed their speed for the horses.

Patting her horse's mane, she said quickly, 'I make scented soaps.'

Samuel turned his head towards her. 'Excuse me?'

'I create and make scented soaps,' she said slowly. 'They are red and I add phenol to them to help keep cuts and scrapes clean from infection. I intend to sell them at my mother's perfume shop and distribute the cakes throughout Great Britain. I hope to use her established export routes to expand the reach of my red soaps to Europe and then the Americas.'

He nodded his head, but did not speak.

'You don't mind?' Frederica pressed.

Turning his head to look at her, he said, 'Would it matter if I did?'

She shook her head. 'No, but I still want to know what you think about it.'

'Soap seems like a clean enough hobby.'

The hairs on the back of her neck stood up when he said 'hobby' but then she realised he was gently teasing her. 'It is not a hobby. It is a profession. How do you feel about your duchess working?'

'The more money the merrier,' he said, angling his horse so his leg brushed against hers. Her heartbeat quickened. 'In case you were not aware, my dearest fiancée, I am rather short on funds. We will have to live quite economically for the first few years.'

Frederica wished she could tell how much Samuel was jesting and which words were the truth. 'Yes, poor us. Living on the cheap in a palace.'

His lips twitched before splitting into a heart-stopping grin. 'Precisely. Oh, Frederica, I knew exactly what I was getting into when I asked you to marry me. I am sure that you will be a magnificent duchess and businesswoman like your mother. You take after her in more than appearance.'

These words ought to have placated her, instead they made her feel worse. Samuel understood her, but she did not know him as well and it irked her.

'What do you want to do with your future?'

Samuel's eyes darted back and forth. From the road to the wooded area to a stone fence. 'I wish to live another month.'

She swallowed her disappointment. He must not

be in a sharing mood today. He had already told her about his father, perhaps he was not yet ready to talk about himself.

Urging his horse to a gallop, Frederica had to focus on her own mount to keep up with him for the rest of the ride to Genappe. The road into the small town felt strangely quiet, like Brussels had. There were no people about. When they arrived at The King of Spain Inn, Samuel dismounted and then lifted her off her horse without a word. Taking her hand in a painfully tight grip, he pulled her into the inn.

The innkeeper met them with his typical low bows and immediately escorted them into the same private parlour. He promised to bring them tea and closed the door.

Unbuttoning her pelisse, she took it off and hung it on the rack. She untied her bonnet and shook her hair out. Her entire person felt sweaty and in need of her stringent scented soap after the long ride. She placed her bonnet on top of her pelisse and went to open the latch of the window.

'Don't touch it,' Samuel snapped.

Spinning on her heel, she turned to look at him. 'Which George died and made you king?'

He gritted his teeth and clenched his fists. 'It is not safe. Back away from the window and do not give anyone a clear shot of you.'

She remembered his warning about the French informant. Frederica touched her neck and felt the steady pulse of her heartbeat. She wished to live another month too. Her shoulders were tight, yet her lips trembled.

Taking a seat on the far side of the table, she whispered in French, 'What should I do?'

Samuel moved his chair until it was right next to hers. He sat down and entwined their fingers, as if they were besotted lovers. 'Act normally, but we will not linger today. I only pray that Grant is timely.'

Frederica wished she knew when Samuel was spy acting and when he was not. The sweet brush of his lips against her forehead felt tender. How much did he care? It seemed like a silly question when both of their lives were at stake, but she could not help but think it.

The innkeeper knocked before bringing in the tea tray, followed by Lieutenant-Colonel Grant. His scarlet uniform coat looked more ragged than ever. His eyes narrowed when he saw them holding hands on the table. Samuel pulled away first and Frederica busied herself making the tea once the innkeeper set down the tray with a bow. Grant also moved his chair from the window. Samuel's suspicions must be correct.

The Scot reached into his coat and slid the letter across the table. Samuel pocketed it as Frederica poured three cups of tea. The liquid burned her tongue and throat as it went down. She ate a couple of biscuits, before draining the rest of her burning tea from her cup. Once her cup touched the saucer, Samuel stood up.

'Thank you, Grant,' he said with a deferential nod, before putting on his hat.

Frederica sprang to her feet and pulled on her bonnet, tying the ribbons haphazardly and slipping into her pelisse coat. She did up the buttons so quickly that they were not in the right order, but she did not care. The feeling that they were in trouble only heightened with each moment. They needed to go immediately.

For the first time, Grant stayed in the private parlour and she and Samuel left. He tossed a coin to the ostler and their horses were brought around to the front of the building. She could see that the mare and the grey had been fed, watered, and brushed. Frederica wished her dear grey could get a little more rest, but it was not to be. Samuel grasped her by the waist and lifted her into the saddle without a by your leave. She was both annoyed and impressed. Frederica was not a feather-weight, but Samuel had lifted her easily. Swinging up into his own saddle, Samuel nodded to the ostler and signalled for Frederica to lead.

She did not have to be told twice. Easing her heels into her horse's flank, she urged her tired mare forward to a gallop. It was bad manners to canter through a town, but she could not shake the feeling that they were in very real danger if they stayed. They had not ridden a mile out of the small town when Frederica heard a shot. She abruptly swerved her horse and fell out of the side-saddle hard into the dirt. She brushed her dress off—at least she had not been hit. She fumbled with the saddlebag for her pistol and pulled it out, cocking it.

After dismounting, Samuel came to her side. 'Are you injured?'

'No, but I thought I heard a shot.'

Frederica looked around at the surrounding fields and a clump of trees thirty feet from the road. She looked back at the trees and caught a glimpse of a man. She pointed her pistol at the spot and shot. The figure ran away. She must have missed. Pulling out her shot bag, she reloaded the pistol as Samuel went for his own gun.

'Do you think you hit him?'

Shaking her head, Frederica said, 'No, he was too far away for my pistol. He must have had a shotgun. Should we go after the man?'

Samuel grunted. 'No. I say we run for it. He might already be reloading the shotgun behind a tree and we will be sitting ducks.'

'Let's ride.'

He practically threw her back onto her horse, her pistol in her hand. Then slapped the rump of her mare to make it run. Glancing over her shoulder, she saw him swing into his own saddle and gallop towards her. Like herself, Samuel had pulled out his gun and was holding the reins with only one hand. His bigger horse quickly caught up with hers.

'Keep your pistol out and your eyes peeled,' he said.

She swallowed as she nodded. Her throat felt tight and drier than the Sahara Desert. For the first time since arriving in Belgium, she longed for the dull, steadiness of the London Season. They ran their horses for over a mile before Samuel deemed it safe for them to walk. She did not think her poor grey could have gone much longer at their previous speed.

Exhaling slowly, Frederica released the hammer of her pistol and placed it back into her saddlebag. She wiggled her clenched fingers before picking up the reins again. Glancing over at Samuel, she saw that he too had stored his weapon.

He smiled as he sighed. 'That was close. Do you still like being a spy?'

Grinning in return, Frederica nodded. 'I like being useful and proving that a lady can be just as helpful as a man.'

'I've never thought about it.'

'Women's rights?'

Samuel cleared his throat. 'Forgive me, I was speaking about myself and not about you. I meant that I had never thought about my future and what I wanted. I suppose that I assumed that it was already mapped out for me. I would take care of my family's estates and preform my duties in Parliament. I have not considered what *I* wanted.'

'You should.'

'I've always wanted to be like your father.'

A laugh broke from her lips. 'But, Samuel, he is terrible at estate management. My mother oversaw our estates before Wick took charge. And I do not think he has attended Parliament more than a handful of times. He only cares about his family and his animals. The rest of the two-legged world is on its own as far as he is concerned.'

He leaned towards her and their legs brushed against each other. It set Frederica's pulse racing again.

'I did not mean that I wish to become a naturalist or a scientist,' Samuel said. 'Rather, I want to be a father like him. He played with his children. Taught them how to do things. And every time that I visited, he always had a line of little ones trailing behind him. Hampford never acted annoyed or impatient. Quite the opposite, he always seemed delighted that his children wished to be with him.'

Frederica laughed with her mouth closed. Her little sisters, Helen and Becca, were Papa's favourites because they loved animals as much as he did. They still followed him around. They were all three probably exploring the local fauna and flora as well as wildlife in Greece. Her chest ached from missing them.

They were quiet on the rest of the ride. Samuel's keen eyes were watching for threats and Frederica's mind spun with thoughts. She sighed with relief when they reached Rue de Lombard just as the sun began to set. Jim moved to help her from her horse, but Samuel was there first. She slid down into his arms and felt safe for the first time that day. Leaning her head against his shoulder, she hugged him tightly.

Samuel rubbed soft circles on her back. 'You're safe now.'

'You are too,' she mumbled into his shoulder. The bullet could have easily hit him, as well. She wanted him to live another month. Hundreds of months.

Stepping back, he released her waist and back, but moved his hand to her chin. 'I want a future with you. I want to live on the cheap in a palace full of our children. I want to teach them how to ride, swim, and hunt with you. And then I want to help you wash them with your scented soaps after they have got all filthy and scratched up from playing together. I would not mind helping you wash either…in exchange for certain liberties.'

Her face felt warm, as did the rest of her body. It was not just his flirtatious words, although she was not a ninny and understood their sexual meaning. It was the pureness of his dreams. Samuel needed to be the father that his own had not been. But most importantly, he said that he wanted those things with her.

'You have beautiful dreams,' she said, grabbing his

wrist and kissing the palm of his hand, before lightly pressing her lips to his mouth. 'Thank you for letting me be a part of them. I shall have Jim bring you over a cake of soap.'

Chapter Seventeen

The next morning, Samuel's nerves were shot and he felt emotionally drained. These were not uncommon consequences of spending time with his betrothed. Although, it would not be fair to blame her for yesterday. He had felt goose bumps on his arm before he even met Frederica that morning. He knew it had been dangerous to make that trip with her. The battle was getting closer. The air felt charged with it.

He was no longer a lad who wished to prove himself to Wellington—another surrogate father figure. Samuel knew that there was no glory and very little dignity in a battlefield death. An officer's body received more deference than a soldier's, but they were still piled together in a barn or a charnel house until friends or family could take the corpse and have it properly buried. The common soldiers' bodies were thrown into mass graves with no names and sometimes without markers.

No mourners.

No funerals.

This would be the end thousands of his men faced after their battle with Napoleon's armies. At seventeen, he had thought that he had nothing to lose. And now he knew that he had everything to lose. Frederica, his family, a future with a palace full of children. Slender Billy was right. He could not wait until after the war to tell Frederica his feelings. She deserved so much more than a death letter.

Exhaling, Samuel sat in the corner of the room, unnoticed. He watched Colonel Scovell bow to the new chief staff officer, Colonel Sir William Howe DeLancey, a man in his thirties with piercing dark eyes and curly hair. The man towered a head over Scovell as he escorted him to Wellington's office. DeLancey stayed at the door and Scovell entered and left the room alone. Samuel would have loved to hear what they were saying. But it was bad form to spy on your own side.

A few minutes later, the Duke of Wellington opened the door and barked an order that all his staff should come immediately for a meeting. Samuel was one of the first of the twenty men to arrive. He sat next to Lord Fitzroy Somerset and Sir Alexander Gordon. Within five minutes all members of the staff were seated around the dining room. In the centre of the mahogany table was a large map of Europe. Strong and powerful like King Arthur of old, Wellington stood at the top of the oval table.

'The intelligence I received last night from Grant suggests that the bulk of the French army is here in Paris protecting it,' Wellington said, pointing to the city on the map. 'He further suggests that over a hundred thousand men have been moved to the north of France and are coming our way with Napoleon to personally command.'

'Then we have the advantage, Duke,' Samuel said.

'We have nearly ninety-two thousand men, and that is not including the Prussians.'

'Napoleon's presence on the field is worth forty thousand men,' the general said gravely. 'And his soldiers are veterans. They have fought before, unlike most of our soldiers, who are green, and the loyalty of the Dutch soldiers is particularly precarious—many are still committed to France.'

Somerset stood up, knocking his chair over. 'The Prince of Orange has suggested that we go on the offensive and surprise Napoleon on his own turf.'

Wellington pressed his long thin fingers together. 'In regard to offensive operations, my opinion is that, however strong we shall be in reference to the enemy, we should not extend ourselves further than is absolutely necessary, in order to facilitate the subsistence of the troops. His Royal Highness, the Prince of Orange, has presented his plan to me, and I do not approve of an extension from the Channel to the Alps, and I am convinced that it will be found not only fatal, but that the troops at such a distance on the left of our line will be entirely out of our position of the operations.'

Picking up his chair, Somerset sat back down. 'What would you have us do, sir?'

Samuel wondered the same thing.

Wellington pulled out several maps of the local area and pointed out the best spots for a defensive action. 'I have sent several spies to watch over Napoleon's army. We must know which road he will take, so that we can choose the best possible ground to meet him. When word arrives, we need to be prepared to immediately spring into action. All men on my staff must be in constant readiness.'

The general then dismissed his staff, but held a hand on Samuel's shoulder to detain him.

'Pelford, I would like you to stay,' Wellington said in his softest, most penetrating tone. 'I wish to have private speech with you.'

Samuel watched Wellington close the door after every other person had left the room and walk around the large oval table.

'You have been a member of my staff since our days in the Peninsula, and you know I consider my staff to be family,' Wellington said and waited for Samuel's nod of affirmation. 'I would not ask this of you if I did not think it was imperative to our success. I would like you and your betrothed to do more than simply courier information for Grant. I want you two to travel deeper into France and learn which generals and what roads Napoleon will be taking. Information that Grant cannot get whilst wearing his army uniform.'

Riding alone with Frederica was pushing the line of propriety. Travelling alone with her would be ruinous to her reputation.

'The Duchess of Hampford would never agree to it.'

Wellington stopped walking around the table and sat next to Samuel. 'Lady Frederica does not need her mother's permission. Only her husband's.'

It took a few moments for his words to sink in. The general meant *him*. Samuel would not have to wait until after his army duties were over to marry Frederica. To bed her. To make her his in every possible way. He wanted nothing more—but then he would be placing her in terrible danger. He was not sure he could endure many more days like yesterday.

'Unfortunately, it will cause a bit of uproar and perhaps some pernicious gossip,' Wellington continued, 'but Scovell thought that if you left with Lady Frederica from my party tonight, leaving a note that you were being married privately, then no one would expect either of you to return for a few days. I, of course, will not court-martial you for desertion either.'

Samuel could not even form a small smile at the poor joke. 'When will we be married?'

The general cleared his throat. 'Tonight. Scovell has arranged for a Belgian minister to meet you at a chapel not far from the fête. That is, if you are willing?'

Samuel's muscles felt tense and his stomach heavy. How could he risk the life of the woman he loved? How could he make such a large decision about her welfare? Blinking rapidly, he realised that he did not need to. The decision was not his in the first place. It was Frederica's. She did not require his or her mother's permission. She was an intelligent and independent woman. Yesterday, she had proved that she was a capable spy.

Taking a deep breath, Samuel sat up in his chair. 'I am willing if she is, Duke. The only permission Lady Frederica requires is her own.'

'Of course. Of course,' Wellington agreed, vigorously nodding. 'But from all accounts she is a formidable young woman.'

That was putting it lightly, Samuel thought.

Chapter Eighteen

Shaking out his clenched fingers, Samuel entered the large ballroom in his dress uniform. The Duke of Wellington's party was stuffed with fashionable people like a London squeeze. Samuel acknowledged several acquaintances with curt nods before walking over to a large circle where the general stood in the middle.

'I say nothing about our defensive operations,' Wellington said loudly, 'because I am inclined to believe that Marshal Blücher of the Prussians and I are so well united, and so strong, that the enemy cannot do us much mischief. I am at the advanced post of the whole, the greatest part of the enemy's force is in my front, and, if I am satisfied, others need be under no apprehension.'

Samuel wondered how much was bravado, for the general complained about everything from his staff, to the equipment, to the soldiers, in private. Leaving the circle, he walked on and spotted his friend the Prince of Orange moving his way. Slender Billy put his arm around Samuel's shoulders and reminisced about the time Samuel had put soap in the officers' wine and when Fitzroy burped out a bubble. It was during this anecdote that Samuel noticed Frederica standing on the side of the dance floor. Captain Wallace was at her elbow, but she was not dancing with him. Even though her left foot was tapping to the beat of the tune. She wore a light green dress that emphasised her lovely, voluptuous figure. He could hardly wait to take it off this night.

'Well, old fellow,' Slender Billy said, giving him a little shove in the middle of his back. 'You'd best go claim the girl if you are going to ignore who you are speaking to and glower.'

Recalled to his senses, Samuel quickly apologised, but the prince would have none of it. Billy shooed him away with one hand. 'Kiss her once for me. Make that twice. She's a looker.'

Trying to suppress a smile, Samuel strode over to Frederica's side. 'Ah, Captain Wallace, I believe the first waltz is mine.'

He abruptly took Frederica into his arms, waltzing her away from him. Frederica's hazel eyes sparkled as she smiled at him. Samuel felt an overwhelming desire to kiss her there and then.

'Poor Mark, I told him that I was not dancing this evening,' she said with a wrinkle of her nose. 'You have made a liar of me.'

Samuel raised his eyebrows. 'Actually, I hope that I am about to make an honest woman of you. Wellington wants us to elope and go farther into France to discover which generals and what roads Napoleon will take. I told him that I was willing, but that you could decide for yourself.'

Her mouth hung open, but she did not speak for several turns. 'It would be very hard for you to take a wedding trip by yourself.'

'And terribly awkward,' he said with a ghost of a smile playing on the edge of his lips. 'Not to mention disappointing.'

Bright red circles formed on her cheeks and Samuel had a pretty good idea what his betrothed was thinking about. It was all that he had been able to focus on all afternoon.

'I shall try not to be a disappointment,' she parried without her usual sharpness. 'Shall I go and tell my mother?'

He scanned the room and easily located the Duchess of Hampford speaking to Lady Richmond. 'There is no need. After we leave, a waiter will give your mother a billet. I have written to inform her of our private marriage and short wedding trip.'

Frederica looked down at the green lace overlay of her dress. 'I do think I might be a tad conspicuous in the countryside in this gown. In your plans, have you provided for proper clothing for me?'

'Colonel Scovell's wife saw to it,' Samuel said, pressing his hand harder against her waist. 'We are to be middle-class French merchants and will be dressed accordingly.'

The musicians struck the final chord. Reluctantly, Samuel dropped his hand from her waist and took her fingers in his other hand. He led her through several couples and an antechamber. Accepting his hat from the servant, he took the wrap and put it around Frederica. Then he escorted her out the door. Frederica lifted her skirt as she walked down the stairs to where a carriage waited for them. Scovell and his wife sat on the opposite seat with their backs to the driver. The couple matched each other in age and reserved countenances.

'Good evening, Lady Stringham, Lord Pelford,' Colonel Scovell said, bowing his head. 'May I introduce my wife, Mrs Scovell?'

Samuel and Frederica greeted the older woman in unison: 'How do you do?'

'Very well, thank you,' she said in a soft voice.

Awkward silence followed and Scovell broke it. 'We do not have a long drive. The chapel is only a couple of streets away.'

Frederica gave a small smile, but Samuel could see that she was nervous. She kept running her right fingers up her left arm, breathing in and out abnormally fast. The coach stopped, and the Scovells exited first. Samuel followed, offering his arm to Frederica, but she leapt out of the carriage and onto the pavement. She then took his hand and they entered the church.

Several candles cast shadows in the large domed room. A man in black robes stood in front of the crucifix and beckoned them forward. Samuel took Frederica's elbow and directed her past the wooden pews to the front of the chapel.

Nodding, Samuel told the minister to proceed.

The minister was a small man with a lined face. He smiled at Frederica and began the wedding ceremony in French. The minister's sermon was succinct, and Samuel almost missed his cue to say 'I will'.

Frederica said, 'I will,' loudly, and her voice echoed in the empty hall.

The minister then declared them man and wife. They both signed the register and then Scovell witnessed the marriage certificate. The spymaster congratulated them and said that his lodgings were only a step away and that he and his wife would walk. He assured Samuel that both of their trunks were in the carriage and explained that they had rooms booked at the Fleur Blanche Hôtel.

The ride to the inn took almost ten minutes—it was on the edge of the city. Neither Samuel nor Frederica attempted to make conversation. His bride appeared just as nervous as he was and not nearly as excited. He swallowed, his mouth dry.

Samuel stepped out of the carriage first. 'I would hate for you to sprain your ankle before your first adventure.'

Clasping his hands around her narrow waist, he helped her down. He could hardly wait to get her into his arms again.

He directed the coachman to bring in the saddlebags and he opened the door into the inn. The Fleur Blanche Hôtel was a modern building of three stories with an elegant exterior of the palest blue. They were ushered in by a landlord impeccably dressed in a simple suit of black. The landlord looked to be at least seventy years old. His hair was white and thin, but worn to his shoulders. His face was wrinkled, but his figure did not slump. He whistled for a servant to carry the luggage, and he begged Samuel and Frederica to follow him.

The proprietor took them to a second-floor room that was richly furnished in shades of gold. A large four-poster bed with gold bed hangings took up most of the room. A bottle of champagne and two goblets were on a small round dining table. The landlord gave them a knowing smile and wished the new couple a happy marriage. The servant placed the saddlebags near the door, before shutting it behind him.

Frederica walked around the room. 'What a charming apartment. I have never stayed in a hotel so fine.'

It was obvious by the way she chattered that she felt ill at ease.

Samuel coloured with embarrassment and disappointment as he sputtered, 'I did not realise that they would only reserve one room. I do not wish for you to be uncomfortable.'

Frederica's neck and face were flushed, but she looked him directly in the eyes. 'We are married after all—to each other. Will you turn around whilst I change my clothes?'

He would have dearly liked to watch, but did as she requested. He had not considered that shyness could be a hidden quality of his bride. She had certainly never been shy before and he found that he did not particularly like it. He wished for his brazen betrothed.

Samuel felt a hand on his shoulder and jumped.

'Would you undo my buttons?' Frederica asked, her neck as red as her cheeks. 'I cannot reach them.'

She turned away from him.

Lifting a curl off her back, he placed it on her shoulder. He breathed heavily as he fiddled with the small ornate buttons. His heart beat furiously in his chest as though he were in a battle for his life. He felt a frantic heat course through his veins. Frederica turned to look at him and took off her dress, leaving only her shift and corset on. She carelessly tossed it to the ground. Like all aristocratic ladies, she was used to being waited on.

'Could you untie my corset, as well?' Frederica asked, and again turned her beautiful back towards him.

Was she trying to seduce him? Or could she truly not untie her own strings?

Samuel gulped and took several tries before untying the knot and slowly unlacing the whaleboned garment. He let it drop to the floor. He placed his hands where the corset had been around her waist and kissed her shoulder. She made a mewling sound that nearly undid him. He nuzzled her neck and let his hands stray upward.

'I—I—I am not ready.'

With what was left of his slipping self-control, Samuel stepped back from her. He had been preparing for this night all day but she'd had less than an hour. From other officers' bawdy talk, he knew that the first time for a lady could be painful and unpleasant. It was not unnatural that she would be scared, and unlike her feminine peers, a Stringham would know exactly how mating was done. She probably knew many ways, but this thought did not cool down his body.

He clenched his hands and exhaled slowly. 'There is no rush. Would you prefer I asked for a separate room?'

'Do you snore?' Frederica asked, blushing fiercely as she stood before him in the thin material of her shift.

'No.'

'Will you steal the sheets?'

'Never.'

She attempted a tight smile. 'Then I suppose there is no reason why we could not sleep in the same bed.'

Samuel agreed with her gravely. Sleeping beside her would be more torture than pleasure. He would have to keep his hands to himself. He had always prided himself on self-control, but that was before a half-naked Frederica would be sleeping beside him.

Wearing only her shift, Frederica slipped into the bed underneath the covers. Her eyes were as wide as guineas as she watched him unbutton his uniform jacket and then his shirt. She did not avert her gaze and he was not going to ask her to. Nor was he going to fully undress before her. He thought it would scare her and remove his tenuous control of his own body. After putting on his nightshirt, he then pulled off his unpleasantly tight breeches. He brought the bottle of champagne and two wine glasses to the bed. He uncorked the bottle and then poured out the bubbly liquid into the glasses.

He handed one to Frederica and then raised his glass. 'To our marriage.'

Frederica raised her cup and echoed his toast.

Chapter Nineteen

Frederica opened her eyes. For a moment, she did not recognise her surroundings. Beside her in bed, softly snoring, lay her husband. The morning sun shone through the curtains and she pulled the sheets up to her neck. She sneaked another peek at Samuel. His chest rose up and down rhythmically. Extending her hand from under the sheet, she brushed his muscled chest with her fingers. How she had longed to touch him the night before. To try out all the delightfully shocking things her mother had told her about. But she had been too afraid. Not of the act. Nor of the pain that might be part of her losing her maidenhood.

She was afraid that she would be a gauche disappointment. Young men were encouraged to 'practise', for want of a better word, before the marriage night. Their indiscretions were socially acceptable as long as they were relatively discreet with a widow, mistress, or at a brothel. Those women knew how to please a man and enhance the sexual experience. Likely some naughty tricks to extend the pleasure. Frederica had no doubt that she would eventually excel at bed games.

She enjoyed kissing very much and she loved kissing Samuel.

Most young ladies did not know how babies were made. The lucky ones like herself were told by their mother before their wedding night. Some brides knew nothing and had to rely on whatever their husband decided to tell them. Or not tell them. Frederica could readily understand how terrifying sexual congress could be for the unprepared.

She was prepared in knowledge. But what if he laughed at her naivety? Her clumsiness? He had laughed at her so many times in the past and each time it had crumbled a part of her soul. Not that she had been innocent. She had wanted his attention too much to be ignored.

Gulping, she could not resist allowing her fingers to run over his smooth, muscled chest again. A large hand caught hers, and Samuel opened his eyes. Frederica felt heat rush to her cheeks.

'You looked just like that the first time I saw you. You were six or seven years old,' Samuel recalled. 'You had on a yellow frock and your hair was in two braids. Your face looked so worried and full of guilt.'

'I was guilty,' Frederica confessed. 'Elizabeth, Mantheria, and Charles said that I was too young to play with you, so I collected spiders and put them in your bed. When you arrived, you gave me a doll with blue ribbons in her hair. I felt terrible, until the next day, when you pushed me into a mud puddle.'

Frederica felt the laugh vibrate in his chest before she heard it.

Samuel smiled at her. 'We were a pair of hoydens. I daresay you remember every awful thing I did.'

She nodded her head into the pillow. 'I do. Every single dead mouse you put in my shoes, every worm you slipped down the back of my dress, and every mud ball you threw at my head. Shall I go on?'

'No, no,' Samuel said, lifting her hand to his mouth and kissing it. 'That list is incriminating enough. I daresay it was a good thing we only visited each other in the summer.'

Squeezing her eyes shut, Frederica said, 'Let us not talk about the past.'

He kissed the tips of her five fingers as he still held her hand. 'You are right. I would much rather talk about the present and you do not need to be sly about your caresses.'

She gulped. 'I do not think that I am ready yet—for, you know.'

Samuel pressed one more kiss into the palm of her hand. 'You might not be, but your hand certainly is. Well, shall we get an early start of it?'

Frederica readily agreed, and with less embarrassment than last night, she managed to give herself a quick sponge bath and put on a fresh shift. She pulled her corset up, but could not manage to tie it from behind. She felt like a cat chasing its tail. Samuel must have seen her struggles and offered his assistance.

Tying the strings, he kissed her bare shoulder. 'Whoever invented corsets should be awarded a knighthood at the very least.'

Frederica laughed silently, for he had squeezed all the air out of her. She walked over to her trunk and took out a plain grey dress made of coarse material. Pulling it over her head, she returned to Samuel to button up the back buttons. Then she moved to the mirror and combed through her long brown hair, while Samuel finished dressing in a simple dark blue suit, suitable for a merchant. Frederica braided her hair and twisted it into a knot at her neck. Wade would be horrified with her hairstyle. She stuck her tongue out at herself in the mirror.

'Another face that I recall you giving me as a child,' he said, peering over her shoulder in the mirror.

She turned to face him and with one gentle finger traced the white scar on his cheek near his jaw. She heard his breath quicken with her touch.

'You did not have this growing up.'

'No, you are not responsible for this scar,' Samuel said with a heart-stopping smile. 'I did not even get it in a battle. Merely a practice skirmish with a friend.'

'How ignoble.'

He laughed and added in a mock-serious tone, 'Please don't give my secret away.'

'Never,' she whispered, realising that they were no longer playing. Samuel's secrets would always remain safe in her keeping.

'Rica, we had better hurry and eat our breakfast. We should have been on the road an hour ago.'

'Yes, of course.'

They breakfasted in a small private parlour and partook heartily of cold ham and pastries.

She picked up a buttery croissant. 'When did I become Rica?'

'You said that you didn't like the nickname Freddie, so I was trying a new one—Rica,' Samuel said, lifting his glass of juice. 'I suppose, if you would prefer it, I could call you Your Grace, Lady Frederica Maria Ada

Isabella Stringham Corbin, Duchess of Pelford, but it is a bit of a mouthful.'

Frederica's eyes wandered to his mouth. 'I do not like either shortened version of my name. They're juvenile… It is as if you still see me as a child.'

'Nothing could be further from my thoughts.'

Frederica felt her neck and cheeks suffuse with colour. Samuel grinned in triumph and took a large bite of an apple Danish. The filling squirted out onto his lapel and Frederica laughed. Samuel wiped it off with his napkin and joined in her mirth.

She could not help but wonder how her mother had felt the morning after she had married a stranger. Frederica had wed her childhood nemesis. Her emotions seemed to roll all over inside of her; she felt—excited—embarrassed—eager—unsure.

Returning to their golden room, Frederica donned a plain black riding habit and dowdy straw bonnet. Samuel settled with the landlord, and a groom attached their saddlebags to two horses. Samuel put his hands on her waist and assisted her into her side-saddle. She felt breathless from the brief contact. He gave her a small smile and started his horse into a trot. Frederica followed behind him, and they left the city of Brussels.

They rode for over ten hours until they passed the border between the Netherlands and France. There were no soldiers who policed the border, and Frederica saw several peasants pulling carts of their belongings towards France.

'Where are they going?' Frederica asked.

'They are French loyalists returning to the safety and protection of their emperor,' Samuel said. 'Our horses are about spent. We will sleep here tonight and allow the ostlers to attend to the horses.'

Frederica nodded and followed him. She had never ridden so many miles in one day in the saddle. She felt sore and exhausted.

It was early afternoon the following day and the sun was directly above them. The French town they passed through was a small one and boasted no more than fifteen buildings in total—two of which were public houses. Samuel pulled his horse to a stop near the first public house and dismounted. Handing the reins to an ostler, he lifted Frederica out of the saddle and led her into the inn.

Only a handful of customers stood near the bar, and the owner, a round-faced man with a leering grin, met them and asked if they would require a room. Samuel answered in French that they were only stopping for luncheon, but would require a private parlour if one were available. The owner ogled Frederica again, then led them to a cramped room. Samuel ordered the meal and shut the door.

'Stuffy, isn't it?' he said in French, opening the small window. Then he added in a soft tone barely above a whisper, 'Remember, we must only speak French while in France.'

Frederica nodded and took off her hat. She shook her head and yawned widely. 'Where are we going?'

'To Paris perhaps,' Samuel said. 'We will ride until we find the army.'

'You were stationed at Paris with Lord Wellington?'

He looked out the window and then walked up behind her and whispered in her ear, 'This is hardly the time or place to discuss my time with the British ambassador to France.'

Frederica bristled, but remained silent. The owner knocked twice and carried in a tray of food and a pint of ale. They ate in silence and when they were finished, Samuel called for the horses and paid their shot. The owner eyed Frederica on their way out and gave her one last leery grin. She shuddered. Glad that she was not alone.

They rode for another three hours before Samuel slowed his horse down to a trot and she followed suit. 'We should give the horses a rest.'

Frederica nodded, but did not speak a word. They rode side by side for a quarter of an hour before Samuel said, 'I am sorry. I did not mean to offend you.'

'Oh,' was all that she could think to say.

Samuel suggested that they dismount and walk for a little while to rest their mounts. Frederica readily agreed.

'I have always wanted to travel,' Frederica said suddenly. 'That is why I persuaded Mama to take me to Brussels. I loved the year that I spent in Italy.'

'After this is over, I will take you anywhere you wish to go,' Samuel said, taking her hand and holding it.

'I should like to see the places you have lived—France, Austria, and Spain. My little sisters are in Greece with Papa and I am terribly jealous. They write of all the little islands that they visit in their boat.'

He squeezed her hand. 'I hope you are not planning on guiding the boat. When we went punting near Farleigh, you hit a tree branch in the water and nearly toppled into the river.'

Frederica laughed at her younger self; she had fallen into the boat and it had left her covered in bruises. 'Well, I think the blame lies squarely with the person who taught me how to punt.'

'Nonsense, I gave very clear instructions.'

'Don't hit the tree,' she mimicked. 'Not one word about how to move the boat in a different direction, going against the current, and after I fell into the boat and quite scraped up my hands and knees, all you said was "I told you not to hit the tree".'

'I was insufferable,' he agreed.

'So was I, but for quite a different reason than you.'

His hold on her hand tightened. 'What do you mean?'

'You were always trying to avoid me or running away from me.'

'Well, I am not running away now,' he said, winking suggestively.

Frederica gulped audibly, and Samuel pulled her into his arms for a brief kiss. He released her, and she felt her heart in her chest beating against her corset.

'I chased you because you ignored me,' she blurted out. Her face and neck growing hot. 'And the more you ignored me, the greater lengths I went to get your attention. Culminating in putting a bear cub in your room and yet you still acted as if I was beneath your notice. I could never decide if I liked or hated you more.'

One side of his mouth quirked up. 'I would ask if you like or hate me more now, but I am too afraid of the answer.'

'And I am still afraid that you will run away from me or laugh at my feelings for you.'

There.

She had said her greatest fear. The true reason why

she kept him an arm's length from her heart. She was so scared of getting hurt again. Of offering her heart on a platter, only to have him refuse it.

'I noticed you that last summer,' he said quietly, his eyes meeting hers. 'How could I not? You had grown breasts. Beautiful large breasts and I could not stop staring at them. I was afraid that you had caught me more than once, so I tried not to look at you at all. I was seventeen and you were only fourteen. You were too young for me then. I was supposed to be the mature one, but the ragamuffin little girl who had chased me and beat me at everything was turning into a lovely young woman. And I did not want to think of you that way. It made me feel dirty like my father. That is why I gave you the chocolates and told you that you were immature. I wanted you to avoid me. To hate me. But in truth, I was the immature one.'

'And now?'

'I still cannot stop myself from staring at your large breasts.'

Frederica giggled and playfully hit his shoulder. 'Do be serious.'

'I am,' he assured her with a saucy grin. 'But the rest of your figure now commands equal attention. I adore the sway of your hips and the roundness of your bottom.'

At least he was attracted to her now and did not try to avoid her. She could hardly expect him to tell a woman he was compelled to marry because of family debts that he loved her. 'So I could be headless and it would not matter to you.'

'Just because your lush lips and sparkling eyes were not in the top three of my favourite body parts does not mean that I do not appreciate them. Only slightly less than other more obvious endowments. I am also enamoured of your wicked roving hands, but again, they are lower down on the list.'

'Your eyes are the top of my list.'

'That is because you have not seen me unclothed yet.'

Frederica gasped in surprise. Choked and then coughed. Samuel's conversation was dripping with innuendo.

'The sun is starting to set,' he said, glancing over his shoulder. 'We have only another hour or two of light, we had best get back on the horses.'

They rode hard until they reached the city of Valenciennes and found a tiny inn. Samuel personally saw that the horses were rubbed down and fed, while Frederica retired to their small chamber. She took off her hat and let down her hair. She combed through it until Samuel arrived with a bottle of Burgundy and two glasses.

'I was hoping you would need some assistance undressing.'

Frederica stiffened and her hazel eyes nearly popped out of her head.

Light-headed, Samuel roared with laughter. 'Just with the buttons you cannot reach. I daresay we are both exhausted after the hard ride.'

For once his mirth did not offend her. Frederica admitted that she was very tired. Samuel expertly unbuttoned her plain dress and untied her corset. He did not kiss her shoulder this time, and Frederica felt keenly disappointed. They ate dinner together in a private parlour before returning to their room and climbing into the narrow bed. Frederica could feel his warm arm against hers. She felt his body twitch as he fell asleep. She lay there for a long time listening to his steady breathing and wondering if Samuel could grow to love her, as deeply as her father had her mother.

Chapter Twenty

They left the inn early the next morning and rode all day until they reached the town of Roye, and the day after that, they travelled until they reached the outskirts of Paris. Frederica felt bone-tired, but her eyes could not stop moving from one building to another. The old city at sunset was an architectural delight. Cut into perfect sections by the rivers. She wished that she could explore it more fully with Samuel. But that was impossible.

Samuel's eyes did not stop moving either. He was looking for potential threats. Soldiers swarmed the streets with ladies on their arms. Every hotel and public house was filled. The French citizens who could afford to had come to the protection of Paris. For Napoleon had highly fortified the city.

They rode past a fashionable section of town with brightly painted buildings and gorgeous architecture. However, Samuel guided them to a quieter inn, far from the centre of town, where they spent the night. Frederica was becoming more accustomed to having another person in her bed. Samuel did not steal the sheets, but despite his denial, he did snore—a low monotonous drone. She tried to fall asleep but could not. She decided to touch him to see if he would stop snoring and placed her hand on his shoulder. He stirred, turned on his side towards her, and slung his left arm over her waist. Frederica held her breath, but he did not wake up. Exhaling, she closed her eyes and fell asleep with a smile on her lips.

Frederica woke up first, even though it was nearly midday, and mulled over a plan. She tapped Samuel on the shoulder and he moaned and turned over. He placed his pillow over his head. She laughed and began to tickle him.

'I surrender,' he said, turning over to look at her. He pulled her against his hard chest and kissed her passionately until they were breathless.

She loved kissing him and snuggling into the crook of his arm. 'I have a plan, but I am sure you will disapprove of it.'

'Well, I have surrendered.'

'I think we should go to a pub tonight with lots of soldiers and partake of nasty tap drinks.'

Samuel sat up abruptly and shook his head. 'I will not allow my wife—'

Frederica placed a finger on his lips. 'You have surrendered, so you must listen to the entire plan. You and I will flirt and mingle and find out what we can. People are much more inclined to speak freely after a pint or two.'

'It is still too dangerous.'

'I will bring my pistol and my husband for protection.'

'My presence might be a deterrent to the French officers,' he said flatly.

'We will never be far from each other.'

Samuel kissed her fingers one by one. 'It is a good plan. If a man were to ask such searching questions, it might be noticed, but to a beautiful woman, no soldier can resist bragging of his consequence.'

'I will need to purchase a suitable dress and make-up for my face.'

They ate a late repast and then explored several shops to find the necessary purchases. Samuel helped Frederica get ready. She only wore one petticoat and dampened her chemise and the gauzy white second-hand dress they purchased so they clung to her. She had never painted her face before and smudged the rouge on her cheeks. Washing it off with a towel, she tried again. She powdered her face white and painted her eyes. Looking in the mirror, she felt her heartbeat quicken at her reflection—her mother would be scandalised.

Samuel did not seem to mind at all.

'Now where to put my pistol,' Frederica said aloud, taking it out of her reticule in a short, jerky movement. She felt a bit jumpy and her nerves were on end.

'You will not be able to hide it on your person. You can see every curve of your body in that dress,' he said. 'I will carry it in my coat.'

Frederica handed Samuel the weapon and they walked out of the rear entrance of the inn. They followed the noise and the lights to a row of busy taverns. Women of ill repute lingered outside in the shadows and beckoned to Samuel. He held her hand tighter. Still her heart palpitated and her hands shook. This was the moment she had been waiting for her entire life. She could do something that truly mattered. She would be a spy that brought back important intelligence that would make a difference in the upcoming battle. Her life would have meaning.

'Blast,' he whispered in her ear. 'I will be the only man without a uniform.'

'Then we must find you one,' Frederica said, in a higher tone than usual. 'Will you hand me my pistol?'

Samuel placed his hand inside his jacket pocket and pulled out her pistol. 'Try not to make too much of a mess. I will have to wear the fellow's jacket after.'

'And you think the French will notice a large bullet hole surrounded by blood?'

His lips twitched. 'Possibly.'

They hid together in the alley and watched several soldiers pass by, but none that were the same body type as Samuel. They were all slim like Captain Wallace. Or short.

'You are too broad-shouldered,' Frederica complained, kissing his ear.

'Look at the fellow who just got out of the coach.' Samuel pointed out. 'I daresay I could fit into his uniform.'

The man descending from the coach was even broader than her husband. 'You and our elephant.'

Frederica did not hesitate. Stepping out of the shadows, she walked stiffly towards the soldier. Her knees kept locking. She pressed her fist against her thigh, trying not to show her fear.

'Pardon me, sir.' She spoke in French, giggling longer than she should. 'My sandal has become untied. Could you tie it for me?'

The beefy French soldier looked her up and down, smiling his rotten teeth at her. *'Oui.'*

Frederica lifted her skirt to reveal her shapely ankle

and put her sandal forward. Her shoulders felt tight and her stomach was rock-hard. A cold sweat covered her skin and she tried not to flinch.

The man got to his knees and took one of his thick fingers and caressed her ankle. The hairs on the back of her neck and arms stood up. Nausea rose in her throat, but she forced herself to swallow it back down. Wellington had trusted her. Samuel needed her. She would not fail either duke.

Frederica brought down the butt of her pistol hard on his head, knocking him out. Taking a deep breath, she took one arm and Samuel the other, and they dragged him into the alley.

'Couldn't we have picked a lighter fellow?' her husband complained.

The Frenchman began to stir and her heart raced. Samuel punched him below the chin and knocked him out cold. Frederica pinched her own skin between the thumb and forefinger. Over and over again. She watched as he took off the man's trousers and uniform jacket. Tugging the trousers up over his own, he tightened the belt to its last rung. He pulled on the jacket and Frederica helped him button the row of gold buttons. Lastly, he put on the man's hat. Samuel looked very handsome in a uniform, even in an ill-fitting one.

'Not perfect,' Frederica said, eyeing the baggy uniform as she rocked back and forth, 'but I think you will pass.'

Samuel offered her his arm and she placed her shaking hand in the crook of it. They walked out of the alley and down the middle of the street. The air was a curious mixture of open sewage and sweet patisserie.

Her stomach roiled and she fought to control her body. They entered the closest tavern.

The taproom was loud and full of people—some drinking, some talking, and some gambling. The roulette table was swamped with people eager to lose their money, or win their fortune. Several tables hosted male card players. The only women in the room appeared to be prostitutes. They were scantily dressed like Frederica and most appeared to have dyed their hair to stick out from the crowd. One woman's locks were a harsh yellow and another's a brashly bright red. Their faces were heavily painted almost like masks and Frederica wished that she had been more generous with her own cosmetics.

She waved Samuel away and she sauntered through the room, circling. The higher the rank of the soldier, the better the information. She felt a hand on her shoulder and resisted the urge to pull away or punch him in the nose. Turning around, she smiled. The man behind her was old enough that he could have been her father—lines mapped his eyes and mouth. His hair and sideburns were tinged with grey. He licked his thin, colourless lips in what might have been attraction. Frederica only felt revulsion, but she forced her mouth to form a smile.

'You appear to be lost, mademoiselle,' he said in an oily voice.

Frederica looked at his uniform and saw his rank—colonel. The same as Samuel. He would know the highest levels of intelligence.

She smiled coyly. 'Only looking for some company, Colonel.'

He offered his arm, and she placed her quivering

hand on it, ignoring the pit in her stomach that was ever growing.

The older man covered her hand with his callused one. 'Shall I get us a room?'

Frederica swallowed down the bile rising in her throat. 'Later perhaps. I should like first to have a drink and perhaps watch you play a little.'

The colonel led her to a table. A waiter immediately came and bowed before them.

The older man touched her knee underneath the table and began to work his hand up. 'My new little friend and I would like a drink.'

Frederica grabbed his hand with hers and pulled it off. She slapped it playfully and whispered in his ear, 'No play until you pay, Colonel. I know how you officers are. Kissing today and leaving tomorrow.'

She saw him stiffen. Instinctively, she kissed his cheek and then nipped at his ear. She hoped it pained him more than pleased. Her own eyes kept darting towards the exit.

He immediately relaxed and guffawed.

The waiter returned with a bottle of red wine and two glasses. The colonel poured and they both picked up their glasses and raised them for a toast.

'Vive l'emperor,' Frederica said.

'Vive l'emperor.'

Frederica sipped her wine slowly and saw Samuel fifteen feet away playing roulette. The colonel downed his wine with a gulp. She poured him some more, this time filling the glass to the top—well past where she should. He gulped it down, as well. Frederica filled his cup again.

'Are you trying to get me drunk, mademoiselle?'

Frederica gave a high false laugh, chewing the inside of her cheek. 'Impossible, Colonel. I am sure you have too hard a head. I am only loosening you up a bit.'

He guffawed again and gulped down another glass of wine. 'I am ready.'

Swallowing down her fear, she forced herself to wink at him. 'But first I should like to discuss my pay.'

'Fair enough,' he said. 'How much do you charge?'

'Are you requesting my company for tonight only or for longer?' she said, giving him a smile and licking her lips suggestively as he had.

'Alas, only tonight, mademoiselle,' he said with a groan. 'We are to march first thing in the morning.'

Frederica leaned closer and placed her hand on his top button and undid it. 'Colonel, who is your commander so that I may ask his permission to steal you away?'

His eyes opened and Frederica pulled his mouth down to hers. She swallowed down the revulsion of his rank breath and pushed him away when she could tolerate no more.

'Marshal Grouchy, mademoiselle. But he will not mind if I am absent from my post for a few hours,' he said, puffing out his chest as if to impress her. 'Napoleon, himself, will lead us to battle.'

Frederica's face lit up. 'Does the colonel know the emperor?'

He shook his head. 'I have yet to have that honour, but I am slightly acquainted with Marshal Ney, who will be going, as well. Now it is time for you to come with me.'

The older man took Frederica by the elbow in a painful hold and guided her towards the stairs. She clutched her glass with the opposite hand. Glancing over her shoulder, she saw Samuel was still playing roulette and he had not noticed her leaving. The colonel led her up the red velvet stairs and stopped in front of a door. He bent down to open the knob and Frederica brought down the glass as hard as she could on his head. The colonel's head was certainly hard, for he shook off the blow and grabbed her by the shoulders and shook her. His fingers dug into her skin. Kicking him in the shins, she tried to bite his left arm. He struck her across the cheek and pushed her to the floor. Her entire body shivered in fear.

'You like to play rough, mademoiselle. Wait until we get inside.'

The colonel lifted his right arm to strike her again, when Samuel ran into him, sending them both sprawling on the floor. Frederica stood up and edged away from them. Samuel hit the colonel with a left hook and then with a right uppercut. The colonel raised his hands to protect his face from the onslaught, but was helpless before the fury of Samuel's fists. Samuel gave a final punch to the colonel's jaw, which knocked him out cold.

He stood up; his knuckles were bleeding. 'We have drawn too much attention. We had better go.'

Frederica nodded and put her trembling arm through his.

They walked down the stairs and through the main room, past the roulette table and out of the door. Frederica's heart beat in her throat and her legs felt so weak that she was glad to lean on her husband for support. She itched all over. Everywhere that awful old man had touched her.

Samuel hailed a cab and gave directions to the driver. The cab dropped them off a street before the inn. Samuel took her hand and led her between the houses. Shrugging off the French officer's uniform, he threw it in a puddle that smelled of sewage. They walked back to the inn without speaking a word. Samuel took a candle from the owner, and they climbed the stairs to their room. He bolted their chamber door and they both let out a sigh of relief.

Pouring water from a pitcher into the washing basin, she washed Samuel's bloody knuckles with the red soap she'd sent to him. It lifted her heart a little that he had brought it with them. When she patted his knuckles dry with a towel, her hands were almost steady. She took the bloody water and dumped it out the window. After closing the single glass pane, she pulled the curtains shut. Frederica placed the basin back on the dresser and looked at her reflection—a large red welt had formed on her right cheek by her eye. She slumped onto the edge of the bed and tears filled her eyes.

Samuel cupped her face in his hands. 'I am so sorry I did not get there sooner... I did not want to arouse attention. I did not think he would harm you.'

'Ney and Grouchy,' Frederica whispered.

'What?'

She cleared her dry and sore throat. 'Those are the names of the marshals who will be in command with Napoleon...and they are leaving tomorrow morning.'

He inhaled sharply. 'Wellington will want to know immediately. I do not think it would be wise to leave tonight—it might cause suspicion, since we have already paid for lodging. We must leave at first light in the morning and get ahead of the army. It will take them much longer on foot and with their equipment. We should be able to beat them by a couple of days.'

Frederica sniffed and twisted her wrists. Her body flushed with an uncontrollable heat as she realised how close her plan had come to disaster.

'Can you hold me?' she asked in a small voice. 'I had no idea it would be quite so awful.'

Samuel took her into his strong arms. She rested her head against his chest, trying to hold in her tears. But still they fell down her cheeks and onto his night-shirt. She shivered and he held her tighter against him.

He patted her hair and whispered, 'No one will ever harm you again.'

Closing her eyes tightly, Frederica wanted desperately to believe him.

Chapter Twenty-One

Samuel woke up with Frederica still encircled in his arms. Her skin felt hot and flushed against his. The angry red welt on her cheek had turned into a purple bruise. He touched it gingerly, and she turned her head away from him and slept on. He watched the lace of her nightgown rise up and down. He could feel his own heart pounding inside his chest. Never before had she needed his help for anything. He was so used to viewing her as a competent minx. Not that she wasn't very capable, but everyone needed help sometimes. And he could not remember ever seeing her scared until last night.

This trip.

Their wedding journey had been eye-opening in so many ways. He had learned so much about Frederica. He had seen her nervous, shy, scared, and vulnerable. All traits he never dreamed his indomitable wife possessed. Samuel now understood why she danced out of his reach in Brussels and made a point to flirt with other soldiers. She'd wanted him to chase her, as she had chased after him. He even supposed that she worried if she let him catch her, that he would lose interest.

There was very little chance of that.

His body was overly warm and stimulated in all sorts of ways that were most uncomfortable with a shy wife. Shaking his head, he could not help but smile. Frederica felt nervous with him. He would not have believed it possible.

Moaning, she stirred in his arms.

Samuel was not yet ready to let go. He had never felt anything like this before. He wanted to hold her for ever. Protect her. Laugh with her. Love her. Slender Billy was right. Frederica deserved to know how he felt and not just through a death letter.

But how to tell her?

She'd lowered her guard with him on the ride to Paris, but it had been firmly back in place since. Sighing, he realised that they were both very careful with their hearts.

Frederica blinked several times and rubbed her bruised face into his chest. 'Is it morning? Should we be on our way?'

'Not quite yet and if we leave before sunrise, it will draw the kind of attention that we don't want. We cannot appear to be in a rush.'

She kissed his neck and then underneath his chin, making a trail of kisses to his lips. He returned her kisses gently, not wishing to scare her with the force of his own feelings. It felt so right to have her encircled in his arms, to touch her satin-like skin with his fingers, and to lose himself in her wicked mouth.

Frederica kissed him once more before nuzzling her head in the crook of his neck. 'I want more than kisses, but I am scared to disappoint you. And I do not want you to laugh at me.'

Smiling tenderly, he caressed her cheek and then her glorious hair. 'Why would I laugh at you?'

She covered her face with her hands, burying her head further against him. 'At my inexperience. What if I am awkward or, even worse, bad at lovemaking?'

His body temperature rising exponentially, he gently pulled her hands away from her face and gazed into her beautiful hazel eyes. 'What if I promise not to laugh?'

'Stop smiling.'

He pressed his lips together in a thin line, but the edges turned upward.

'You are still smiling.'

'We are in bed together, Frederica,' he said with a light laugh. 'And you said that you wanted me to make love to you. It would be a miracle if I was not smiling.'

Shaking her head, she gritted her teeth. 'I do not know what to do—I mean, I do know, but I have never done it before and I could not bear it if you mocked me.'

He brought her hands to his mouth and kissed her wrists, her palms, and then the tip of each little finger. 'I do not want to mock you. I want to worship you. And you need not worry about being compared to previous experiences. I have never done it before either.'

Pulling her hands away from him, she sat up in bed. The covers fell from her chest, revealing her thin chemise. 'Do not lie to me. I know gentlemen are not supposed to be virgins.'

Scraping his hands through his hair, Samuel sat up in the bed. 'I know, but I could not be like other young gentlemen. I did not wish to get the pox or bring some other bawdy house disease home to my wife like my father did. I should have already told you, but my mother has the French pox too and it's in the latent stage where there are no symptoms. Our family doctor says that the longest time he's seen a patient stay in the latent stage is thirty years. It has been fifteen for Mama and every day I fear that the disease will return. At the most, she will have another fifteen years to live before her organs deteriorate and she goes mad. It will probably be sooner and it is all my lecherous father's fault.'

Placing a hand on his shoulder, she swallowed. 'I did not know that about your mother. I am so sorry. How long have you known?'

'Since I was ten years old,' he said, his voice tight. 'Mama used to say that she depended upon me. Then she called me her sweet baby angel Sammy, but her confidences were crushing. I could see the sores on her hands and mouth and I did not know what or how I was supposed to help her. And after she passed the first two stages of the illness, there was always the worry about my father and his many mistresses. I tried to be the best son I could for her. To do well in school and not chase petticoats or give in to my base desires. So that I wouldn't add to her worries.'

She inhaled deeply. 'That is why you hate that nickname. I wish you would have told me sooner. What a terrible burden for a child to bear.'

Samuel could no longer meet her gaze. 'It was. That is the true reason that I joined the army. Yes, my father's pox coming back contributed to it, but mostly I could no longer live with our family's secrets. I abandoned my mother to deal with it alone.'

Placing her hand on his back, she rubbed circles against his nightshirt. 'I love your mother, I truly do. And I have said it before, she is a very capable woman. But she was wrong to put so much pressure on a child. And you need not remonstrate with yourself any longer—she wasn't alone. After you left, she turned to my mother, who was more than capable of helping her take care of your father and the estates. You are not responsible for your father's, nor your mother's, choices.'

Frederica's words and her touch seemed to ease the tenseness of his muscles. She had given him absolution for his greatest regrets and deepest sorrows. The Duchess of Hampford was nearly the same age as his mother and a much better confidant. She was an adult with experience and resources. Samuel did not blame his mother for depending upon him at such an early age; she must have felt as if she had no other choice. She didn't want society to know the truth. But he also knew that he would never put such pressure or expectations on a child of his own. He would never expect a boy to bear the burdens of a man.

Exhaling, he felt the rest of the tension leave his body. 'You're right. You are right. I am only responsible for my own choices.'

'And do not feel guilt for choosing to leave a difficult situation. When someone is drowning, they cannot save another swimmer. Sometimes, you have to keep yourself afloat and there is no shame in survival.'

Her words were like a balm on his wounded soul. He had done his very best for as long as he could, and when it became too much, he had left. And he hadn't completely abandoned his mother. He wrote to her regularly and came home after his father's death. He'd even promised to marry Frederica because of his mother's pressure. Slightly smiling, he did not hold that particular offence against Mama any longer. Frederica was the greatest joy in his life.

'You saved me once when I was drowning.'

She let out a gurgle of laughter. 'After I pushed you into the river.'

'True.'

And they laughed together.

Frederica leaned her head against his shoulder and her hand brushed across his torso. He was no longer thinking about his parents or his past. His mind and body were focused on his beautiful wife in bed next to him.

'Is it terrible for me to say that I am glad that it is your first time too? That I am the only one that you have been with intimately, so you can't compare me to anyone else, and that you are not diseased.'

He encircled his arm around her waist and pulled her tighter against him. 'No. I am glad that I am your only one too.'

'How do we start?'

He stood up, shucking off his nightshirt and tossing it on the floor. 'Although we do not have any practical experience, we are both bright people. I am sure we can figure it out between the pair of us and I am certainly eager to try.'

She clapped her hands over her mouth and he realised that she was covering a giggle. How quickly their conversations went from serious to silliness. Coming back onto the bed, he moved her hands a second time and kissed that wicked, laughing tongue. Their hands gently explored each other, unsure, but each touch burned. And they came together slowly, tenderly, and thoroughly.

After, he held her in his arms, feeling happier than he had ever been in his entire life. His limbs felt weightless, but full. He couldn't help but hum his favourite bar tune about a buxom maid named Nelly. He was sure that the mythical barmaid had nothing on his wife.

Frederica rubbed her face against his chest and laughed.

'How come you can giggle during the entire act, but if I crack so much as a smile, I am in trouble?'

She giggled again.

How he loved that sound!

All the little noises that she made before, during, and after.

Frederica kissed his bare shoulder. 'Because I cannot help myself. I am too joyful to merely smile—I must laugh.'

Leaning towards her, he brushed her satin lips over and over with his own. He wanted nothing more than to stay with her in this bed. In this room. For ever.

But the sun was rising. It was time to leave. His general and his friends were both waiting for the information.

His wife.

Samuel wanted a lifetime with Frederica and a family. But one short wedding trip might be all the time that they had together. He could not wait any longer. He needed to tell her the truth—that he loved her. Loved everything about her. From every stubborn hair on her head to her sharp heels that she had stomped on his feet with. She had well and truly caught him this time and he would never let her go if the choice were merely his.

But it was not.

He heard his wife moan as she pulled the dress

over her head. The coarse material must have brushed against the bruise on her face. She walked towards him with her shiny brown curls tumbling over her rounded shoulders.

'I finally understand why men as a whole rule the world.'

Samuel pulled up his other boot. 'And why is that?'

She turned around and glanced over her shoulder coquettishly. 'They can do up their own buttons. Men's buttons are on the front of their clothes, and a lady's buttons are always on the back, making them eternally dependent on another.'

Moving his hands to her shoulders, he carefully buttoned her dress up. His fingers shaking a little. 'That is why God made man and woman. To button for each other what the other cannot button. I solemnly promise to always unbutton your dress for you.'

Giggling, she spun around in his arms to face him. 'And button it back up?'

He kissed her hard on the mouth. 'Well, eventually.'

She made a trail of kisses from his mouth to his ear. She licked it and then nibbled on the end. 'That's more than fair.'

They dressed in a hurry and ate a small breakfast, before Samuel paid their remaining shot at the inn. The ostler brought their horses and they were fresh. Samuel helped Frederica onto her grey and then mounted his own mare. They trotted down the street slowly, as if they were not in any hurry to beat an entire army to Brussels. Frederica was unusually quiet as they rode and Samuel felt light-headed. The air felt charged with lightning. The hairs on his arms stood to attention like an ensign before a quartermaster.

Samuel leaned over nearer to Frederica. 'I am going to take us another way. If someone should question us, let me do all the talking. And if I say to make a run for it, do so immediately. With or without me.'

'Yes, of course.'

She would never have agreed to such terms in England. Nor would he have asked them of her, if their situation was not fraught with peril.

They passed several soldiers. Samuel lifted his hat to them, and Frederica waved merrily. She even blew a kiss to one of the soldiers with a shaking hand and a tremulous smile. He could tell that she was scared, yet she still put on a brave face. His bride was truly the most remarkable of women.

They rode under the gates of the city and onto the road that led to Brussels. They urged their horses to a canter and eventually a gallop. After two hours of hard riding, Samuel told Frederica to slow her horse down to a walk for a mile or so. She did and directed her grey close to Samuel so that their knees were touching, a small, but helpful, comfort. He was beginning to depend on her presence. He did not wish to live in a world without her. He needed to get her to the safety of Brussels as quickly as possible.

'Where did you learn to fight like that? With the French colonel?' she asked with a small smile. 'I doubt that it was covered at Eton. You could not even beat Matthew in fisticuffs then and he isn't very good.'

He shook his head, his own lips twitching. 'Your brother is several years my senior, but I learned how to improve my fists and my swordsmanship from an army guide in the Peninsula.'

'You would pummel Matthew now.'

Her brother was an amusing fellow whose best weapon had always been words. 'Seven years. I suppose Matthew has changed a great deal.'

'Not a whit,' she assured him with a chuckle. 'He is still quite nutty about steam locomotives and you should never trust him with a pen. He will write the stockings off your toes and charge you double for them.'

His heart lightened. Matthew had always been a clever cove, but a kind one. 'Didn't he get married a few years back?'

Frederica beamed at him. 'Yes. To Nancy. She is one of my dearest friends. She taught me how to wield a dagger and twirl it between my fingers.'

'A paragon,' he quipped, knowing that weaponry was indeed the way to Frederica's heart.

'She used to be a part of a criminal gang.'

'I look forward to improving my acquaintance with her,' Samuel said and he was not lying. He had forgotten how wonderful it was to be a part of a large and loving family. He had missed the Stringhams in all their absurdity, criminality, and animality. Smiling, he looked forward to being among them again. To belonging.

'And Wick's wife, Louisa, is very nice too,' she added conscientiously. 'She doesn't wield a knife, but she is quite wicked with a sewing needle.'

'You said that Wick has taken over the estate management.'

Biting her lower lip, Frederica nodded. 'Yes, Papa still cannot see past the end of our elephant's trunk.

His animals and his studies are all that he cares about. And Matthew has partnered with our grandfather in his business.'

'He's a businessman?' Samuel tried to keep his tone even, but there was a note of surprise in it. Most gentlemen knew only how to spend money, not earn it.

Her eyes narrowed and she gave him a scowl of disapproval that he recognised all too well. 'Yes, and I mean to be a businesswoman.'

Samuel cleared his throat. 'I remember. Your red soap.'

Frederica's face turned redder than any soap. She looked adorably guilty. 'But I did not tell you everything… It is not just our mothers' fault that you had to wed me. I could have refused to accept the arranged marriage, but I did not.'

'I could have refused my hand, as well.'

She lowered her head, shaking it back and forth. 'Not very easily. I knew that you were in a tight pinch and I wanted you to finally choose me. Not to be forced into proposing to an almost stranger. I told my mother no at first to the arrangement, but then she promised to give me half of her company now and the other half—you know, after she dies.'

His throat felt unaccountably dry and it was difficult to swallow. 'You married me for *perfume* bottles?'

'A lot of perfume bottles. And a company that exports its product to most major cities in Europe,' Frederica said and gulped. 'As you know, I mean to expand the business into red scented soaps.'

He did not speak for several minutes. His mind whirling with these new revelations.

Of course the strong-minded and independent Frederica would not have accepted his proposal of marriage simply because her parents wanted her to. Even if she both liked and despised him, in equal measure. She would have been too proud and obstinate. No, he should have realised that Lady Hampford had sweetened the pot. Frederica was no fool or simpering society miss.

Throwing his head back, Samuel laughed out loud. 'At least we will always be clean and smell good.'

Frederica giggled, covering her mouth with one hand. 'I could use some perfume and soap about now myself. I smell strongly of sweat and horse.'

'Me too,' he said, winking at her.

Her colour was still high in her cheeks. She looked flushed and ready to be kissed. 'Do you mind terribly that I married you for a perfume company? I should have told you before we spoke our vows.'

'Not at all,' he said and meant it.

Samuel would have been too stupid to seek out her company again. Before seeing her, his mind had entangled Frederica and the Stringham family with his father's expectations. And he had not wanted to do anything to please the lecherous old man who was his sire in name only. He might have missed the love of a lifetime by holding on to old grudges. Plus, she had not kept her ambitions from him a secret. She'd told him about her scented soaps and even sent him one that his valet had packed for this very journey. It was very red and strong smelling.

Turning his head, he saw that Frederica was still gazing at him intently. 'At least you did not buy me cheaply. I daresay it cost at least a hundred thousand pounds. And any person would be flattered to be purchased at that price.'

She snorted and then laughed. It was inelegant and utterly adorable. And she was his.

His.

He did not care that his parents had planned the union whilst he was in short coats. Or that his father's debts had made the match inescapable. Or that his bride was bribed to marry him.

How they arrived here did not matter.

She laughed again and he smiled at her. 'I see a town not a mile off. Do you mind if we stop for a few minutes? I have need to—well, you know—'

Samuel readily agreed, and they cantered into the hamlet and found a small, dirty public house. He assisted Frederica to dismount and tied both of their horses to the hitching post. Tossing a coin to the ostler, he asked the lad to bring their mounts some water.

A haggard woman with a scowl and greasy black hair was the proprietor of the public house. Frederica followed the woman to the privy. But something felt off—wrong. Samuel ordered some ale and waited for his wife. Frederica joined him in the taproom, where they quickly drank the ale. He placed a few coins on the bar and led her out of the door by her elbow.

He untied the horses with efficiency, and both were mounted and riding in less than two minutes.

'Why the hurry?' she asked.

'That woman suspected us.'

'How do you know?'

'A feeling.'

He led them away from the road through several wheat fields. He changed directions three times and they did not stop when it became dark. After dismounting, they passed by an apple orchard which cast grotesque shadows in the moonlight. Frederica picked a couple of red apples and tossed one to Samuel. They both ate theirs eagerly. Then they crept through the orchard and towards the large shadow of a barn.

Frederica touched his arm. 'I can't hear any animals.'

Samuel handed her the reins to his horse. 'I will go check it out.'

Opening the barn door as quietly as possible, Samuel blinked to accustom his eyes to the darkness. His other senses came awake. He could smell manure that was not more than a day old. His feet stepped on grain, loose on the floor. There were no animals in any of the stalls. Nor chickens wandering around.

He returned to Frederica. 'Someone left in a hurry. All the stalls are empty and there is a sack of grain spilled on the floor. They were probably trying to avoid having their animals stolen by the army.'

Frederica wrinkled her nose. 'I hope that we are not sleeping on the floor.'

'Nonsense! Only the best for my wife.'

He could see her smile at the comment. It felt unaccountably right to call her *his* wife. To be *her* husband.

Samuel found a few bales of hay, and he cut them open with a knife and spread the clean straw on the dirt floor of the barn. Meanwhile, he heard Frederica feeding the horses apples.

He could tell she was smiling at him in the darkness. 'They are as hungry as we are.'

'I'll fetch them some water,' he said.

She nodded. 'I'll put them in the empty stalls and brush them down.'

It did not take long to locate the well, about twenty-five yards from the barn. He heaved out a bucket and brought it back to Frederica. They both drank first and then washed their faces. Then he fetched two more buckets of water for the horses, before collapsing beside Frederica on the hay. They did not undress, but lay together, huddling for what little warmth they could find.

'I always wanted to sleep in the hayloft as a child,' Frederica said, snuggling up to Samuel. 'But perhaps you could warm me up first?'

He enthusiastically accepted this challenge and after only a few minutes, they were both quite hot. He placed his arm underneath her head and kissed her brow. He felt her body twitch a few times, before she settled into a sleep.

Samuel prayed that he could keep her safe.

Chapter Twenty-Two

Samuel woke up before Frederica. He fed and watered the horses and saddled them up. He touched her shoulder to wake her. Opening her eyes, she smiled at him. He could get used to waking up to her smiles.

'We need to leave before sunrise, just in case this farm isn't abandoned like I thought,' he explained.

Frederica stood and brushed the hay off her riding habit. Samuel gently picked several pieces of hay out of her hair.

Her cheek was still puffy and purple as she touched her disordered brown locks. 'I am sure I look a fright.'

'I think you look beautiful.'

And he meant it. Heaven help him, he meant it.

Frederica only laughed and he led the horses out of the barn, latching the door behind them. Samuel led them back to the road and they made good time until late afternoon. He could see the outline of the city of Valenciennes. Glancing over to Frederica, she gave him a wan smile. He heard his stomach rumble. They were dirty, tired, and hungry. His instinct was to circle around the town instead of going through it, but he could see Frederica's shoulders sagging, her face pale. She was exhausted.

He gently pulled on the bridle to slow his horse to a walk. 'Let us dine in Valenciennes and perhaps stay the night. I think we are both done in.'

She did not respond, only nodded. As if too tired to speak.

They rode slowly into town and there were only a few people in the street. There was an unnatural quiet about the town. The silence before a battle. Samuel stopped at the first inn and helped Frederica dismount. He tied the horses to the hitching post and he watched her stiffly walk in. The owner, a rail-thin man with a skull-like head, met them at the entrance. His dark eyes took in the state of their clothing. He gave them a sinister smile and asked how his humble inn could serve them. Samuel ordered a dinner and asked if there was a private parlour.

'This way, monsieur, mademoiselle,' the owner said with sinister courtesy. He led them to an adjacent room with a dirty square table and four shabby chairs. The owner shut the door with a thud.

Samuel shook his head. 'I am sorry, Freddie. I did not think a nicer inn would allow us in.'

She walked around the table several times. 'No indeed. And there was no other inn on the street. If this place were nicer, we would have been refused entry.'

He watched her touch her reticule for her pistol. Instinctively, he checked his coat for his knife and his pistol. They were there and ready.

Frederica circled the table again, but did not sit down on a chair. 'Something doesn't feel right.'

'I agree. Let us leave,' Samuel said, his stomach roiling with a mixture of fear and hunger. 'We are close to the border. Mons is only another twenty miles, and there are British soldiers there. We will be safe.'

Samuel cautiously peeked into the taproom—he counted ten heavily armed Frenchmen. He closed the door softly and told Frederica to take out her pistol. She did so immediately and cocked down the hammer on it. Pulling out his own weapon, he raised his finger to his lips and then threw open the door.

'Come on!'

Frederica followed him out of the small room with the musket poised in her arms ready to shoot. They ran across the taproom without a word and out the exit to their horses, which were whinnying and fretting. The animals must also have sensed the danger. Samuel pocketed his pistol and started to untie the knots. Glancing over his shoulder, he saw that a Frenchman had followed them and was pointing a pistol at him. He heard a shot and braced his body for the bullet, closing his eyes momentarily. But he felt nothing. The air cracked with a second shot. He opened his eyes to see Frederica standing between him and the body of a dead Frenchman. She clutched her side, which he saw was wet with blood seeping through her gloved fingers. His wife must have stepped between him and death.

Behind her, he could see more men coming towards them. He tossed her onto her horse as she gasped with pain. He mounted his own mare and led both animals in a dead run out of the city. They had to get to the border before the soldiers could stop them. Sweat poured off his face and the horses' bodies. Glancing over his shoulder, he kept making sure that Frederica was still on the back of her grey.

Once he was sure that the soldiers were not following them, he veered off the road and into a small forested area. He didn't stop until they were no longer visible from the path.

After slipping off his horse, he lifted Frederica gently to the ground and helped her lie down. Her legs were too weak to hold her upright. 'Let me see the wound.'

She moved her hand from her side and it was wet and red. Her blood had dripped down her clothes all the way to the hem. Unsuccessfully, she tried to unbutton her riding habit. He brushed her hand aside and quickly unbuttoned it and then took off her dress. With only her shift and corset on, he could see that the bullet had gone clean through her side. Her stays had partially protected her skin, but he still thought that she would need stitching. The fact that she had been able to stand after being shot was incredible. Most soldiers would not have been able to. Nor would they have been able to stay atop a mount for a several-mile ride.

'Bandages. I need bandages,' he said in an undertone to himself.

Frederica swallowed, her face pale and strained. Closing her eyes, she said, 'You can use the bottom of my shift.'

He kneeled down beside her. This delightful garment only grazed the top of her knees. Tearing off the bottom four inches of her shift, he ripped the fabric into long bandages and tied them tightly around the wound at her waist. He lifted her back gently with each wrap. He hoped that would stop the wound from bleeding. Leaning back, he got an eyeful of her long, shapely legs and had to remind himself that she had just been shot. This was not the time for longing thoughts.

'Freddie—I…I…uh…do not know what to say,' he whispered, exhaling slowly. 'You took a bullet for me. I do not think anyone else would have done that for me. W-why did you do it?'

Frederica's lips were nearly as white as her face, but they smiled slightly. 'You cannot bring up the bear cub any more.'

He let out a wet chuckle. 'I won't.'

'And I mean to guilt you about it for the rest of our lives. If ever I am losing an argument, I will say, "Remember that one time in France when I took a bullet for you?" And then you'll humbly let me win.'

A tear slid down his cheek, he was so worried for her that he could barely breathe. She had lost a great deal of blood and they were still several miles away from Mons and safety. He brushed her hair away from her face. 'I will always let you win.'

'Liar.'

Bending forward, he pressed a kiss against her brow. It felt strangely cool. She reached for him and he wrapped his arms tightly around her. She felt fragile to him for the first time and he realised that if the bullet had been a few inches closer to her stomach, that he would have lost her for ever. His fiery, fierce, and formidable Frederica.

Rubbing his face into her hair, he spoke into her curls, 'I am not worth it, darling.'

'You are to me.'

Those four little words nearly undid him. Never before had someone loved him so purely. Not his parents. Not his friends. Not his general. None of them would have sacrificed their lives for his.

Tilting his head back, he brushed his lips against hers before saying, 'Promise me that you will never risk your life for mine again?'

'It is just a flesh wound. I could stitch it myself if I could sew a straight line.'.

He squeezed his eyes shut trying not to picture her dead and in a coffin, but the image stayed in his mind. 'Promise me, Freddie.'

She pressed a kiss to his ear. 'I cannot. You know that I cannot.'

Another tear slid down his cheek. 'If you love me, you will live.'

Frederica kissed the tear away. 'I love you and I hate you, Samuel Corbin, and I will do whatever I think is best at the time.'

Samuel wanted to argue with her, but innately he could not fight with her when she was injured for him. When her very life was in the balance. All he could do was ensure that his wife received medical treatment and safety. He had to get her back to Brussels. England would have been better.

Gingerly, he helped her put back on her dress and riding habit before lifting her up into the saddle. Her face paled another shade. Samuel could not meet her eyes. His mouth was dry and his heartbeat raced. He felt so inadequate. The woman he loved had taken a bullet for him, and yet he still could not ensure her safety. Mons was still over an hour's ride away. A hard one.

Samuel leaned closer to her. 'Would you rather ride with me?'

She clenched her teeth together, grimacing and shaking her head. 'The horses are already spent. It would be easier for them if we rode separately.'

Swinging up into his own saddle, he said, 'We will take it slowly. If you need to stop or rest at any time, just say the word.'

Urging his horse into a gentle canter, Samuel's muscles were tensed and his teeth clenched. His eyes kept darting all around to ensure that no danger lurked in the shadows of a tree or a rock. They rode that way until he reached the edge of the city of Mons at dusk. Frederica had not asked to halt, nor had she spoken at all. He thought that she must be using all of her considerable willpower to simply stay on top of her grey. Samuel was in pretty bad shape himself and he did not have a bullet wound.

The road into the city was blocked by British officers wearing dusty scarlet uniforms that would have been all the better for a washing. They pointed their bayonets at them and what was left of Samuel's patience evaporated in the hot air. He needed to get his wife help immediately.

'For heaven's sake get out of my way,' Samuel yelled in English. 'Are you blind? My wife has been shot and needs medical attention immediately.'

The six soldiers looked at each other dubiously. They must have all been of the same rank and it was obviously not a high one. Common soldiers, even cavalry, were often brainless sheep to be herded.

'That is an order!' Samuel yelled, urging his horse closer to their line to intimidate them. 'I am Colonel Lord Pelford and I will see each and every one of you court-martialled, if you do not obey me instantly.'

The officers parted, and Samuel rode through them, pulling the reins of Frederica's horse. Glancing back, he saw her swaying in her seat. They could not arrive soon enough at a respectable inn.

He pointed at a spotted young man on his right. 'I want a surgeon at that inn in less than ten minutes. Do you understand me?'

The spotted young man nodded vigorously, and Samuel rode twenty more feet to the hitching post. He slid off his horse and carried Frederica's limp body in. She gave him a feeble protest, but did not fight him. That worried him more than the bullet wound. Holding her close to his chest, he hollered at the innkeeper in French to take him to a room. The stout man immediately led the way up the stairs to a small room that had a narrow bed, a wooden chair, and a table. The furnishings were humble, but clean, which was all that they needed. The innkeeper pulled down the blankets on the bed and Samuel gently laid Frederica on it. She mumbled something, but it was incoherent. He hoped it was an insult. She was strongest when she was fighting him.

The stout innkeeper went to the door and yelled to his wife in French to come quick and then in broken English. Moments later, a sturdy woman with a kind face and an abundance of red hair came through the entrance.

Her large green eyes widened, and she pointed a stubby finger at her husband. 'Put a kettle to boil, Janssens, and I will get some fresh linen. You can speak English to me, milord. I were born in Dover. Now take off her boots and help your wife get comfortable.'

Monsieur Janssens and his wife immediately left the room. Samuel set about the task that he had been assigned. Perhaps he was a mindless sheep of a soldier after all. As gently as he could, he pulled off her boots and stockings. They were covered in dirt and flecks of blood. Slightly smirking, he remembered that it was not an uncommon state for his bride. During their entire childhood, she'd always had a layer of mud on her boots and often on the rest of her person. She had been an indomitable explorer and a fearless friend. He could not imagine a world without her in it. Telling him what to do. Teasing him. Kissing him. The fear that gripped his heart now was tenfold what it had been during their escape. She simply lay there. Not moving. Not speaking.

Sitting on the edge of the bed, Samuel stroked his wife's hair. 'Just hold on, Frederica, and think of the most marvellous scar you will have. It may be even better than the ones I received from the bear cub's claws.'

He thought he saw a ghost of a smile on her lips. Even wounded, Frederica was the most competitive person that he had ever met. He felt empty at the thought of living without her challenging and loving presence.

'Care to see my scars?'

Her eyes were closed, but his wife only nodded her head slightly. Her countenance was even paler than before. Her wicked fingers had skimmed over his scars on their travels to Paris. His body had tingled when she touched him, skin to skin. Then he had made her his wife. It had been the most transcendent experience of his life, well worth waiting four and twenty years for. There could be no other woman for him.

Mrs Janssens returned first with a stack of linens and a nightgown. She placed them on the table by the bed. Then pointed at him like she had at her husband. 'Milord, would you kindly leave the room?'

'I am not leaving my wife,' Samuel said flatly.

Mrs Janssens nodded and her hair flopped back and forth. 'Wash your hands and help me undress her then.'

She shut the chamber door. Samuel assisted Mrs Janssens in gently taking off Frederica's bloodstained riding habit, dress, and shift. He had never seen her completely unclothed before. She'd kept her chemise on during their first lovemaking; he'd quite enjoyed working around it. And their second time had been in a dark barn where they both had been fully clothed except for the essential areas.

He noticed that Frederica's pale, curvaceous body was covered with sticky black and red dried blood. She seemed smaller and more vulnerable without her clothes. Mrs Janssens lightly touched the bullet wound at her waist and Frederica's body twitched as she cried out in pain. His own chest mirrored the ache. If only he had been faster. If only she had not stepped between him and the man with the gun. If only—

There was a knock at the door and Mrs Janssens took the kettle of hot water from her husband.

'Now I need a basin of cold water,' she said, firmly shutting him out. She cast Samuel a look that seemed to say, *Give me any trouble and you will be kicked out, as well.*

As gently as he could, he washed the dried blood off his wife's body, careful to keep clear of the gaping wound. The blood was brighter there, even if it had coagulated. The skin around it was already red and angry. He hoped and prayed that it would not become infected. In his army experience, infections killed more soldiers than bullets.

Then he remembered her red scented soap. Dunford

had packed it in his saddlebag. He excused himself to go and fetch it. He prayed it worked as well as Frederica said that it did.

When he returned, Mrs Janssens set the kettle near the linen and took another towel, dipping it into the scalding water. She held the rag in the air for a few moments to allow it to cool before she expertly wiped away the dried blood from the wound. Frederica's eyes popped open and she said a few choice words that would have shocked most ladies. She had probably learned them from her father or brothers. Samuel put an arm around her shoulders, wishing that he could give her more comfort. Or laudanum for pain relief. When the rag was saturated, Mrs Janssens took a new towel and dipped it again in the hot water. He had been right. The bullet had only nicked her side.

Samuel held out the cake of red soap. 'Please use this to clean the wound, ma'am.'

The older woman brought the bar to her nose and gave it a sniff before dipping it into the water and lathering it over the wound. The soap smelled of rosemary and an astringent odour that he did not recognise. He hoped the little cake could fight any infection that was beginning to set in. His wife was nowhere near out of danger yet.

Once the area was clean, Mrs Janssens asked, 'Shall I sew you up, milady? I reckon I will do a better job of stitches than the doctor.'

'Y-yes,' Frederica said in a pained whisper.

The Englishwoman glanced at Samuel for his approval too.

'Please. I will pay any price.'

Mrs Janssens left the room with the soiled rags and

returned with more hot water to sterilise the needle. He had to turn his head away as the point of the needle entered Frederica's skin. He expected her to scream, but instead she fainted in his arms. Another thing he could add to his list of surprises. Frederica could faint. *Unfathomable.* He did not try to rouse her immediately, assuming that her consciousness needed a respite from the pain.

When Mrs Janssens finished stitching, she bid Samuel lift Frederica, while she wrapped the bandage around her. Once she secured the bandage, Mrs Janssens directed Samuel to cradle Frederica's head so that she could put the nightgown on her. Mrs Janssens gently placed Frederica's feet underneath the sheets and covered her with the blanket.

There was another discreet knock at the door.

Mrs Janssens rushed over and opened it to take the basin of cold water from her husband. She set it on the table next to the bed. 'Now, milord, let her rest and I will make some broth for when she stirs. Take one of those cloths, dip it in the cold water, and dab at her face. We must prevent her body from becoming feverish, if we can.'

'Yes, of course,' Samuel said, swallowing down the sour taste in his mouth. 'Thank you, ma'am. I cannot tell you how much I appreciate all that you have done for my wife. You are most skilled.'

Mrs Janssens gave him a sad smile. 'You cannot have lived in Europe during the last twenty years, without taking care of a fair share of bullet wounds. Mind you, do not let the doctor bleed her again when he comes. Them doctors is as bad as the leeches they use for sucking blood. And your wife looks as if she has already lost too much.'

With that, she left the room.

Samuel pulled the chair next to the bed and sat down. Dipping a fresh cloth into the cool water, he wiped at Frederica's pale face. She lay so still. He placed his hand on her throat and could feel a light pulse. He took her hand, rocking in his seat. Unable to hold still. Fear gripped his heart and his mind. Not even in the midst of battles in Spain, had he ever felt so powerless and scared. His eyes grew wet and his vision blurred.

Squeezing her hand tighter, he said, 'Do not leave me, Frederica. Please do not leave me. You promised me a lifetime of bickering and I really must insist upon it.'

Frederica's eyes did not open, but her lips moved. Samuel moved his ear closer to her face to hear her say one word: 'Bossy.'

A wet chuckle escaped him and he wiped at his watery eyes, the weight in his chest lightening now that she had regained consciousness. It was a small step, but it gave him hope.

'You also promised me a palace full of children,' he reminded her, watching her lips twitch slightly upward. 'Wild, badly behaved little Stringhams that will probably be covered in mud at least half of the time, and the rest, jumping into rivers fully dressed. Or pushing each other in. I hope our children will be just like you. Just as brave, headstrong, argumentative, and imaginative. And I cannot deny that I am particularly looking forward to the creation of the children.'

She gave a soft, breathy laugh and opened her eyes. 'As am I.'

Leaning forward, he brushed a gentle kiss against her brow. Her temperature was closer to normal now. He hoped that was a good sign.

Mrs Janssens gave two knocks before re-entering the room with a harried man with a small black bag who Samuel assumed was the doctor. 'Monsieur Dubois, the surgeon, milord.'

Samuel stood and held out his hand to the doctor, who reluctantly gave a limp one for him to shake.

'My wife was shot by French soldiers,' Samuel explained, trying to keep his voice even. 'The bullet grazed her side and Mrs Janssens cleaned the wound and sewed it.'

Dubois looked over his long, thin nose at Frederica's still form. He opened his black bag and took out a metal horn-shaped instrument and placed the rounded part against her chest and his ear against the top. He listened to her breathe for a few moments. Then he picked up her wrist and held the pulse, timing it with a golden pocket watch. 'Well, monsieur, if the bullet has already been taken out and bandaged, I think it is best to leave it to heal. I will just take a pint of blood and check on my patient tomorrow.'

Frederica's eyes flew open again. 'No.'

Samuel looked from her to Mrs Janssens, who shook her head slightly.

He swallowed heavily. 'No, doctor. My wife has lost enough blood.'

Dubois gave an exasperated sigh and threw his hands up in the air. '*Sacré bleu!* I was dragged by a British cavalry soldier out of my home, and if you refuse to allow me to bleed her, I will no longer attend the young woman.'

'Do you have any laudanum?'

He shook his head. 'No, monsieur. It is hard to come by these days.'

Without medicine, the doctor would not be of much help.

Glancing at Frederica, she nodded her head forward with a grimace. She did not wish to be bled. Samuel turned back to the doctor. 'Go then. You will have plenty of other patients before the week is done.'

Mrs Janssens and Dubois both looked aghast.

The innkeeper's wife grasped her chest, her face paling several shades. 'Then the rumours are true? Napoleon is coming?'

'You have a day. Possibly two.'

Dubois gave a curt nod and left the room, slamming the door behind him. Samuel wondered if the doctor would try to flee or help. After the battle, every church, school, and public building would be full of wounded soldiers in need of medical attention. Death was often a slow and painful process.

'Samuel,' Frederica said in a weak voice.

Moving to her side, he took her hand with one arm and gently caressed her brow with the other. 'What can I do for you?'

She gave him a small smile, but then winced. 'I am so hungry and everything hurts. And you know that I do not like to miss meals.'

Mrs Janssens cleared her throat and curtsied. 'I'll get milady some broth and bread.'

She left the room.

Perching on the edge of the bed, he continued to stroke her hair and cheek. 'I am so very sorry. I feel terrible that you were hurt under my protection.'

Frederica gave him another pained smile. 'No more sorrys. It was brilliant. You were brilliant. *I* was brilliant.'

This drew a reluctant laugh from Samuel.

She closed her eyes and gasped. 'Except next time, I will try my best not to get shot.'

He kissed her forehead and then her cheek. How he loved her. 'I would prefer that.'

Mrs Janssens returned with a candle and a tray. 'Milord, I prepared the room adjacent to this one for you to freshen up, and Mr Janssens has your dinner in hand. I shall look after the madam.'

Samuel glanced at Frederica, who gave him another weak smile. He thanked Mrs Janssens again and left the room. He found the horses in two stalls in a barn behind the inn. They appeared to have been fed, watered, and brushed down. He was grateful that Monsieur Janssens had taken care of them. The poor animals had run their hearts out for them. Patting his horse's head, he took off his saddlebag. Then he did the same for Frederica's grey.

After returning to the inn, he brought their meagre packs upstairs. The room for him was slightly smaller than Frederica's and not as well aired. Pouring water from a pitcher, he washed his arms, hands, and face. He wished he could wash away the image in his mind of Frederica's blood on his hands. He knew that he should leave her and take the information on to Wellington. It was his duty. But Frederica was his heart.

Chapter Twenty-Three

Frederica ached all over. She felt worse than she did last year when she was kicked in the stomach by a zebra. Clutching at her side, she groaned and tried to sit up gingerly. Falling back on her pillow, she decided to stay exactly where she was. She looked around the room and saw Samuel asleep in a chair by her side. How uncomfortable he must have been! Only an exhausted person could sleep on a wooden chair. His head hung to one side; his jaw was shadowed after several days of growth and no valet. It made him look older, rugged, and even more handsome. He was her husband and even if he did not choose her, Samuel wanted a life with her. A family. She warmed at the thought of it.

'Samuel?'

Blinking, his eyes slowly opened. He leaned forward and took her hand, caressing her knuckles with his strong fingers. 'Can I get you anything? Water? Breakfast? A chamber pot?'

'I am fine.'

He snorted, shaking his head. 'You are a terrible liar.'

'I feel awful,' Frederica said with a grimacing smile. 'How are you?'

Yawning, Samuel shrugged his shoulders. 'Stiff.'

She picked up his hand and brought it to her dry lips, brushing a kiss on the back and then in the palm. 'Please tell me you haven't slept in that chair all night? You must be exhausted.'

'No, no. Only half of it. Mrs Janssens, the innkeeper's wife, took the first shift. She is a most redoubtable Englishwoman and I am sure that you will like her.'

Biting her lower lip, Frederica remembered the red-headed woman who had sewed up her side. 'Yes. How lucky we were to have found her. Will you see if she is willing to help me dress? I do not think I could do it on my own this morning. I cannot even sit up by myself.'

He smiled down at her tenderly. 'And where do you think you are going with a bullet wound in your side?'

Frederica's breath hitched and she wished she didn't have to breathe, for every movement hurt her wound. 'We have to get back to Brussels and warn Wellington about the French generals that Napoleon is bringing with him.'

'We can go tomorrow.'

Squeezing her eyes shut, she shook her head against the hard pillow. 'There is no time to delay. Napoleon's forces are already marching towards us. If our mission is to be a successful one, we must get the information to Wellington as soon as possible, so that he can prepare his plan of attack. You need to leave me.'

'I will not,' he said quietly. 'It isn't safe for you.'

Of all the times for Samuel to be stubborn.

'It isn't safe for you to stay. You know that you should go. You are Wellington's ADC. You are on his staff and he trusts you to bring him this information.'

Moving to the bed, Samuel put his arm around Frederica's waist and kissed her cheek. 'Your health and safety are more important to me than a few hours' notice for a general. And whether that makes me a fool or a traitor, so be it.'

She threw her arms around his neck and pulled him down to her on the bed. Even though it hurt like she was being stabbed repeatedly, she hugged him tightly. Frederica felt alarmed at the thought that he belonged there. She had tried not to let her feelings for him deepen. He already had the most frustrating hold over her heart and mind. Yet here he was, choosing her over his general. The man who had become a father figure to him. A man whose respect he had earned. Samuel was putting her needs above that of his soldiers and his country. She never dreamed that he would be that devoted to her. To anyone. It filled her with a wonder that helped dim some of the pain.

Her eyes watered with unwanted tears. 'Why are you so difficult to hate sometimes?'

Frederica felt his laugh rumble in his chest before she heard it. The warm air brushed her ear and she shivered in his arms.

'Then it is settled. I will go and fetch you some breakfast.'

She nodded her face against his scratchy cheek and watched him leave the room. Slipping one foot and then the other onto the wooden floor, she forced her sore body into a sitting position first and then to standing. She couldn't allow Samuel to betray his general. He would be burdened with guilt for the rest of his life and the poor man already had enough memories that brought him pain. She limped to the window and stared out into the bright morning. Her vision must have been affected, for something large and black clouded the corner of her view. Rubbing her eyes, she opened the window and peered out of it. The black swarm was still there and it was moving.

Swallowing, her mouth went dry as she realised that it was the French army. Napoleon and his generals had taken the same road as Samuel and herself. Her husband had been right. It was not safe for her or for him to stay in Mons for another hour. Let alone another day. She would have to find the strength to leave.

It took several halting steps to make it to the narrow wardrobe where her only other plain dress was hanging. Riding her horse today was going to be a misery, but if Samuel was willing to sacrifice his career for her, she could endure some pain. Mrs Janssens must have cleaned and pressed her gown, because it looked as good as new. Pulling it over her head, she could only be grateful that she was already wearing a shift, for to lift her arms twice would have been torture. She sat on the floor and pulled up her stockings and laced up her boots.

Touching her wild curls, Frederica could not help but wish that Miss Wade was there scowling at her. She had such a way with hair. One that Frederica did not. Lifting both arms again, she braided her curls. She had to hold her breath to stop herself from crying or swearing. Probably both. She tied the end and dropped her arms, gasping in pain.

Frederica was still sitting on the floor when Samuel re-entered the room with a breakfast tray.

Gasping in surprise, he set it on the side table before stooping down beside her. 'What are you doing out of bed? Did you fall?'

She exhaled shakily and pointed to the wall. 'We must go this very morning. Napoleon's army is hot on our heels. Look through that window.'

Samuel moved swiftly to the open window and leaned his head out of it, holding on to the casing.

'Do you see the army?'

She watched him shade his eyes with one hand and lean out even farther. 'I do see a glimpse of something dark. But it is a great distance from us.'

Her eyesight must be sharper than his. 'Help me to my feet. I want to get something in my stomach before our long ride. I will need every bit of strength that I possess.'

Samuel put his hands around her arms and lifted her to her feet. Frederica was relieved that he did not touch her waist. It was smarting something dreadful. She hoped her movements hadn't caused the wound to open and bleed again. Samuel helped her across the room and into the chair that he'd spent half the night in.

She picked up a piece of toast. 'Go and have Monsieur Janssens prepare the horses and supplies. We should leave in a quarter of an hour.'

He placed his hand on her shoulder and gave it a light squeeze. 'Very good.'

Frederica forced herself to eat the toast and eggs, as well as the cherry water and lint weed tea. She'd learned from her mother that they had medicinal qualities. Even if she had no appetite now, she would need her strength for their hard ride. Draining the last of the tea, she felt her chest palpitate and her muscles quiver. She touched her chest and let out an airy laugh. After one and twenty years of age, she was finally behaving like a heroine in a novel: scared and silly.

She cleared her throat—she had no time for such theatrics. She was a spy after all. Frederica got to her feet and left the room, taking the stairs one at a time. The main floor of the inn was as clean and as inauspicious as her bedchamber. There were a few wooden tables, chairs, and a tap. Mrs Janssens bustled out of the kitchen door and bowed to her.

'Is there anything else you'll be needing this morning, milady?'

Frederica put a fist by her sore side. 'Might I have a bonnet? I must have lost my hat yesterday in the scuffle. I promise that my husband will pay for it.'

'Now, never you mind that, milady,' she said, waving her hand. 'Milord has been most generous in settling his accounts. The least I could do fer ye, is give you an old straw bonnet to keep the sun off your face.'

The good woman fetched the hat and even tied it around Frederica's chin. Frederica thanked her profusely before walking outside, grateful not to have to lift her arms again. Samuel stood near both horses and was speaking to Monsieur Janssens. She could see that their packs had been tied to their saddles and that their water jugs were refilled. The innkeeper doffed his hat to her and Samuel kneeled, cupping his hands. Taking a deep breath, she put her boot in his hands and allowed him to lift her onto her grey. She felt a jolt of pain when she sat down in the side-saddle, but forced herself to take the reins. Her fingers closed tightly around them.

Samuel mounted his own horse and they rode to the gates of the city, where several cavalry officers stood guard. They halted for a moment and she heard her husband warn them that the French army was coming and to prepare for battle. He saluted the captain in charge and then urged his horse forward. Frederica followed behind him. The up and down movement caused her wound to throb, but they had to continue. A young woman was not safe near an army, even if she had a bullet hole in her side.

After an hour, she sagged in the saddle and Samuel took the reins of her horse and guided both animals. She could no longer control her grey. It took all her stubbornness to stay seated. More than once, she had to catch herself from slipping off. Placing her hand on her wound, she felt a little blood seeping through her wool dress. She prayed that the stitches would hold a little longer.

How she remained on the back of her horse for another four hours, she did not know. All that she did comprehend is that by the time they reached the edge of the city of Brussels, each and every part of her body ached.

Samuel brought their horses to a halt. 'Shall I return you to your mother's house?'

Frederica shook her head roughly. 'I do not think that I am strong enough yet to deal with her wrath.'

Taking off his hat, he raked one hand through his hair. 'I confess I have always been a little afraid of your mother. Would you mind staying in my room at headquarters until you have been rested? I am sure that it is not as large or as fine as yours.'

Bile rose in her throat and her head felt dizzy. 'At this moment, I could happily lie down in the middle of the street.'

He touched her leg and rubbed it gently with his hand, like you would to calm a spooked horse. 'Hold on for just a little longer.'

With a click of his tongue, he guided their tired mounts through the city to the Rue Royale. Several guards were stationed outside of it and then pointed their weapons at the pair.

Samuel took off his hat again. 'I am Colonel Lord Pelford reporting to General Lord Wellington. Go and fetch a surgeon at once.'

The guards lowered their weapons and two men moved forward to take the reins of their horses. Samuel easily slid out of his saddle and moved to help her down. He put his hands on her thighs, rather than her waist, to lift her off her spent mare. His arms moved to encircle her as her knees gave way. She could not stand or walk. Her head felt like a horse had sat on it. There was not a spot on her body that did not throb in pain. Touching her temples, she winced.

Samuel lifted her up into his arms and carried her into the large house that Wellington and his staff occupied. Several soldiers saluted her husband as he weaved through the hall and up the stairs to presumably his room. He kicked open the door and then set her gently on top of the bed.

'Close your eyes. I will be back in a few minutes to take care of you,' he promised. 'I must first tell Wellington that Napoleon has brought with him Marshal Grouchy and Marshal Ney to command. And that the wily little emperor has taken the path through Mons.'

For the first time in her life, she obeyed him. Closing her eyes, Frederica let oblivion take her.

Chapter Twenty-Four

Samuel waited the next afternoon for the doctor to arrive and check on Frederica again. The night before, all the man had done was prescribe laudanum. It had eased the pain a little, but Frederica said that the hot bath and her red soap had helped more. She ate breakfast with him in bed, but was taking a nap now. Her colour was much better and he hoped that she would make a full recovery. All he could say for certain was that her tongue and wit had returned in full force. When Mr Dunford had found her in Samuel's bed, she'd teased his poor valet until the man was as red in the face as a bowl of cherries and he'd fled the room like a delicately nurtured debutante intent on keeping their reputation unsullied.

While looking out the window, a soldier tapped him on the shoulder and told him to report to Wellington's office. Samuel did so at once, along with several other staff members. The general told them to sit down around the table.

'The Prince of Orange writes that his troops have not been engaged, but the town of Binche is now occupied by the French and the Prussians driven out.'

Slender Billy.

He said a silent prayer of gratitude that his friend was not harmed.

DeLancey breathed in deeply. 'It has begun.'

'Ah, this letter from the Prussians explains that their first corps was attacked around Charleroi shortly after dawn, before five o'clock in the morning,' Wellington said, stabbing the paper with his pointer finger. 'Damn me, this dispatch is vague. Not a word about the size of the French force. This strike could be a trick, a feint, to pull us away from his real target. I dare not offer aid to the Prussians until I am sure of Napoleon's position.'

DeLancey stood. 'Lord Wellington, every ranking officer has been invited to the Duchess of Richmond's ball tonight. Shall I instruct them not to go, but to stand to ready for orders?'

'No,' Wellington said authoritatively. 'All members of my staff will attend the Duchess of Richmond's ball. If we were to cancel it, it would only encourage the Belgians who are loyal to France. No, we will go. We will smile and we will hearten our soldiers. DeLancey, have any dispatch brought directly to me at the ball.'

'Yes, Your Grace.'

Samuel did not think he could dance the night before a battle.

Wellington glanced at the other three men. 'The rest of you, go and put on your best dress uniforms, and I will meet with you again at the ball, where I will give you further orders.'

He would have no choice in the matter.

Samuel walked up the two flights of stairs to his bedchamber. He was met at the door by his valet, Dunford, an impeccably dressed and manicured gentleman in his late thirties. He had a high forehead and his ears pointed at the tips.

Dunford swept his employer an exquisite bow. 'Your Grace, I could not lay out your dress uniform for this evening because your bedchamber is occupied. I have been polishing your boots in the kitchens. The *kitchens*.'

Samuel could hear the indignation in his servant's tone and forced himself not to smile. 'Dunford, I apologise. I will be returning Lady Pelford to her mother's house this very afternoon. I will call for you when I am ready to dress for dinner. I shall be attending Lady Richmond's party this evening.'

The valet swept another perfect bow. 'Of course, Your Grace.'

Samuel opened the door to his room to find Frederica yawning. He shut the door and then rushed over to her. She placed her arms around his neck and pulled him down to the bed, covering his neck and face with kisses.

'Frederica, I am to fight tomorrow.'

She wrapped her arms around his back, pressing all ten fingers against him. 'Hold me.'

His heart pounded as he kissed her hair, her ear, and her neck. 'I would hold you for ever if I could.'

Frederica kissed his shoulder that she was leaning her head on. 'You *will* hold me for ever. That is an order. I am a duchess now and you have to do what I say.'

'Yes, Duchess.'

Bending his head, he kissed her with all the passion in his soul. Knowing that he might never see her again. Hoping to have a lifetime with her. Wishing for more hours in this day. Realising there was no greater pleasure than holding her in his arms. Knowing that she was his.

Out of breath, he leaned his forehead against hers. 'I am to attend the Duchess of Richmond's ball tonight. The Duke of Wellington insists that all members of his staff attend. I wish— I would rather spend the evening with you. Please forgive me, but I must take you now to your mother's house. We have run out of time.'

Frederica nodded her head against his. It took all of his willpower to sit up and stop holding her. She meant more to him than anything in the waking world.

Clutching her right side, she tried to sit up but was unable to. Gently, Samuel took her by the shoulders and helped her to a sitting position. He picked up her newly pressed, but still ugly, gown and eased it over her head, not bothering with a corset. He buttoned up the back, before sliding on her stockings and newly polished boots.

She giggled softly. 'You remind me of a prince in a fairy-tale story—*Cinderella*.'

Looping the lace, he smirked. 'My dear wife, your boot looks absolutely nothing like a glass slipper.'

Frederica gave him a playful push on the shoulder. 'In some renditions, her slipper is made of fur.'

Shaking his head, he tied the other lace and held out his hands to her. She allowed him to pull her to her feet and steal another kiss. Each one could be their last.

Frederica picked up her straw bonnet that was smashed beyond recognition. 'Perhaps you ought to take me out the rear entrance. I daresay I look a fright. Poor Miss Wade. She will be mortified on my behalf.'

He took her elbow. 'She can commiserate with Dunford.'

She laughed as he led her out the door and asked for a servant to call him a carriage. Since the back door led to an alley, they were forced to walk out the front entrance in all their rumpled glory. Samuel found that he did not care. What did wrinkles matter when there was a war to be fought? And a brave and beautiful wife at his side?

He directed the driver to number fourteen Rue de Lombard. Frederica snuggled up next to him, her head resting on his shoulder. Their legs touched. Their arms were entangled and yet it still was not enough for him. He needed to be nearer to her. He could never be close enough.

The carriage stopped abruptly and Samuel cursed underneath his breath. The ride had been entirely too short. He stepped out of the carriage and then helped Frederica out. Holding hands, they walked up to the door of her mother's rented house and he knocked on it. She leaned against him as if standing was too great a task. He hoped that her wound had not begun to bleed again. He regretted having to move her again so soon after their long ride. But she would be safest and best cared for at her mother's house.

Frederica stiffened and stepped away from him, dropping his hand. 'Goodbye, Samuel. I would rather you did not come in. I do not think I could bear to say goodbye to you again.'

His own throat seemed to have closed. He could not manage even the smallest syllable of farewell. Samuel nodded and turned to go. But something pricked from behind his eyes and he knew that he could not leave without saying the words that had been on the tip of his tongue for days.

Pivoting on his toes, he glanced back at her. 'I—I love you.'

Her hazel eyes widened and she opened her mouth, but before she could speak, the butler opened the door.

'My lady! Wade, come at once. Lawson, go and fetch Her Grace and tell her that her daughter is home.'

Mr Harper put his arm around Frederica's shoulders and ushered her through the door without another word.

Samuel's heart fell to his feet. He hoped that his wife loved him more than hated him in this moment. For there was no more hate in his heart.

Love had taken its place.

Chapter Twenty-Five

M ama let out a shriek of relief and ran to embrace her daughter. 'I feared the worst, my dearest.'

The tight hug pulled against her stitches, but Frederica sagged in her mother's arms. 'I am so tired, Mama. Spying is not as glamorous as it seems in trashy novels. I was hit in the face by a nasty French colonel and I got shot. It was not pleasant at all.'

Her mother kissed her cheek and held her tighter. 'I should imagine not and I know about your wound. Samuel sent me a note yesterday. Had you not been staying with a general, I would have stormed through the doors and demanded to see my daughter. Now, let us get you up to your room.'

Her mother put Frederica's arm over her shoulder and helped her up the stairs, not saying a word about Frederica's clothing, nor her hasty marriage. She helped her daughter to the bed as Miss Wade arrived. Together they took off the ugly dress and helped Frederica into a nightgown. Mama tucked her under the covers, like she was still a small child.

Frederica blinked, her eyelids heavy. 'All I have done

for the last twenty-four hours is sleep and yet I cannot keep my eyes open.'

'Then close them.'

And she did.

Frederica slept fitfully for several hours and awoke to see her mother reading in a chair by the window. The sun had gone down, but it was not dark yet. It must have been five or six o'clock in the evening. There was still time to see Samuel again. Time to tell him that she loved him completely. The words that she had not been able to say quickly enough before he'd left earlier that day.

Groaning as she sat up, Frederica said, 'Mama, have you been invited to the Duchess of Richmond's ball?'

Mama closed her book and set it down on the table beside her. 'Yes, of course. But I do not plan on attending with you being indisposed.'

Frederica slid her feet out from the coverlet. 'But I wish to go. I must go. It might be the last time I see Samuel alive.'

Her mother looked at her intently for several moments. The concern in her eyes easy to see, but also respect. Frederica was a grown woman and capable of making her own decisions. 'I will tell Wade to dress you in the white satin frock, and I will lend you my diamond tiara and necklace. We will miss the early dinner, but if we are to go, you will look like a duchess.'

Frederica managed to get to her feet and she hugged her mother, gritting her teeth at the ache in her side. 'I love you, Mama.'

She kissed her daughter's forehead. 'I love you too. But you need a bath and perfume, badly.'

Frederica was too exhausted to laugh, but she man-

aged a small smile. Her mother left the room and the
two footmen returned with a metal tub of water. Half
of the servants in the house carried hot buckets to fill
it. Wade assisted Frederica in removing her nightgown
and helped her into the bath. Frederica would have
loved to soak her sore body for hours, but now was not
the time. She washed herself with the red soap. Her
lady's maid put a poultice on her wound, before wrapping it tightly. Then she helped Frederica put on fresh
undergarments, and Frederica howled in pain as Wade
pulled up the corset, even if it was not tight.

'Should I stop, my lady. I mean, Your Grace?'

'No, no. I want to look my best.'

Wade slipped the delicate white satin dress over
Frederica's head and buttoned the round pearl buttons.
Then placed the diamond necklace around her throat
and the matching tiara in her curls. Frederica gazed at
her reflection in the mirror. She looked like a princess.

Like a bride.

Her maid held up a jar of powder. 'Your Grace's
mother said that I ought to put some powder on your
face to cover your bruises and the circles underneath
your eyes.'

'Yes, please, and some rouge.'

Wade held Frederica's train as she walked carefully
down the stairs. Her mother sat in the sitting room
waiting for her. She wore a black gown with a set of
rubies. As always, her mother knew how to best show
her daughter to advantage. Mama had dressed as her
foil. Together they would catch every eye in the room.

'Are you ready, my dear?'

'Yes, Mama.'

Her mother took her arm and helped her out of the

house and to the carriage. When they arrived at the party, they were directed into a large anteroom with a thirteen-foot-high ceiling. The walls of the room were covered in rose trellis pattern wallpaper. It was hard to believe that a few months before, this had been a storage shed for coaches.

The butler announced, 'The Duchess of Hampford and the Duchess of Pelford.'

Several eyes turned towards the entrance, and her mother took her arm and escorted her into the room near a crowd of foreigners watching the Gordon Highlanders dance a Scottish reel in their tartans and kilts. Her eyes fell on Mark Wallace, who waved to her merrily from the floor. He was dancing with a pretty blonde who no doubt had a generous dowry.

Georgy took her other arm, her countenance wan and sorrowful. 'I cannot believe that you did not invite me to your wedding.'

'Nor I,' Mama said, releasing Frederica's arm.

'It was sudden.'

Her friend pouted and her mother sighed. 'I will go and pay my respects to Lady Richmond, do keep an eye on her for me, Georgy?'

'I will. Two of them.'

Frederica patted her friend's hand that was on her arm. 'I am sorry, Georgy. It was very small and private. Nothing at all like tonight. It looks like every officer in the Continent is here, including General Lord Wellington. What a triumph for your mother.'

She saw that her friend's eyes were filled with unshed tears. 'I sat by your duke and the Duke of Wellington at dinner, and the duke gave me an original miniature of himself painted by a Belgian artist.'

'Which duke?'

Her small jest made Georgy release a watery laugh. 'Wellington, of course.'

Frederica nudged her friend with her elbow. 'I am so relieved. I was about to call you out for a duel.'

Her friend rubbed her already red eyes. 'How can you jest at such a time?'

Frederica let out a shuddering breath. 'What else can I do? If I do not smile, I will weep. If I do not dance, I will drop to the floor.'

More tears fell down Georgy's cheeks. 'I do not think I can dance. All the troops, saving my father's regiment, which is to guard Brussels, have orders to be ready to march before first light.'

Frederica gulped. It was exactly what she expected, but the reality overwhelmed her. If she did not find him at the ball tonight, she might never see Samuel again. She checked her own tears, but others could not or would not. All around her fathers, mothers, sons, daughters, wives, and husbands openly wept and embraced their loved ones with a final goodbye. She watched them leave the ball and prayed that Samuel had not already gone.

She pulled Georgy around the room, searching for Samuel. They passed the Duke of Wellington, who lacked his usual composure. A matron asked him about the rumours.

'Yes, they are true, we are off tomorrow.'

The matron began to sob. 'Oh, my sons! God protect them!'

Frederica steered Georgy away from Wellington and to the door, where several officers were already leaving the ball to change out of their dress uniforms. At last, she saw the broad shoulders and strong back of Samuel.

She dropped her friend's hand. 'I am sorry, Georgy. But I have seen my husband, and I dare not waste another moment in conversation.'

Frederica practically ran to Samuel, ignoring the throb of pain in her side. He turned around at her approach and without a thought to their surroundings took her in his arms and soundly kissed her. He held her in his strong arms, so tightly she could barely breathe. She wished that she could stay encircled in them for ever.

His hands moved to cup her face. 'What are you doing here? You ought to be in bed. How is your wound?'

'I had to see you again,' Frederica explained. Her eyes on him, oblivious to everyone around them. 'I began to worry that I'd missed you. So many officers have already left the ball for the front.'

Samuel dropped a kiss on her hair. 'Wellington requested I remain with him. I suppose I shall fight tomorrow in my evening costume. Now turn around and let me look at you.'

He gently released her. Frederica smiled wistfully and slowly circled. Her nerves felt like pistols all firing at the same time.

Samuel whistled. 'Beautiful. You look like a princess. Like a proper Cinderella. You should always wear white, like a bride. *My* bride.'

But she had no time for flattery. Clutching the lapels of his shiny red coat, she stared resolutely at the top brass button. 'I wanted to tell you that I love you and that I do not hate you even a little bit.'

He lifted her chin with his finger so they were eye to eye. 'I could not quite hear that. Could you say it again?'

Frederica grabbed his finger on her chin and kissed it. 'I love you.'

Samuel gave her a roguish grin and her heart hammered in her chest. 'I still couldn't quite hear that over the din of the crowd.'

With a sobbing laugh, she spoke in a voice loud enough that everyone standing within six feet could hear her. 'I said, I love you!'

Samuel gave an exultant laugh and kissed her brow. A feeling of euphoria settled upon her as he gently pressed her head against his chest, calming her tense nerves. 'I heard you all three times, but I couldn't resist the pleasure of having you repeat it.'

'Be careful, won't you?' Frederica begged, pulling herself tighter against him as tears began to spill down her cheeks. 'Do not take any foolish risks.'

'Never.'

Frederica gave a small watery chuckle. 'I want to grow old with you.'

Samuel ran his palms up and down her back, sending shivers over her skin. 'We will travel the world together and you can take over your mother's company.'

'Where will you take me first?'

'Do you fancy a trip to Scotland? I have a little castle up there on a loch, very private, the perfect place for a wedding trip. That is of course if your mother has not already sold that property. Perhaps we'd better check with her before we set off?'

Frederica let out another watery chuckle. 'A prudent idea.'

Samuel looked past her to the Duke of Wellington, who waved one hand at him. 'I must go, my darling.

We will be marching in front of your house. I will look for you at the window.'

'I will be there.'

He took both of her hands in his and kissed one and then the other, squeezing them before he released them. Frederica watched him walk to Wellington's side, and they left the ball together. It took all her strength to stay standing upright on her own two feet, holding on to her painful side. It felt like he was walking away with her heart and leaving her chest with a large gaping hole. The tears that she had not allowed to fall streamed down her cheeks and onto her white bridal gown.

Mama put a gentle arm around her shoulders and held Frederica for several minutes while she sobbed. She accepted a handkerchief from her mother and wiped her eyes and nose with it. Glancing around the large room that had been full when she arrived, she realised that more than half of the guests had already gone.

'The soldiers are going to march past our house,' Frederica said, sniffling. 'I should like to see them.'

'Then we will leave at once.'

Mama shepherded Frederica to the entrance, where they waited only a short time for Jim and the driver to arrive with their carriage. And back at their house on Rue de Lombard, her mother asked Harper to move two chairs to face the front windows.

They sat together, mother and daughter, watching regiment after regiment pass by—the Brunswickers, Scotch, and English. Frederica did not think she could have slept through it even if she had wished to. Noises filled the air: carts and wagons clattering against the stone road, soldiers blowing bugles and beating drums, horses neighing, and people shouting farewells. Frederica recognised the Gordon Highlanders at once by their tartans and kilts. They marched by in perfect formation and fearlessness. Standing before them was a trio of bagpipe players that played a lively Scottish jig. She saw Mark riding a horse. She waved and smiled. He tipped his hat to her.

Shafts of light peeked through the chimneys and over the rooftops—morning had come. Mama retired to bed, but Frederica stood at the window, determined to stay awake until Samuel came by.

At last, she saw the unforgettable face of the Duke of Wellington, and on his right, mounted on his exquisite mare, rode Samuel. He was still dressed in his bright red dress uniform coat. Frederica tapped against the glass and waved furiously. Samuel kissed his hand to her and was gone from her sight within moments.

Slumping down into her chair, she fell fast asleep.

Chapter Twenty-Six

General Wellington led his staff to Quatre Bras. When they rode into the small Belgian town, Samuel felt the hair on his arms rise—it had already begun. He saw the French army charge against the Dutch Belgians. Instead of holding their positions in the abandoned houses and sheds, the soldiers fled for the Bossu wood in a panic. Samuel saw his friend the Prince of Orange raise his sabre high in the air and yell for his troops to turn and fight, but the soldiers did not heed him.

Wellington swore in disgust.

The Prince of Orange turned on his horse and saw Wellington and Samuel. He galloped towards them in a fury, his thin face red from a mix of exertion and embarrassment.

''Pon my soul, my men were holding fine, returning shots, until the French cavalry charged with their shouts of *"Long live the emperor!"'* Billy explained, 'and my force buckled.'

'Obviously,' Wellington said dryly. 'We have no time for excuses. Go back to the woods and rally your troops to fight man to man in the trees. You will hold the French at Bossu woods.'

Billy saluted Wellington and galloped back to the forest with the same fury he had come with.

Wellington waved Samuel forward with a hand. 'Pelford, we must find some way to hold our position. I have no great confidence in the Dutch Belgians. We cannot lose possession of the Nivelles-Namur road, or we will lose contact with the Prussians.'

Samuel pointed. 'Lord Wellington, look. Picton's forces are not a half a mile down the road. All is not lost.'

Wellington took a small spyglass from his pocket and looked through it. Samuel saw his mouth move as Wellington counted the infantry and light cavalry brigade divisions.

He closed his spyglass. 'Pelford, you must tell Picton that he has to hold the French. No matter the cost.'

Samuel saluted the general and urged his tired horse towards Lieutenant-General Picton and his men. He relayed the message and the Welshman let out a string of vile curses.

'Get on with you, Pelford. Tell Wellington that we'll hold the line.'

Nodding, Samuel returned the same way he came. Glancing over his shoulder, he saw Picton leading his cavalry to charge. He'd been that close to the fighting. The sound of a single bullet pierced the air by his ear. He ducked, only to realise that it was his horse and not himself that had been hit. His beautiful mare stumbled to her knees and fell on her side, with Samuel's left leg beneath her.

Samuel tried to pull his leg out, but the weight of the dead horse felt like a boulder. Looking around him, he saw several other bloody bodies on the ground.

Some were as still as death, while others twitched and moaned waiting for help. If he did not move soon, he might be joining the dead. Touching the buttons on his jacket, he thought of Frederica. He did not want anyone else to help her with her buttons. No one but him.

With a surge of adrenaline, he used all his strength to lift the horse's carcass and shimmy his leg out from underneath it. Samuel rolled to his knees, but his left leg would not bear his weight. Placing his hands on his leg, he felt down it. Nothing felt out of place, or broken, but it hurt like the devil. His knee was bruised and his ankle sprained.

He managed to get onto his feet and swayed in a standing position. Turning slowly, he saw that the French soldiers were swarming the Bossu wood like ants over a crumb. They would reach him in minutes. He stumbled forward and joined other Allies running towards the British line. Samuel met a group of Gordon Highlanders.

Samuel held his side with his hand. 'They are coming.'

He felt a hand on his back and looked up into the face of Mark Wallace, who gave him a crooked grin.

Wallace handed Samuel a flask of whisky. 'Looks like you could use a drink.'

The Scottish whisky burned down Samuel's throat, but it revived him. He stood tall and handed the flask back to Wallace. 'Thank you. Tell your men to get into position, the French will be here any minute.'

Wallace turned to the Gordon Highlander Brigade, wearing their clan tartans, and he yelled in a loud voice for them to make ready for battle. The air echoed with 'ayes' and a trio of bagpipe players situated at the back of the brigade began playing a bonnie tune. Samuel watched each man kneel to prepare to shoot their muskets. Wallace walked through his men giving encouragement.

'First line, fire!' Wallace commanded.

Gun smoke filled the air, and the first line of Highlanders ducked and fell back to reload.

'Second line, fire!'

Several French soldiers fell to the ground, but countless others took their place and continued to charge.

'Third line, fire!' Wallace yelled, lifting his sabre. 'The rest of you, get out your sabres and get ready to charge.'

The third line of Highlanders shot their muskets and fell back in their ranks.

'Charge!'

The Highlanders yelled and held their sabres high above their heads, the silver blades reflecting the sunlight. They charged only ten feet before they met the French soldiers. Samuel stumbled to his feet, raising his sabre to block a blow from another French soldier. He continued to fight, but it didn't seem to matter how many French soldiers they killed or wounded, more continued to pour out of the Bossu woods. The Highlanders fought with fury to the music of the bagpipes.

He stabbed a man through the neck and saw Wallace crumble to the ground, his lower leg bleeding freely. Samuel yelled, stumbling towards the French soldier who had stabbed the captain. The enemy soldier parried a few blows, but was no match for Samuel's strength and speed. Samuel ran him through the stomach. Wallace moved his head and moaned. With the last of his strength, Samuel picked Wallace up by the middle and slung him over his shoulder.

'Fall back!' Samuel yelled to the Highlanders, limping his way back to the crossroads.

He set Wallace's unconscious body into a wagon for the wounded and took off his uniform coat to wrap his leg. Samuel had barely tied the arms together when the driver set off for Brussels. Hopefully the young captain would be operated on by a doctor there.

Glancing around the battlefield, he saw that the British Ninth, Forty-Second, and Forty-Fourth Brigades were putting up a good fight, but that they were greatly outnumbered. British soldiers were falling back to the crossroads. If they retreated farther, they would lose communication with their allies the Prussians.

Samuel looked down the road and to his relief, he saw Colonel Alten leading the Third Division. The troops ran to join the battle. But they were falling like flies. In that moment, Samuel realised that life was fleeting and precious. He wondered if the dead soldiers had sweethearts and wives waiting at home in England. Frederica was only in Brussels, but it felt like a world away from him now. How badly he wanted to make it home to her. He'd give everything to see her smile once more.

He found Wellington mounted at La Haye Sainte farm near the centre of the Allies' position. He thought of Frederica's kisses and their picnics together. Those memories were bittersweet. Samuel borrowed the horse of an officer that had already been killed. Smoke from Hougoumont hung over the field between the two armies. Beneath the smoke, Samuel saw the helmets and feathers of the cuirassiers moving quickly towards them. Cannon and artillery fire fell upon them like rain.

'Hard pounding, gentlemen,' Wellington yelled to the British gunners from his own mount. 'Let's see who pounds the longest.'

Samuel saw a long line of wounded soldiers on the road behind La Haye Sainte. He looked in the other direction and saw the French preparing for another attack—Samuel guessed that they had seen the wounded men and assumed the British were retreating. The French cuirassiers and infantry yelled loudly and ran towards La Haye Sainte farm. They swept past the guards and slaughtered all the British inside. The French now held the centre position of Wellington's line.

'The Brunswickers must fill the gap,' Wellington yelled. 'We cannot let the French break the line and get control of the Genappe road.'

Samuel galloped towards a group of reserves dressed in black uniforms with tall collars and black trousers with a blue stripe down the side. He saluted the captain and relayed to him Wellington's orders. The Brunswickers made four columns and marched to fill the gap on the Genappe road.

'They are fleeing,' Wellington yelled. 'Come, Gordon, Pelford. We must rally the Brunswickers.'

The three men galloped towards the retreating men, and Wellington rode in front of the line, cutting off their path.

Wellington held up his sabre. 'My men, follow me!'

The general then led his horse through them and charged the enemy alone. Samuel spurred his horse to follow and held up his sabre and yelled, 'To Wellington!'

He heard the gallop of Gordon's horse beside him and, for a moment, thought that they were going to be a three-man charge against an entire column of French infantry.

Then he heard the Brunswickers echo his call. 'To Wellington! To Wellington! To Wellington!'

Samuel turned to see the black cloud of Brunswickers running towards him, and he continued onward. He rode straight into the enemy's line and began to stab at every man in his reach. He ducked and heard a bullet sail over his head. Turning his horse around, he circled back towards the Brunswickers, who were slaughtering the enemy before them.

He heard Alexander cry out in agony. His friend had been hit by a bullet in the leg, but he could not stop to help him.

'Go on! Go on!' Wellington yelled. 'They won't stand. Don't give them a chance to rally.'

A bullet whizzed by Samuel's ear.

'Sir, you need to retreat back to safety,' Samuel insisted. 'You're within firing range.'

'Never mind, let them fire away. The battle's gained, my life's of no consequence now. We must clear the field and keep the French retreating.'

Samuel raised his sabre above his head and charged one of the few remaining French squares of soldiers. He stabbed two men, and then he felt a bullet hit him high in the chest. His hands slackened on his sabre and on the horse's reins. Sliding off the horse, he fell face down into the mud and blood. He lifted his head up and fought to keep consciousness. He'd promised

Frederica to do everything in his power to get back to her. Memories of her flashed in his mind: summer days swimming at Hampford Castle, bread and cheese picnics, kissing in the orchard, waltzing at balls, and their precious time as man and wife. Then the darkness consumed him.

Chapter Twenty-Seven

A group of Highlanders yelled in broad Scottish accents, 'Boney's beat! Boney's beat! Boney's beat! Huzzah! Huzzah! Boney's beat!'

Frederica turned to look at the window and saw Highlanders throwing their bonnets in the air and yelling again. She looked for Mark, but did not see him.

It was over.

After months of preparation and days of fear, the great battle was finally over. Great Britain and her allies had defeated Napoleon a second time. Clutching her side, she exhaled with relief. They had been victorious and now all she needed was to see Samuel. To make sure that he was okay. She wanted her quarrelling-ever-after ending. He'd promised her that even girls who do not follow the rules of society could still have happy endings.

'I must obtain news of Samuel.'

Mama was already dressed in her pelisse and bonnet. She kissed Frederica's cheek. 'I will send Jim. I wish I could go for you, but there are so many wounded officers that need my help at the hospital. It is a good thing we brought plenty of your soap. I am almost down to my last bar.'

She didn't doubt that Jim would do his best to find out what he could, but a duchess would learn a great deal more than a footman. 'I am well enough to walk, Mama. I promise you.'

Sighing, her mother nodded her head. 'At least bring Jim with you. The streets are still not safe.'

Her chin quivered and she tugged at her collar. Mama and Miss Wade had spent the previous day from dawn to dusk at a makeshift hospital in a church, whilst she had lain in bed to recover. Mama told her last night that there was so much to do. Men to feed. Wash. And write to their loved ones. Some would survive with missing limbs, others would not. Frederica should be helping them this morning, but her mind and heart were focused on Samuel.

When Harper opened the door for her, Jim, the footman, waited outside. She noticed that he carried a pistol. She wished she had thought to bring her own.

'We'll have to walk, Lady Frederica,' he said. 'Her Grace let the men driving the wagons of the wounded borrow our horses.'

She nodded her head to him. 'On foot is fine, Jim.'

The footman took her elbow and they wandered slowly through the crowded streets of Brussels. Many of the wounded soldiers were still able to walk and they filled the roads with their bloodstained clothes and pale, haggard faces. Frederica thought that half of the city seemed to be standing in the streets waiting for news of their loved ones. She saw women of rank beg eager questions to the lowliest of foot soldiers. Strangers conversed together like friends. There was no ceremony, no false dignity, it was humanity at its core caring and sharing with each other.

A beautiful young woman with a halo of gold hair grabbed the reins of a horse that Frederica recognised. It was Mark's cousin's magnificent black stallion, but a different man was astride it. A boy really. He could not have been more than eighteen or nineteen years old. The brown whiskers on his face were sparse.

'My husband, Colonel Sir Alexander Gordon, have you heard anything of him? This is his horse.'

'I am so sorry, Lady Gordon,' the young soldier said, 'but your husband died this morning in Doctor Hume's arms.'

The young woman's lower lip began to quiver. 'Do you know where his body is?'

The soldier saluted her. 'At Wellington's headquarters in Waterloo.'

He tried to urge his horse forward, but Frederica stepped right in front of the horse's snout and it recognised her scent.

'You were at Wellington's headquarters? Do you know aught of my husband? Colonel Lord Pelford. He is an aide-de-camp to the general.'

The young man would not meet her eyes and shifted in the saddle.

'Tell me!' she shouted over the noises in the crowd. 'You must tell me.'

His eyes were wet when they finally met her gaze. 'He was shot and is currently missing, presumed dead. The general does not know where his body is.'

Stumbling away from the soldier and the horse, she would have fallen over if Jim had not caught her. She felt as if she had been shot a second time, through the centre of her chest. The pain was real and excruciating. She kept swallowing, but nothing seemed to open her constricted throat.

She did not cry.

She could not cry.

She would not believe it.

The possibility of life without Samuel seemed inconceivable.

Who else would annoy her to exasperation?

Disagree with almost everything she believed in?

And kiss her until her toes curled?

'Let us get you back home, my lady,' Jim said, steering her back towards their rented home on Rue de Lombard.

Her own mind was so foggy that she could not have found her way to the rented house. Jim did not leave her at the door, but escorted her inside the parlour and to a chair. He told Harper to make her ladyship some tea.

'Master Samuel? Pelford?' Harper asked.

Jim did not say a word. He only shook his head.

Frederica tried to swallow once more. 'No tea. I just want to be left alone.'

The butler gave her a sympathetic look and then both he and Jim exited the room. Once the door closed, the tears that she had held inside of her spilled out in muffled sobs. Never in her life before had she experienced such despair and it consumed her. She felt as if her head was under the water of a cold river and there was no way for her to breathe as the current dragged her away.

The next morning, her mother came into her room to check on her. Frederica lay in bed. She had no energy and her head felt dizzy. She had dreamed of Samuel dying over and over, until she woke up in a cold sweat. How she wished that her sisters were there with her! She could have used a cuddle from Becca or a blunt observation from Helen. Mantheria would have tried to counsel with her about the proper ways to grieve, but she was not ready to be wise. Touching her swollen eyes, she winced. They were dry and achy like the rest of her body.

Mama lifted the lid of her meal tray. 'You have not touched your hot chocolate nor breakfast.'

Squeezing her eyes tightly shut, Frederica shook her head. 'I am not hungry.'

'That is a first.'

A snort escaped her lips, before she could stop herself. How could she find her mother's wit amusing the day after she learned Samuel was dead?

Anger built in her belly. 'How can you make a joke at a time such as this?'

Her mother placed a gentle hand on her shoulder. 'It was more a dry observation. Dearest, Samuel would not mind you laughing. Even when you were little, he liked nothing more than to make you smile. Whenever he told a joke, he always looked at you to see your reaction.'

Shaking her head, Frederica said, 'He preferred to make me shriek with fury.'

One side of her mother's mouth went up into a half smile. 'That too. The both of you could not bear it if the other one ignored you. Oh, the lengths you two went to for the other's attention. Remember the time when you put salt into his tea?'

Another chuckle escaped her lips. 'It was brilliant. Samuel spat the tea out across the table and it hit both Matthew and Wick.'

Glancing up at her mother, Frederica saw that her eyes were filled with tears. Samuel was not merely a suitor. Her mother had seen him grow up. Not that her mother's pain could reach the depths of her own, but Frederica was wrong to assume that she was not grieving deeply.

She placed her hand over her mother's. 'I am sorry to be snappish, Mama. I know that you loved Samuel too.'

Mama nodded and kissed Frederica's curls again. 'I did and I love you, my dear girl. And although I do not know what it is like to lose a husband, I do know what it is to lose a loved one. My own mother and two of my beloved children. That sort of pain does not go away after days or months, even years. But they are not gone entirely. You carry them with you in your heart wherever you go. So please laugh at salt in tea, bear cubs in bedchambers, and every other happy memory you have of Samuel. It is in your memories that you can keep them alive.'

A sob broke from her throat and her mother wrapped her arms around Frederica as she wept. She cried and cried until she could no more. And then she laughed and snorted.

Rubbing her wet nose with the back of her hand, she said, 'Remember when I was eight and he dared me to eat a grasshopper?'

Her mother cringed. 'I can still hear the sound of you crunching on the shell. I nearly lost the contents of my stomach.'

'He paid me a guinea.'

'You could not pay me a hundred guineas to eat a grasshopper,' Mama said with another shiver of dis-

gust. 'And when I complained to your father, he assured
me that it was perfectly good for you.'

Frederica sniffed. 'I'd forgotten. Papa ate a grasshopper with me.'

'And I could not kiss him for a week.'

Leaning her head on her mother's shoulder, she let
out another watery chuckle. 'I wish I could kiss Samuel again.'

'Did his skills finally surpass the Italian count?'

Another laugh tore through her. 'Yes. Yes, they did.'

Her mother dropped another kiss on the top of her
head. 'I would like nothing more than to relive memories of Samuel with you all day, but I must go. There
is too much to do at the hospital. So many men have
been wounded and need my help. And you will be helping too. I believe we will go through every bar of red
soap that you made.'

Pushing away from her mother's arms, Frederica
felt herself snapping out of a trance. 'Just give me five
minutes to dress, Mama, and I will go with you.'

'You are still recovering from your wound.'

Frederica shook her head, pushing off her coverlet
and forcing her sore body to stand. 'I want to be too
busy to think.'

'Well, I can certainly promise you that.'

Her mother helped her change her shift and gown.
It made Frederica feel like a little girl again. But after
Waterloo, she knew that she had left all childhood behind. Even for a wild young woman who grew up in a
castle with exotic animals life was not a fairy tale. Terrible things happened to everyone and all she could do
now was save another woman's sweetheart.

They walked down the stairs arm in arm to the land-ing where Miss Wade stood waiting. She took Frederica's other hand, and they walked in a line down the street to the church. A servant opened the door, and Frederica saw an immaculately clean room with rows of camp beds and each held a soldier—officers and privates mingled together. There were nearly one hundred men in the large room. Most of the men were missing an arm or a leg, besides flesh wounds. Mama put on a white apron and handed one to Frederica and Wade.

'The surgeons are gone,' a woman said in a tired voice. 'They have done what they can do for the men. All we can do now is make them as comfortable as we can.'

Her mother touched the other woman's shoulders. 'Yes, of course. Go home and get some rest.'

'I will return this evening to trade places with you.'

Mama bowed to the woman of inferior rank. 'I do not doubt it.'

Her mother then turned and led Frederica and Wade to the cloister, which was being used as a kitchen. Frederica recognised the cook, for he was their own cook. He stood stirring three large pots of soup that looked to be mostly chicken broth with a few herbs. And one pot was full of tea.

'The tea needs a little more time, but there is no reason why the men cannot drink spirits to celebrate their victory,' Mama said. 'Frederica and Wade, set out the wine that is currently being stored in the confessional booth and help Miss Brady and the other volunteers distribute it.'

Wade and Frederica immediately pulled back the curtain of the confessional booth and saw six cases of wine. They each carried one case back to the cloister and then returned for the other four. The dark-haired woman had already opened the four cases and was efficiently doling out the bottles to the volunteers.

'Start down that line there and only fill the glasses halfway,' the woman said in a businesslike tone. 'We need to make sure that there is enough for everyone.'

Frederica continued to pour wine, until she reached the second to last man in her row. He was not wearing a shirt, and his chest was covered in bandages, his left arm a stump from amputation. She gently touched his shoulder but no response. Touching him again, she realised that he felt cold. She would tell her mother that he was dead, as soon as she served the last man—he was missing his right leg just below the knee. A bandage covered half of his face and his middle.

She looked closer and recognised the face. 'Mark, it is me, Frederica.'

There was no response. His wounds had been attended to, but when she put her fingers on his arm, his skin was on fire. She moved her hand to his forehead, which burned to the touch. If she could not relieve his fever, Mark wasn't going to live through the day. She brought a fist to her chest at the pain and anguish. Looking around her at the hundred other wounded soldiers, she realised that she would not be able to help them all.

Yet, she could not bear for another friend to die. She placed the wine and the glass on the floor near his camp bed and ran back to the kitchen. Grabbing a bucket, she went outside to fill it with fresh cold water from the well. She came back inside and found a stack of clean linens. She took the top few and headed back to Mark. She dipped the first linen in the cold water and laid it on his face where there were not bandages, but without covering his mouth or nose. She unbuttoned his shirt and placed another wet cold linen on his chest.

Mama signalled to her to come. Frederica assisted in serving the soup and changing the bed linens.

But every quarter of an hour, Frederica would take the bucket back to the well for fresh water and reapply the compresses to Mark's hot body. She sat hard on the stone floor next to Mark and breathed in and out. She was so physically exhausted that she could not keep her eyes open. She felt a hand on her head, and she looked up—it was Mark's. He was finally awake.

She scrambled to her feet and poured him a glass of wine and held it to his lips.

He sipped it slowly until it was gone. 'Your husband carried me off the field. Pelford saved my life.'

Frederica nodded and felt a tear slide down her cheek—then another.

Numbly, she went to help another wounded soldier. If Samuel had saved lives, so could she.

Chapter Twenty-Eight

The next day, Frederica slept late. She'd overdone it the day before. Mama and Wade had already left the house for the hospital. Along with Mr Harper and all the kitchen staff. The only servants that remained were the grooms. Jim waited patiently to escort Frederica to the church that was a temporary infirmary. She had not got much rest the previous night and her mother had insisted that she sleep in before coming to help. Frederica still had no appetite and very little energy. She rubbed her chest, but nothing alleviated the heavy sensation in her heart.

There was a knock on their front door.

Jim cleared his throat, shuffling his feet at the bottom of the stairs. 'Should you like me to answer that for you, Your Grace?'

Her new honorific.

Samuel's title.

Chills covered her body. 'Yes, please, Jim.'

She slowly walked down the stairs. The footman, with considerable grace, opened the door for a military man and brought him into the parlour. It took her foggy mind a moment or two to recognise the man. It was Colonel Scovell, the spymaster who had attended her wedding and made the arrangements for her and Samuel to go to Paris. His hair and beard were longer and his uniform a bit ragged.

He bowed to her and she curtsied with shaking knees.

'Lady Pelford, I am afraid that you were misinformed. Colonel Lord Pelford is still alive, but I am afraid that he is not long with us.'

Frederica felt numb and she collapsed to the floor. Bile rose in her throat and she was glad that she had not eaten breakfast or she would have lost it. Her voice cracked as she asked, 'Where is he? Is he at a hospital in Brussels?'

Scovell shook his head, his expression grave. 'Lord Pelford was taken to a small farmhouse in Mont-Saint-Jean near Waterloo. I saw him there this morning and rode immediately to inform you of it. And if it is agreeable, I will escort you there this very moment. In such cases as these even the smallest delay...'

The spymaster did not finish his sentence, but Frederica knew what he meant. She was going to lose Samuel all over again. Yet she would do anything for a few moments with him. For more memories of her husband to hold in her heart.

'Jim!' Frederica said.

The footman rushed to her side and carefully helped her to her feet.

Frederica grabbed his hands. 'Did we get our horses back from the wounded wagons?'

'Yes, my lady.'

'Please, harness the carriage at once.'

Scovell cleared his throat, giving Frederica a pitying

glance. 'A carriage will take more time and the roads are not good.'

'I need to be able to convey his body back with me,' she whispered in a weak voice, touching the column of her throat to feel her own steady pulse. She needed to know where Samuel was. Always. She could not allow his body to be sent to a charnel house and be piled in a large unmarked grave.

Jim bowed to her. 'As you wish it, Your Grace. I will bring the carriage around at once.'

Spinning on her foot, Frederica took the stairs two at a time. She grabbed the last bar of red soap from her room and then she opened the linen cupboard and took out three clean white sheets, placing them in her portmanteau. Going to the kitchen, she took a tea kettle and the remainder of the bread and cheese. She wrapped them up and placed them in the small trunk. She looked around wildly. What else would he need?

Scovell entered the kitchen. 'Excuse me, Lady Pelford. All the wells at Waterloo are spoiled, for soldiers have thrown bodies in them. Fresh water and wine would be the most advisable to bring.'

Frederica thanked him, opening the door to the cellar before carrying out four bottles of spirits. She took the kettle out of the portmanteau and filled it with water. She added lint weed leaves to the concoction. They would be bitter without the cherry water, but she did not have time to ask Jim to fetch some from the market. Nor could she be certain that it would be available with so many wounded soldiers. She packed a jug of water.

Scovell picked up the portmanteau, and Frederica carried the full kettle. She led him through the front door where the carriage stood waiting. Her mother's usual coachman was perched in the driver's seat and Jim sat beside him holding a gun. Recognising Frederica, Jim relaxed his hold on the weapon. She recalled her mother saying that the horses had to be guarded from thieves when the battle began. So many people were trying to run away by any means possible.

Holding her neck again, Frederica said, 'I need to get to Mont-Saint-Jean as quickly as possible.'

Scovell loaded the portmanteau and begged to be excused to retrieve his horse from the hitching post. Frederica thanked him and entered the coach carefully, as to not spill the precious water or lint weed in the kettle. She sagged back against her seat. She felt like Pandora trying to hold on to her small box of hope despite all the terrible calamities in the world.

What if Samuel were already dead before she arrived?

Why hadn't she, like Sir Alexander Gordon's widow, begged for information from anyone about her husband and the location of his body?

He might have suffered less and they could have spent a day and a half more together.

It was not the lifetime that she had hoped for, but at least she could have been with him. Eased the pain. Impatiently, she scratched at her face.

If only.

Leaning out the window for some fresh air, Frederica saw a shocking sight. Rows of soldiers' bodies were being drawn along by fishhooks. The Belgian peasants were dragging them to a large hole in a field to be buried. Frederica covered her mouth with her hand as her stomach roiled. She swore to herself that Samuel would not suffer such an ignominious end. She would bring his body home with her and have him buried where she could visit often. They would never be parted again.

The coach came to a stop beside a wooden farm-house with a garret, a stable, and a row of cow houses. Scovell dismounted and opened the carriage door. Frederica walked down the steps and saw soldiers using French shields as frying pans over small fires to cook their beefsteaks. Not even the smell of smoke could cover the stench of death.

Scovell picked up her portmanteau and begged her to follow him. He did not lead her to the farmhouse, but to the closest cow house. He opened the door with his free hand. Again, Frederica had to fight not to vomit. The cow house floor was covered in straw and blood, and carrion flies swarmed over the line of wounded soldiers. Infection seeped through the dirty rags that bound their wounds. It was a dirty place not even fit for cows. Let alone soldiers. The brave men who had fought for their country.

She did not see Samuel.

Frederica looked eagerly to Scovell. She was having difficulty breathing. It felt as if her throat was com-pletely closed. Had she been too slow in coming to see him? Her chest felt tight and she struggled to find air.

'They might have moved him inside the farmhouse, Your Grace,' Scovell said, glancing at her. 'When I rec-ognised him this morning, I requested that he be made more comfortable.'

Taking her elbow, Scovell led the way back out of the door of the cow house across a short path to the farm-house. The air was only slightly less pungent outside.

They were met at the door by a wiry woman with a

mop of grey hair and a lined face. Her simple brown dress was covered in dust, and she had a dazed look in her eyes. 'I stayed the whole battle right there, miss, in that there garret.'

Scovell tried to push past her, but she blocked the door-frame resolutely and repeated herself. He set down the portmanteau, and Frederica thought he was going to forcibly remove the poor, deranged woman.

She placed a hand on his shoulder and asked the woman in French, 'Why did you stay here?'

Her eyes lit up with a wild look. 'I have got a great many cows and calves and poultry and pigs. They is all that I have in this here world, and if I did not stay to take care of them, they would be all destroyed or carried off.'

Frederica gave the woman a friendly smile. 'I promise I am not here to steal your cows or your calves or your poultry or your pigs. I am here only to see my husband. Would you be so kind as to move so that we may look for him in your house?'

The woman's eyes darted back from Scovell to Frederica, then from Frederica to Scovell. She stuck her thin gnarled fingers on her chest and repeated the same phrase.

'Of course you did,' Frederica said soothingly, taking the woman's arm and escorting her into the house. 'Now, why don't you step inside your kitchen, and I will make us a pot of tea while you tell me all about it.'

She did not resist her, but allowed Frederica to pull her into the kitchen. There were bodies of wounded men packed closely together. A lone doctor gave them a nod, but continued to help the soldier in front of him. There were three rooms in the lower part of the house, and the woman proudly showed each to Frederica, as if she could not see the wounded bodies in the first two rooms.

Frederica recognised the faces of Major-General Cooke and Major Llewellyn. The woman opened the third room, which was the size of a closet. She saw Samuel's face on the pillow of a narrow cot—it was devoid of colour. Frederica set the kettle on the table near the bed and took his hand in her own. Scovell quietly placed the portmanteau on the floor. He took the overwrought woman by the elbow and escorted her out of the room, shutting the door behind them. Frederica did not have time to help her right now.

Stepping closer, she saw that Samuel still had both his legs and his arms, but across his bare chest were bandages tinged with a yellowish green. Frederica laid her head on his chest next to the bandages and listened to his laboured breathing. He was burning up and she felt cold all over. But he was alive!

She heard his breathing quicken and she raised her head.

Samuel opened his eyes and looked at her. 'Freddie?'

Her heart lifted at the sound of his voice. She touched her cool fingers to his hot lips and kissed his clammy forehead. 'It's *Frederica*, as you well know.'

'You should not argue with a dead man,' he said in a croaky voice.

A sob escaped her lips, but she quelled her tears. 'If you die, I will kill you.'

A crease formed on his forehead as his eyebrows pulled close together. 'That does not make any sense.'

She brushed his fevered mouth with hers. 'Loving

you does not make any sense and I have never let that stop me before.'

Opening the portmanteau, she pulled out a bottle of wine. She uncorked it with shaking hands and held it to Samuel's chapped lips. She cradled the back of his head as he drank greedily from the bottle and then closed his eyes as if the effort took too much out of him. Setting down the bottle of spirits, she got to her feet and picked up the kettle. She opened the door and Scovell stood right outside it, and she asked if he would boil it for her.

'And please request the surgeon to come as soon as he is available.'

He merely nodded in reply.

She walked over to the bed and carefully took off Samuel's soiled bandages—the stench was overwhelming. She gagged. There was a bullet hole on the right side of his chest just below his shoulder. The wound looked an angry red and a yellow pus oozed out of it. Infection was setting in. She remembered hearing Wick say that spirits could ward off infection, so she poured the rest of the bottle of wine over them. Then she pressed out the pus and scrubbed the wound with her red soap and the small jug of water. Taking out a clean sheet from the portmanteau, she ripped it into two-inch scraps. Once she had a pile, she wrapped them tightly around Samuel's chest and over his shoulder.

Samuel's eyelids fluttered and his breath was shallow and gasping. 'I—I did not know if I would see you again. I—I prayed that I would.'

Frederica kissed his bare shoulder and then his cheek and then his brow, before covering him to his chin with the blanket on the bed. It was slightly cleaner than the rest of the farmhouse. She wished that they were back at her mother's rented house on Rue de Lombard.

Caressing his cheek, she said, 'You will see me every day for the rest of your life. We are going to grow old together, remember? And you are going to take me around the world. You promised.'

He shook his head slightly on the feather down pillow. 'I have run out of time, Frederica. It has taken almost all my will to live this long. I was waiting for you.'

Frederica gulped down a sob and laid her head lightly against his good shoulder. She needed to touch him. To feel his feverish warmth. Now that she had seen him, she could not let him go. She would fight with the devil himself to keep her husband.

'Then you must borrow some of my will. I have enough for two people. Possibly three. I am not losing you again. Do you hear me? Never again. You are mine and I don't share.'

She heard a light tap on the door. Frederica sat up, and Scovell entered the room with a kettle in one hand and a small cup in the other. Taking them from the colonel, she thanked him for brewing it.

Frederica set down the cup and poured the hot liquid into it. 'This will help with the pain.'

Holding his head with one hand, she helped Samuel sip it slowly. His skin was still pale, but she fancied he did not look quite as grey.

'I don't think I can sip another bit of that awful stuff.'

'You will. I brewed it myself.'

'Hire a cook.'

Frederica gave a watery chuckle, but forced him to finish the first cup and drink a second one. His body needed to be cleansed both inside and out. If only she could give him a proper bath. She would burn the clothes he was in.

Samuel gave her another weak smile and closed his eyes. His pulse slowed down and he no longer felt as hot.

He was slipping away from her.

She cupped his prickly cheeks with her hands. 'If you think after all these years, I am going to let you have your way and die, you are most certainly mistaken, Samuel Corbin. You are going to live. And I am going to frustrate you for the rest of your life... You—you are going to exasperate me to no end. And we—we are going to be *so blasted* happy, that we only fight part of the time, instead of all it.'

He nodded so slightly that she almost missed it.

Grabbing his wrist, she eagerly felt for his pulse. It was still there. Samuel had only fallen asleep. Relief flooded over her from her head down to her toes. Where there was life, there was hope. She was a Stringham and they were used to getting their own way.

She intertwined her fingers with his and kissed his hand. 'This is one argument that you had better let me win.'

Chapter Twenty-Nine

Samuel's eyes burned as he opened them. He hoped that this was not hell.

He did not recognise the small room he was in, but he did the woman sleeping next to him on top of the coverlet. It was his wife, Frederica. For a moment, he feared it was a dream. Perhaps he had made it to heaven after all. But then his own odour hit him. He smelled of blood, booze and cow. Turning his head to the side of the bed, he saw a bottle of wine. He picked it up, only to find it empty. It was probably on his chest with the rest of the spirits.

'Did you have to dump out the Bordeaux?'

Frederica's eyes popped open and she sat up next to him on the narrow cot. He felt her cold fingers touching his neck for a pulse. 'Would you have preferred I used a less expensive wine?'

He nodded, but his face was on fire. Grabbing her wrist, he pulled her hand to his forehead. Her cool skin felt better than a wet rag there.

'I boiled the surgeon's instruments in what was left of the tea. He was angry with me, but he got most of the bullet out of your chest. The rest of the shrapnel pieces he said could stay there. Then I washed your chest again with spirits and soap and sewed you back together. My sister-in-law Louisa will be so proud of my needlework.'

'Why the Bordeaux?'

She shook her head and kissed his brow. 'You are very obsessed with the Bordeaux, but I suppose that is a good thing. You have decided to live. I will search Mama's cellars for some after I help you with a proper bath. The sponge bath I gave you did not get every-thing.'

Despite the agony of pain, his body felt strangely light. Frederica's every touch and kiss filled the empty hole in his chest.

'I smell like a cow house.'

She smiled at his words and a shot of pure joy went through him. He watched as she dipped a cloth into a bowl of water and placed it on his brow.

'That's where Scovell found you.'

Samuel smirked, even though he felt like he was lying on a bed of nails. 'It serves me right for taking off my officer's coat. My body was thrown in with the reg-ular foot soldiers. Will not Grant be pleased to hear that not wearing my uniform landed me in a cow house?'

Frederica shook her head, smiling back at him through tears. 'Oh, no, Samuel. Whatever you do, do not start Lieutenant-Colonel Grant on his diatribe about intelligence agents and uniforms.' She paused and sniffed. 'I am so sorry that I did not find you sooner. I was told by one of Wellington's staff that you were dead and I foolishly believed them.'

He blinked rapidly. The general thought he was dead. Samuel felt a pang of guilt. The poor man would be mourning him and all the other lost officers. Perhaps feeling that he had played a part in their deaths. He was their leader. Their general.

'I ought to go see Wellington and tell him that I am alive. He has been like a father to me and a much better one than my own.'

'Excellent idea, my love.'

He tried to sit up and fell back against the pillows, gasping in pain.

Frederica pressed another kiss to his brow. 'Wellington will have to wait. Besides, you would not wish to see him smelling of cow. Let us just try to get you into the carriage. You can have a bath when we arrive at my mother's rented house and then I will send a note with Jim to the general telling him that you are alive.'

He watched her go to the door and call for a servant. A tall muscular man who looked like a groom entered the confined space. Samuel vaguely recognised the fellow. Somehow, Frederica and the male servant got him to his feet and together they helped him from the house and to the carriage.

Glancing around, he saw that the sun was setting. It would be night soon, but not even darkness could cover the smell of death that hung in the air.

Frederica climbed into the carriage first and the male servant lifted Samuel like a sack of wheat up to her. She placed his head in her lap and his body lay on the seat beside her. His wife stroked his hair and whispered sweet nothings. He closed his eyes for several minutes to regain his strength. The carriage jostled back and forth, but he could not complain about his current location.

Fighting to open his eyes, he said, 'Do you know that I nursed you once?'

She caressed his brow and cheek with a cool hand. It felt wonderful. She smiled down at him. 'When?'

'I brought measles home from Eton when I was thirteen and kindly shared them with you.'

He felt her smile as she pressed another kiss to the side of his head. 'Measles were probably the only gift you gave me freely growing up. Besides the chocolates, when you told me that I was immature.'

Samuel felt his lips twitch into a smile, the pain in his chest subsiding a little. 'My mother and your mother didn't want your sisters to catch the illness, so I was tasked to help with the nursing.'

'That sounds about right. Was I a good patient?'

'Of course not. You dumped the chamber pot on my head.'

Frederica broke out into laughter. His chin jiggled in her lap from her mirth. It hurt his aching head a little, but her pleasure was worth any pain he felt.

'And was it full?'

He closed his eyes again, unable to keep them open despite himself. 'Very.'

Chapter Thirty

It was a week later before Samuel could walk down the stairs with assistance and he no longer smelled like a cow. Happily, his wife and Jim had bathed him with generous amounts of red soap before General Lord Wellington had come to visit. He had embraced Samuel like a son. Samuel had never received so much as a handshake from his own father and was deeply moved by this brief sign of affection.

That was why he was insisting on attending the Duke of Wellington's dinner party despite the objections of both his wife and his mother-in-law. Neither thought that he should leave his bed yet. It was a miracle that he was alive. Samuel ascribed his recovery to his wife's love. Whereas Frederica was certain that it was the anti-infection qualities of her red soap. Either way, his wife had saved his life.

Dunford made sure that Samuel's military uniform and appearance were perfection, but his wife eclipsed him. Frederica wore a sombre grey dress with a delicate black lace overlay. Diamonds hung from her ears and wrists and neck. She was more beautiful than a queen and by some stroke of fate, and a contract involving a large amount of shares in a perfume company that was about to expand to red scented soaps, she was his wife.

Freddie insisted on holding his arm as they walked together down the stairs at a very slow pace. Her hold on him tightened with each step and he was relieved to reach the bottom with circulation still in his fingers. Lady Hampford stood in the entry waiting for them to leave. Raising a hand, she wiped a tear from her eye. It was the most emotion that he had ever seen her display. His mother-in-law was usually as cool as a cucumber and as direct as a drill sergeant.

'Frederica, you look stunning,' she said with a sniff. 'And, Samuel, you look very handsome. I always knew that the two of you would make the perfect pair.'

Releasing her death grip on his arm, Frederica grinned and twirled around for her mother. 'Thank you, Mama.'

Pride filling his chest, Samuel pulled out his pocket watch. 'We had best be going. Wellington is a military man and expects people to be on time. He did say nine o'clock and it is a quarter till. Goodnight, Lady Hampford.'

He surprised the duchess by kissing her cheek and then held out his arm for Frederica. He leaned on her for support, even though they both had bullet wounds. Once they were alone in the carriage, he showed her just how beautiful he thought she looked. He kissed her eyes, her cheeks, her nose, and her mouth. His wife must have thought he cleaned up rather well too, for she returned his kisses with the great enthusiasm of hers that he had grown to love. And he no longer minded that she had to have the last word—or kiss, in this particular instance.

When they arrived at Wellington's headquarters,

Samuel fixed a few of Frederica's curls that had come loose. Nothing he did could dim the glow in her cheeks and the light in her eyes, nor the slightly swollen nature of her lips. They did not detract from her beauty, but added to it. She looked like a woman who was well loved. And he meant to love her well for as long as he lived.

Longer even.

Together, they entered the house and were led to a parlour. He walked slowly like an old man, but Frederica stayed near him. Her bright smile infectious to every person that they passed.

They overheard the Duke of Wellington speaking to Colonel Scovell. 'This is too bad, thus to lose our friends.'

Scovell gravely shook his head. This was the man to whom he owed his life.

Wellington sighed, bringing a fist to his chest. 'I trust it will be the last action any of us see.'

'I hope so,' Frederica whispered into Samuel's ear. It tickled and sent a shiver of pleasure down his spine. He felt recovered enough to help his beautiful wife in their heir-begetting efforts this very evening. He had promised her a palace full of children and by golly, he was going to enjoy every minute of it.

Wellington moved to welcome each of his guests. He kissed Frederica's hand and squeezed Samuel's hand tightly. 'I am honoured that you would come, Pelford. You always were such a dependable member of my staff. Like a son to me.'

Samuel felt too pleased to speak, so he smiled. His own father may not have been worthy of the title, but he had been *fathered* by great men. First, the Duke of

Hampford. And second, the Duke of Wellington. Both men had helped him reach his potential as a man and as a soldier. He did not need to worry any more about becoming like his father. He never would. Samuel would be a father like Hampford and Wellington. One who taught, lifted, and praised.

They sat down at the dining table that had been used to plan the battle. Samuel could almost imagine that was their purpose, for Frederica was the only woman among them. He hoped that she did not feel out of place. But she had helped earn the victory just as much as any man in the room. She had spied on the French and taken a bullet to bring back that important information.

Despite the delicious food and victory fanfare, there was a sober feeling in the room. Samuel was certain that he was not the only person who felt it.

Too many seats were empty.

Too many of their friends would never see their families or homes again.

Frowning, the general twirled his wine in his glass. 'Nothing except a battle lost can be half as melancholy as a battle won.'

'What do you reckon our losses were?' Scovell asked.

Wellington shook his head, setting down his wine glass. 'It has been a damned serious business. Blücher and I have lost thirty thousand men. It has been a damned nice thing—the nearest run thing you ever saw in your life... By God! I don't think it would have done if I had not been there... Indeed, the losses I have sustained have quite broken me down, and I have no feeling for the advantages we have acquired.'

Samuel could not have agreed more. The battle had been closer than anyone liked to admit and without the steady guidance of the general, the result might have been quite different.

Placing both of his hands on the table, Samuel pushed his sore body to his feet. He lifted his glass in the air. 'To Lord Wellington, who held his line like iron until the victory. To the Iron Duke.'

Every person at the table, including Frederica, stood and raised their wine glass and repeated, 'The Iron Duke.'

Epilogue

Frederica and her husband stood on the stony shore of a Scottish freshwater loch, surrounded by green mountains. It was a glorious sight and she eagerly turned her head to see every angle. The glen was bathed in sunlight and she was glad to be carrying a white parasol that matched the little flowers on her blue morning gown of figured muslin. Her parasol had a dual purpose: to block the sun and to use as a weapon.

The wife of the Duke of Pelford always needed to be prepared.

Samuel wore a plain brown jacket and buckskin breeches. He had taken off his boots and his feet were bare. From his clothing, no outsider could have guessed that he was a decorated soldier and duke. He was so rugged and handsome that it took her breath away and butterflies danced in her stomach. She watched him untie the rope from a post and step into a small rowboat. Once he found his balance, he held out his hand to her.

Cautiously, she took his hand and put one foot into the boat, then the other. All her senses were on high alert. Neither she, nor her husband, could be trusted near bodies of water. 'I do not want to get wet. You must promise not to push me in.'

He gave her a roguish grin that set her heart thumping. 'You pushed me into a river and I did not even know how to swim.'

She had been ten years of age at the time. Frederica might have felt bad if Samuel's younger self had not got his revenge the next day by flinging a pile of elephant droppings at her. They had been a pair of rapscallions.

Lifting her nose in the air, she sniffed, trying not to remember the pungent smell. 'Promise me.'

He gave her another raffish grin that put her on her guard. 'I promise that I will not push you into the loch. We will have a nice little sail to the castle.'

Frederica had barely sat down when Samuel shifted his weight back and forth, causing her to lose her balance and teeter from side to side. Before she fell into the cold water, Samuel placed his hands around her to steady her. One hand covering the puckered scar at her waist. A small price to pay to have him by her side. Even if he meant to dump her into a cold lake.

She kissed his cheek. 'I hope this is not going to be a repeat of the punting lesson.'

Frederica felt his lips grin against her own as he lightly kissed her. Then he pressed his mouth harder against hers to deepen the kiss and she felt it all the way to her toes.

All too soon he lifted his lips from hers. 'I still maintain that my directions were very clear.'

'And yet, I ended up covered in bruises.'

'You were going to hit the tree in the river and I told you *not* to hit the tree.'

She laughed merrily and he helped her sit down on

the seat in the small boat. She pushed open her parasol in front of her, *accidentally* knocking Samuel's oar out of his hand, and into the freezing water.

Frederica placed a gloved hand over her mouth. 'Oh, dear! How clumsy of me.'

Samuel pulled the oar out of the cold dark blue water, his sleeve wet to the shoulder. 'If that is the worst thing that you do to me on this trip, I shall consider myself lucky.'

Feigning innocence, she twirled her parasol. 'You *are* the luckiest man alive. You married *me*.'

The smoulder he gave her caused her pulse to race and heat to pool in her belly. 'Luckier than I knew.'

Samuel began to row the boat towards a small island with a castle. According to Samuel, it was six hundred years old. She could well believe it. The narrow structure was three stories tall and made from grey weathered stones. Green moss grew up the walls, and a large stone staircase led to the front door. It was truly magnificent, like something out of a fairy tale or a Mrs Radcliffe novel. But *The Romance of the Forest* had nothing on her own love story, and she was living her very own happy ending.

Frederica dipped her free hand in the icy water and let it slide through her fingers. 'I am glad Mama didn't sell your Scottish castle after all.'

'So am I,' Samuel said soulfully. 'I shall finally have you to myself. There will be no carriages. No friends stopping by at all hours to visit. No relatives inviting us to never-ending dinner parties. No mother-in-law in the same house only a door or two away. No father-in-law giving me a herd of pigs as a wedding gift, or plenty of practical advice on the use of their dung.'

She giggled, making her shoulders shake. 'I thought that was a very conservative choice for Papa. I was expecting an alligator.'

'You come from a family of alligators,' he retorted. 'Each and every one of your brothers and sisters threatened me.'

Frederica could not help but beam at him. 'With their teeth?'

Samuel continued to row. 'No, Wick threatened to throttle me with his bare hands if I did not treat you right.'

She spun her parasol, laughing. Her eldest brother was quite handy with his fists. 'Well, your past treatment of me was not the best. He did see you push me out of the hayloft.'

'You were eleven and you had put a snake in my bed. I am sure Helen helped. Besides, you are interrupting. No Matthew trying to get me to invest in steam locomotives and railroads.'

Her second brother was a businessman who never seemed to take a day off. 'It is fine that you did not. I already own five percent of the stock in his company and I will share a portion of the proceeds with you when I make my fortune.'

Samuel huffed, lifting his eyebrows. 'No Mantheria, giving me lessons via correspondence on how to be a duke.'

Frederica continued to twirl her parasol. Her eldest sister was married to the Duke of Glastonbury, who was in poor health. She ran his estates with the exactness and efficiency of a good housekeeper/steward. 'I hope you kept all of her notes and study them regularly.'

'No Helen writing me letter after letter from Greece

trying to convince me to take you on a wedding trip to South America, with herself as your companion.'

Her younger sister and her snakes. She missed them both. Helen was one of a kind. 'I hear that there are lots of very interesting reptiles there. I am sure she would love it. But I do not know if we will be able to get her to leave.'

Samuel gave an exaggerated sigh. 'No Becca, sending caricatures of me caught in a spider's web or with a yoke on my shoulder like a pair of oxen.'

'I thought her drawings of you were terribly clever and rather accurate. You are trapped in my web for life.'

'And you in my yoke,' he said, giving her a warm look. Then he ruined the moment by adding, 'Nor my little brother pestering me for every detail of the battle.'

Jeremy had been more persistent than a dog with a bone wanting to know every detail. He'd even got on Frederica's nerves. 'You cannot blame him for wanting to know all about the most famous battle of our age from the ADC to the Duke of Wellington, himself. And, you have not mentioned your mother at all. I love her dearly, but she cried on my shoulder no less than ten times. Thanking me for saving your life. I wish she would have shown my favourite dresses more consideration and saved *them* from wet spots.'

Samuel waved this aside with his oar. 'Like I said, it will finally be only the two of us.'

She had been looking forward to their wedding trip as much as her husband, but she could never resist teasing him. Frederica held out her lace gloved hands and began to count. 'There will also be your butler, the housekeeper, Mr Dunford, Miss Wade, a couple of footmen, various maids, and the cook.'

He continued rowing as if he had not heard her. 'Only the two of us…on an island, in a lake, surrounded by massive mountains. Alone, in a castle, with nothing to do.'

Tilting her head to one side, Frederica licked her lips suggestively. 'Oh, I am sure we can find something to entertain ourselves with. I brought several good books.'

Samuel laughed and scooted forward on his seat. Frederica leaned forward too and brushed her lips against his. Her limbs tingled with joy and her heart sang. Samuel sat back on his seat and began to row more vigorously towards the castle, causing her to laugh.

Once they reached the island, he placed the oars in the bottom of the boat and jumped out into the shallow water of the shore. Grabbing the rope, he pulled the boat onto the sand and tied it to the post so it would not float away. He held out his hand to Frederica and she stepped out of the boat. He lifted her up by her waist and twirled her around and around. She felt as if she were flying. Like one of Papa's birds.

Samuel set her feet down on the sandy beach and whispered, 'Only the two of us.'

Frederica placed his hands on her still flat stomach. 'Only the three of us…'

His eyes widened and his mouth dropped. She had finally succeeded in surprising him. Her husband let out a loud whoop and he picked her up again, spinning her around once before carefully setting her on the sand.

'Should I not lift you?' he asked, his tone filled with concern.

Throwing her arms around his neck, she shook her head. 'No, you should kiss me instead.'

Slanting his lips towards hers, Frederica knew that she was living her very own happily-ever-after.

* * * * *

*If you enjoyed this story
why not check out one of
Samantha Hastings' other great reads?*

The Marquess and the Runaway Lady
Debutante with a Dangerous Past

#2199 A PLACE TO HIDE
Lookout Mountain Mysteries • by Debra Webb
Two and a half years ago, Grace Myers, infant son in tow, escaped a serial killer. Now, she'll have to trust Deputy Robert Vaughn to safeguard their identities and lives. The culprit is still on the loose and determined to get even...

#2200 WETLANDS INVESTIGATION
The Swamp Slayings • by Carla Cassidy
Investigator Nick Cain is in the small town of Black Bayou for one reason— to catch a serial killer. But between his unwanted attraction to his partner Officer Sarah Beauregard and all the deadly town secrets he uncovers, will his plan to catch the killer implode?

#2201 K-9 DETECTION
New Mexico Guard Dogs • by Nichole Severn
Jocelyn Carville knows a dangerous cartel is responsible for the Alpine Valley PD station bombing. But convincing Captain Baker Halsey is harder than uncovering the cartel's motive. Until the syndicate's next attack makes their risky partnership inevitable...

#2202 SWIFTWATER ENEMIES
Big Sky Search and Rescue • by Danica Winters
When Aspen Stevens and Detective Leo West meet at a crime scene, they instantly dislike each other. But uncovering the truth about their victim means combining search and rescue expertise and acknowledging the fine line between love and hate even as they risk their lives...

#2203 THE PERFECT WITNESS
Secure One • by Katie Mettner
Security expert Cal Newfellow knows safety is an illusion. But when he's tasked with protecting Marlise, a prosecutor's star witness against an infamous trafficker and murderer, he'll do everything in his power to keep the danger—and his heart—away from her.

#2204 MURDER IN THE BLUE RIDGE MOUNTAINS
The Lynleys of Law Enforcement • by R. Barri Flowers
After a body is discovered in the mountains, special agent Garrett Sneed returns home to work the case with his ex, law enforcement ranger Madison Lynley. Before long, their attraction is heating up...until another homicide reveals a possible link to his mother's unsolved murder. And then the killer sets his sights on Madison...

**YOU CAN FIND MORE INFORMATION ON UPCOMING HARLEQUIN TITLES,
FREE EXCERPTS AND MORE AT HARLEQUIN.COM.**

HICNM0124